Cassandra

Lottie Winter

ISBN -10:1493622293:
ISBN-13:978-1493622290

For JJ
'as is everything I do'

ACKNOWLEDGMENTS

Thank you -Kieran Martin for his 5% and talents as a sounding board, Tia Lockwood for being the woman with the fine tooth word comb and for waging a war against the scourge of the 'and' and Michael for his patience and tea.

CHAPTER ONE

Cassandra

Tucking a stray hair behind my ear, whilst at the same time wiping a tear discreetly from my cheek, I found myself allowing the sound of Reverend Sand's funeral liturgy fade away. I glanced about the gathered congregation, half of whom I knew were there to take a look at the soon to be destitute unmarried daughter, their chatter being, if I could keep my composure long enough for the funeral to be over. There were as many hoping I would crumple as there were those willing for my back to stay straight and my countenance strong.

My fall from grace had been swift and absolutely not of my own doing! My mother had died some ten years ago, when I was just twelve years old. I could still remember her smile and the way her hair tickled me when she grabbed me and scooped me up into one of her huge unladylike cuddles. I felt safe knowing she would never let me go. But lots of the details were getting fuzzy, every now and again, I would smell something; a flower perhaps or the honeysuckle scented perfume she wore and those half-forgotten memories, would briefly wash over me. After my mother's death my father, a celebrated conductor, fell into his brandy bottle. For a few years his reputation had carried him and society had allowed him to falter, but eventually the jobs dried up as orchestra's stopped using him. It had been at this point, of apparent rock bottom, that I had witnessed what I had thought was my father rallying and reinventing himself; the drinking ceasing and the music back in his life.

It was not until his death just nine days ago, that the truth had finally made itself known, my father had been secretly drinking, gambling and spending his time in places no respectable man should ever been seen. As soon as his creditors realised he had died, they were scrambling around looking for the money they were owed. The house and all the contents would have to be sold, I would be lucky to still have the clothes on my back when they had finished. I fingered the hem of my cloak, my mother's jewellery having been sewn in there by Mrs Suggins, our housekeeper. The very moment she realised what was happening, she had gathered up the small amount of jewellery my mother had possessed and had hastily sewn it all into the hem of my cloak, the creditors would not be taking that! I had since added to the hems of my day dresses all my own jewellery, and a few gold sovereigns. In fact anything that was small enough, with any notable value currently inhabited the thick hems and linings of my dresses. Not worth a fortune, but enough I hoped to keep me off the streets, there were even diamond earrings sewn into the lace of my nightgown.

The thought of being a walking money box made me break into a small smile, and as I did I glanced up, saw the sour face of my Aunt Celia, and the smile turned very quickly into a frown. Of course, I knew I would never actually be homeless, my Aunt Celia was my father's older sister, and she would never see me out on the streets. This was not through a jot of kindness on her behalf, but Celia was a woman for whom reputation was everything. To say my father's antics both during his life and now after his death had already placed quite a dent into her place in society was an understatement. So should she allow her only niece to end up in some bad part of town, in lodgings amongst other women who had either fallen from grace, or for whom grace had never a part of their lives, the dent would become a gaping hole. At least I knew I would always have a place to stay, regardless of the welcome I wouldn't really end up homeless. The thought of living with Aunt Celia, a spinster for whom charity work, gossip and judging others were, and not necessarily in that order, her life was a really rather horrible thought. I sighed softly and took stock of what was occurring in the funeral service, not having heard a word of it since the first few utterings, I was pleased to note that we were almost coming to an end.

I kept my head down as I walked through the church, whilst hearing my own footsteps echo with each step on the stones. I didn't look about at the eager happily grieving faces, I didn't need to, I knew exactly how they would look, all so happy to be grieving as long as the grief wasn't really too close to home. They didn't really have to feel anything, but were able to take full advantage of the good bit of 'being in mourning'. Of course for myself I was really feeling something, despite all his failings and my goodness despite what I had so very recently learned about him, I had loved my father. He was after all my papa, the man who had dried my tears when I was tiny and who had dabbed at bruised and battered knees during my tom boy stage. Both my parents had been warm and caring, unlike most of my counterparts, my parents had both done their bit in bringing me up. As a young child my father would read to me whilst my mother had braided my hair. I had wonderful memories of a safe, loved and secure childhood. Being artists and musicians, my parents although celebrated, had always been on the edge of good society and therefore the way they brought their only child up was also on the edge of good society. My nanny may have got me ready for bed, but my mother always tucked me in, and my father would slip in to kiss me goodnight when he returned from the orchestra.

Feeling my Aunt Celia's claw like hand grabbing at my elbow as we moved away from the grave, the sound of the clods of earth being shovelled in reverberating around the silent graveyard, I realised I had once again, not heard a word the vicar had said. I had thrown in a handful of earth when prompted to do so but then just drifted away again to my thoughts. My head was full of thoughts of the past, of what would be in the future, and of course the present moments of grief and loss. I acknowledged to myself, it was not just the loss of my father but also the cold hard realisation that as an only child, and being an unmarried woman over the age of 21, I was most definitely on my own. Aunt Celia, who was now clinging to me like algae to a rock, was my only living relative. Sighing knowing that I could no longer remain in my own head, and that I would have to acknowledge my Aunt, and whatever it was she thought was so important, smiling I turned my head towards her.

"Aunt Celia, it was a lovely ceremony wasn't it, Reverend Sand did a good job didn't he?" My voice was purposefully light and non-committal, knowing she was looking for some emotion, a weakness the old crone could leap on. Surprisingly, she didn't say anything for a few moments. She just kept her gaze on me, her face looking almost sympathetic, she nodded but didn't let go of my arm. Instead, her hand gently tapped mine, in what almost seemed a comforting gesture. I found myself caught off guard. I almost flinched and pushed her hand away, barely managing to continue walking. It wasn't until we had reached her carriage and were both safely ensconced inside, that she started to speak, continuing as we made our way back to what was still, for now, my home.

"Now Cassandra dear, I have been giving some thought to your future, I know you will have been too stricken with grief and of course with shock at the most recent events, to have done much of that, so I have made some arrangements for you". At these words, my head flipped up and my mouth opened almost like a fish floundering for air as I grasped for the words needed. Taking a deep breath, I steeled myself to remain calm the carriage air seemed thick, laden with the silence between us. Aunt Celia's falsely benign smiling face looking over at me blandly, just waiting for my response. When I finally spoke, I had calmed enough to keep the panic from my voice.

"Arrangements Aunt Celia? What kind of arrangements?" She looked up almost incredulously, as if I should just know her plans. Her faint smile, showing the effort in that seemingly benign act.

"A governess my dear, you will of course be a governess, what else is there for a young woman in your somewhat precarious position. I would of course love to have you come and live with me but we must think of you and your reputation, and this will be best served by you going away for a while to the country. I have found you a perfect position, as a nanny to two young children whose mother died in a tragic horse riding accident some five years ago. All in all you couldn't be luckier, Pembroath Estate is vast and Lord Pembroath is a man of high morals, who will expect his children to be brought up perfectly".

CHAPTER TWO

Thorpe

Stretching in what I knew was a languid fashion, I had totally forgotten about the little wench laying next to me, and it wasn't until I inadvertently kicked her that she awoke and wriggled about. She poked her head out from under the sheets, a warm smile and an endearingly freckled nose greeted me but I really wasn't in the mood, instead I groaned and turned over ignoring her. I remembered vaguely that she was Martha, one of the kitchen maids, she wasn't someone I would normally come across but drunk, horny and on the prowl she had taken very little in the way of persuasion to accompany me and as I recalled it. The little slut had moved well, I most certainly wasn't her first. She had squealed at the right times, seeming more than happy when I slipped silk scarfs around her wrists and ankles while pulling them tightly together, rendering her helpless and ripe for the taking.

And now she wasn't giving up, or taking the hint, I could feel warm hands snaking their way around my body, slipping between my legs and without a moment's hesitation wrapping around my semi erect morning cock. At that I growled and slapped her hands away.

"Has a night with me, not taught you anything girl?" Although she shrunk back from me, I could see a grin still on her face, the knowing little slut was well aware of what she was doing. Embracing that look, I raised myself out of my bed, pausing for just a second to grab at the goblet of water on my bed stand, I took a long gulp to slake the thirst born of far too much wine, whisky and brandy the night before.

I grabbed her roughly, spinning her about so her head and neck dangled over the edge of my bed, this not being the first time I had indulged myself in such things. Although I wasn't short by anyone's regard, at just under 6", I knew my bed was far too high to allow me comfortable purchase, so leaning under I pulled out a small stool which was set there just for this purpose. Pushing the practical thoughts from my head, I got back to the business at hand, or more aptly I got back to the young woman currently squirming under my strong grasp.

"Open your mouth and open your legs" I commanded her, my voice as stern as I could muster. If truth be told I knew I felt a little lacklustre, but I strangely felt as though I owed it to her to stick with what I had started.

With a tiny whimper she instantly obeyed, shuffling her round arse slightly before her legs fell open and at the same time she opened her mouth. With a short grunt I thrust my now erect cock straight into her mouth, leaning over, I ignored her protestations and the choking I could hear, I proceeded to use her mouth in the same way I would any warm wet hole belonging to a slut I was using. I thrust my cock in her mouth, pushing down, thoroughly enjoying her discomfort, relishing the choking and the long wet breaths when I pulled out allowing her to breathe briefly. Leaning myself down so I could see her shiny little clit, still a little swollen from last night's fun, now I could see the fresh wetness appearing on her open lips, leaning down but not touching her I blew softly, her moaning muffled by my now quickly thrusting cock. I knew the poor girl was aroused and needy, yet also slightly scared while trying to keep calm. With each thrust of my now rock solid cock into that warm wet mouth, I choked her enough so that she wanted to cough and splutter. She couldn't as there was no time before I again pushed the tip of my cock towards the back of throat, every few thrusts I pulled myself out briefly allowing her a few ragged breaths as spittle ran down her face so much now it was dripping on the carpeted floor. But still I didn't touch the girl, instead I propped myself up on my elbows and enjoyed watching her cunt quiver and her hips move up to try and meet my mouth. However, I had no intention of touching her again this was, as always, about me. She was there to be used and if her pleasure gave me pleasure then so be it, but this morning, I just needed a warm wet hole to cum into and her mouth had been my hole of choice. I blew again letting the breath run up and down her pussy lips, swollen, wet and split apart and at the same time, I pulled out one final time letting her gather her breath. Giving her time to calm down for a few seconds as I knew it wouldn't now take me long and she would need to be in control of herself to not end up passed out on my bed.

It was with a low grunt that I again lowered myself down into her mouth, without another word or sound I thrust deeper and stronger with each passing second by now holding myself up on my palms. I fucked her mouth not caring about her discomfort, my mind only on the goal only seconds away. She was now squirming under me, her mild panic only serving to heighten my excitement and little did she know, shorten her own discomfort! Another grunt came forth as I finally came, my seed spilling into her mouth and as I climaxed, I called out.

"Swallow it, every last drop" I shouted, as I heard her spluttering making to spit it out. The words instantly had the desired effect and she was now greedily sucking on my cock swallowing everything I had produced.

Pulling my now rapidly softening member from her mouth, I laid back down on the bed and sighed. I looked over seeing the realisation on her disappointed face that that was it. As there was no more for her she sat up, wiping her mouth with the back of her hand, before grabbing a hold of the corner of the bed sheet and wiping her neck and breasts. She looked over at me wordlessly and I grinned at her, loving the look of undisguised discomfort, she had of course been expecting her time to come. I ignored the look and spoke to her in an even tone.

"That will be all Martha you can go now, we don't want the rest of the household staff noticing you are missing". She nodded slowly, almost regretfully.

"Yes Sir', she whispered.

"And Martha....not a word of this to anybody, I mean it, keep your mouth shut girl". She again nodded and said the same words;

"Yes Sir".

Deciding I needed to hammer the point home, I leaned over and grabbed hold of her wrist, my other hand pulling her chin up to meet my gaze.

"I mean it girl, and it's for your own good. I am the Lord here, what do you think would happen if it got out that I had fucked a kitchen maid, hmmm? Nothing, that's what, it's what is expected of me, the housekeepers may tut a little, but they would keep their counsel and know their place. This is my kingdom, I can do as I please with a little wench like you, and not one person would dare pass their judgement in my presence. But you Martha, your life would be ruined, you would be out of this house without a reference quicker than your feet could move. No one would think you anything other than a ruined girl without a future. So for your very own good not a word to anyone, do you understand"? To seal those words, I leaned forward and kissed her hard on her plump rosy coloured lips, before pushing her from the bed and slapping her round rump once, leaving a bright red hand print there within seconds.

She gathered up her clothes and I watched her only half interested as she scrabbled about getting dressed. It seemed to take her an age, by the time she was done I had lost that half interest and was almost surprised when I heard her speak as she let herself out of the door of my bedchamber.

"Yes Sir, M'Lord, I understand". I sighed as the room finally fell quiet, leaning up to pull on the long red velvet bell pull, summoning my valet who of course knew after many years, that I was not to be disturbed until that bell was pulled.

A few moments later Simmonds entered my chamber, a large tray laden with breakfast carried with ease. The big man said nothing, obviously seeing the disarray and the various implements laying about. But he had been my valet for over a decade and never once had he commented, he knew his cushy life depended on it.

He laid the tray down, poured me a cup of tea and handed it to me, before finally speaking, as he started to tidy away the horse whip, paddle, and various sized silk scarves, placing them all in the large chest at the foot of my bed.

"Good morning Sir, I see the new governess has arrived, she looks a little young but has her wits about her. Hopefully she will last a little longer than the previous ones have. For some reason, I get the feeling, she won't take any nonsense"

I nodded as I slowly drank the tea, having of course forgotten the children even needed a new governess, let alone that I had at some point nodded an acquiesce at the suggestion of this latest one.

"Well no doubt I will meet her at some point soon Simmonds, they always feel the need to tell me what I apparently don't know about my own flesh and blood". Simmonds smiled wryly, never a man of too many words he just nodded and muttered.

"Aye m'Lord", before heading off to run my bath.

A few minutes later as my aching bones were soaking in hot water the steam serving someway to clear my head, I grinned knowing each governess had told me with some authority all about my own children and how they would and should be brought up, and how they were the ones for the job. I had at the time of course agreed. The governesses never lasted, but my children were the lights of my otherwise dark life, a reason to continue, the reason I never totally gave up and became nothing but a drinking, debauched walking cliché.

My late wife Eleanor may have been a bitter hateful woman whose early death at the hooves of a highly strung horse had been mourned by few, but she had given me the gift of a son and a daughter. James and Charlotte now aged 9 and 11 were a never ending worry, but also a delight. But they had both inherited my stubborn streak, they saw every new governess as a challenge, trying to get rid of each hapless woman quicker than the previous one. So far the children had won and I didn't ever have the heart to stop them. Having decided some time ago, that I would be the kind of father that the children were always pleased to see. I have plenty of money, and certainly more than enough to ensure that there was always within the household's employment, a governess, or tutor who could take care of a disciplined side of things, whilst I was happy to be the beloved Papa.

CHAPTER THREE

Cassandra

The journey had been a long one, leaving London had felt such a huge wrench. In all of my 23 years I had hardly ever had cause to leave the city and now I was leaving with no idea of when I might be back again. The further we had travelled the more bleak the landscape and countryside had become. Having finally reached Dartmoor, my heart had sunk a little travelling across the moors, we saw not a person, building or dwelling sometimes for many miles. I had travelled by train, my only belongings packed into one trunk, it contained all of my clothing still with mine and my mother's jewellery sewn into the hems, with as many gold sovereigns and other small items of value I could find. The bailiffs had taken virtually everything. I had been pleased to retreat to my aunt's house, the sight of the men stripping my house; which had been a happy home shared with my parents, was too much to bear. As predicted I was left with little more than the clothes on my back, along with the rest of my somewhat meagre wardrobe. I had thanked Mrs Suggins warmly, she had been part of the household since before I was born, and like the rest of staff was now faced with finding another position. I had persuaded her to take several sovereigns from me, this seemed like the least I could do! She told me she was going to Brighton where she had a maiden sister who ran a guest house. She planned to help her sister who was older than her and live out her retirement, as she was now calling her enforced departure, by the sea.

I was met at the station by a young man who introduced himself as Jarvis apparently he was the under butler, I found him to be a surly young man who made no attempt at conversation for the entire journey. I watched the bleak countryside as it sped by, whilst being taken by trap to the hall. It was cold and the wind whipping around seemed to freeze my clothes to my body. I felt myself shivering more and more as the journey went on, it seemed to be never-ending, the vista becoming bleaker, starker and more empty. Finally after what seemed a small age, we arrived at the beginning of a long driveway. Jarvis muttered almost under his breath that we were here, and that soon I would be able to warm myself by a roaring fire. His words of almost kindness startled me for just a moment. Looking over I realised the surliness was in fact shyness on his part, and he had blushed a little after mustering the courage to speak as he had done. I smiled warmly and nodded.

"Yes, that will be most welcome, I fear I am almost frozen to my seat". As we drew up in front of the house, I stepped from the trap almost gingerly because the house, if you could even call it that, was vast. My own home in London had been elegant and of course fashionable, but it seemed tiny, and even pokey compared to what was now in front of me. I took a deep breath and made my way up the large stone steps. I hadn't expected a welcome party and was relieved to see that the door was tightly shut, reaching up I hammered loudly on the large brass knocker. Loud footsteps quickly sounded and the door swung open, a man of about 60 stood facing me. He was brisk and brief with his introductions and, having very little interest in me as the governess he dispatched me as quickly as he possibly could into the care of the housekeeper Mrs Simkins, who after a very brief tour of the kitchen, and the servants hall, instructed a young maid named Martha to show me to my room and of course the children's nursery, which was directly adjacent to my room.

Martha scurried away as quickly as she could obviously intent on not engaging me in conversation. As I walked into my room, I could hear the sound of two children playing loudly and rather roughly their nursemaid was with them, I first took stock of my new room, it was large and slightly shabby, but I knew it would be far superior to anything any of the servants, even Mrs Simkins would have. The rugs on the floor were well worn, but warm underfoot, the bed was large and as I perched myself down upon it, rather comfortable. There were two chairs set by the fire which had been lit and gave the room welcoming warmth. As the governess, I knew I was free to make my room as comfortable as I wished, and looking about I saw a small side table near to the fire where I would place my precious porcelain miniatures of my parents. There was an almost empty book shelf, which I guessed would soon be full with books acquired from the library, there being little else for a respectable young woman in a position such as my own to do in the evening beyond reading and sewing. My trunk had been placed in the middle of the room and I made rather quick work of unpacking my clothing and few belongings. I make a mental note to begin the laborious task of removing everything that was currently sewn into my clothing. I would need to find a safe and secure home for it all, as inside dress hems was not a suitable permanent home.

A knock at my door, brought me quickly out of my thoughts, Martha made a surprise return, carrying a small tray, it was set with sandwiches and a pot of tea, it was only then that I realised just how hungry I was.

"Mrs Simkins thought you would be hungry, dinner is over, but cook had a nice bit of ham for these sandwiches". I nodded and smiled as she placed the tray down on the small table by the fire. I continued my job of unpacking, making myself finish before I set about devouring the sandwiches. As I looked up Martha was still stood there.

"Thank you so much Martha, Mrs Simkins was right I just realised how very hungry I am". Still Martha didn't leave, instead rather than wanting to be out of the room quickly as she had done earlier, this time she plonked herself down on one of the chairs and said,

"So, you come down from London Miss, what on earth would make you want to do that, it's a godforsaken place, I would be off to the big city soon as I was able, not leaving it".

Not answering her, I merely smiled and nodded again, I quickly changed the subject I asked her a question she knew I knew the answer to, but I couldn't think of anything else to say.

My room, it is next to the children's?" Now was her turn to nod, and she did so vigorously.

"Yes Miss, the nursery is next door", she pointed at a door, which I had yet to make my way through and which I had assumed went into a changing room.

"You can get right into the nursery through there Miss, their ole nurse she used to sleep in here, but now she sleeps down the hall, it's a nicer and bigger room and she took it for herself".

Finally after I had said little more than a thank you and had continued my unpacking, Martha took her leave.

Once she left I stood up and went over to the fire, sitting down I munched the sandwiches, and made quick work of a cup of tea. It was only then that I felt brave enough to take a deep breath and walk through the door leading to the nursery, my new life as a governess had officially begun.

CHAPTER FOUR

Thorpe

I stretched, and rubbed my hands and feet, it was that time of month already. Each month seemed to go by so slowly, and then all of a sudden it was that time again, and here I was once again at the top of the staircase, looking out at the large window, ostensibly just watching the world go by. In fact my mind was full of thoughts of what was to come that evening. As I allowed my mind to wander and meander in a most pleasing manner, an unknown figure caught my eye. A young woman, she couldn't have been much older than twenty-one, and she appeared to be wandering around the Rose Garden. Having never seen her before, I hollered for Giles, the old man seemed to get slower and slower as the days went by and it was an age before he finally arrived next to me. Without bothering to acknowledge him, I pointed towards the young woman.

"Who is that woman? She appears to be wandering aimlessly around the Rose Garden".

Giles merely glanced out the window.

"She is the new governess Sir, her name is Cassandra. I am given to understand that when the children are not in her care, she does sometimes wander the grounds. Is she bothering you?, Your guests are due to arrive soon, if she's bothersome, she can spend her free time elsewhere".

I shook my head.

"Her wandering in the garden has little effect on me, but tell me, how is she getting on? She looks young", Giles paused for a moment, nodding softly as he appeared to think through the question.

"Yes she is young, however it would appear that the children have met their match, they seem to adore her, and hate to ever do anything to upset her. She comes from a musical background and the children have been putting on concerts for the staff, very talented they both are too, if I may say so Sir". I nodded slowly as I listened, the skeleton of a plan forming in my mind.

"Well in that case, I think I should meet this young woman. The timing is perfect, I have a little time to kill before my friends arrive, have her sent to my study and do it with a solemn face, there's a good fellow, there is nothing like a slightly frightened young woman to get one in the mood for a fun few days". Giles nodded and scurried away, not amused that he would have to go outside on such a cold day.

I sat down behind the large desk, it had been my father's before me, as had the chair and it always brought an amused grin to my face when I thought of how un-approving the old man would have been at many of the antics that the chair, and in fact the desk had seen. The leather was now well polished and looked in very good condition, it would appear that the various bodily fluids which had been liberally spilled over the chair in the last few years had served only to enhance it! I chuckled quietly to myself as I mulled over perhaps bringing to the market a new polish for leather! I was brought out of my daydream by a sharp knock on my study door, followed swiftly by Giles, who was preceded just as quickly by the same young woman I had seen a short while ago wandering my gardens. I nodded to Giles, who quickly, well as quickly as the old man could muster, left the room slamming shut the large oak door with rather a lot of dramatic presence.

I said nothing, taking my time watching the dark haired young woman. I noted how she met my gaze, appearing full of confidence but as I watched a little longer, my eyes raking over her body, I was pleased to see how she held her hands together a little too tightly one finger nail picking at her thumb. She was trying too damn hard to appear a woman in control which meant she of course appeared to me to be a woman almost not in control! Long dark hair, with what looked, from what I could see spilling out of the tight bun she had pulled it into, a natural curl or wave gave way to a most pleasing face. If you were being highly critical and I always was, one could say her nose was a little on the squashed side and her eyes set just a little too far apart. Looking closer I could see a small scar on her bottom lip. As I watched her mouth, her full lips parted just a tiny amount so I could see her tongue running over her teeth, I knew this silence and realised my gaze; which ran from the top of her head, to the tips of her toes was unnerving her. This of course, was only serving to excite me, just a little. This weekend was going to be such fun and how could I deny myself this little starter, a tiny morsel of delight before I started on the banquet.

Finally, when I had taken my fill of simply looking at her, and when those large brown eyes finally pulled from mine and she set her eyes to the floor, did I speak.

"So, you are the new governess, I have heard many good stories about you, it would seem you have won over my wayward children, when no other could, do tell me Cassandra, what is your secret"?

She pulled her eyes up meeting mine again, she visibly took a deep breath before she spoke. Her voice instantly enthralling me, softly spoken yet with an almost hardened edge, it was instantly easy to see why my children loved this woman so quickly and so easily.

"Well Sir I am not really so new, I have been living here looking after the children for nearly five months now, it is just that you have shown no interest in knowing what your children are doing, that our paths have taken this long to cross. As far as having as a secret, I have none, the children are bright and intelligent, with minds that want to learn, I have simply fed their interest while not for a moment mistaking them for lesser individuals. And music, how they love music, both are learning and loving the piano so much. It is hard for me to get them to stop practising at times, I fear you may have two concert pianists on your hands", she smiled somewhat ruefully as she looked up again at me.

"Of course Sir your children would never need anything such as an honest profession, but they will be accomplished".

I snorted with laughter hearing her words, now this one, this girl I liked her, no- one had spoken to me with such honesty or in fact such impudence for a long time. Governess she might be, but she was still in effect a servant, which meant, of course, I owned her.

"Well Cassandra, it seems you would like to put me in my place, but what you forget is that I regularly spend time with my children, who are more than able to tell me what they are up to, I don't need to refer to the hired help for that, and as for an honest profession, I seem to remember a letter begging me to take you on, from your Aunt, who explained in great detail how your father had fallen so hard from grace, straight into a bottle of whisky which had finally done for him. Now let us not quarrel or have cross words on our very first conversation, I am grateful you are looking after them both so well."

I smirked as I paused briefly, in truth having only just found the letter a moment before she entered the room, watching her turn the colour of an over-ripe tomato at the mention of her father, and then her shoulders relax a little at my final words. Pleased with the reaction, I continued.

"Now, you are a young woman, living in my household, yes you are in my employment, but you are well brought up, and able I have no doubt to conduct yourself well in polite company....yes ?" I asked

She nodded her head looking confused
"Yes M'Lord, of course".

"Right then, servant or not" I said, loving the way her shoulders now sagged at the word,
"You shall come tonight to dinner, I am having guests and you might enjoy yourself, good food, plenty of wine and of course good company". Up went those shoulders again, as she smiled.

"Yes Sir, thank you so very much, I should be honoured." Nodding again like a benevolent old Uncle, I smiled.

"Dinner at eight it is then, but mind yourself young Cassandra, dinner will be fun, but the entertainment afterwards will likely be nothing like you have ever seen, but fear not the first time for everyone is scary you will, I am sure be joining in and panting with anticipation for the next time, just like the rest of us".

Looking confused, and a little worried at my words, she went to start talking again, but waving a hand I dismissed her.

"Until later Cassandra, and wear something which might show us something of what promises to be a half decent pair of bosoms."

Blushing the colour of the red carpet she raced away, her good manners and upbringing forbidding her from saying another word. I chuckled again as I swung about on my chair, looking up at the clock and spying the time, I stretched before heading off to bathe and get ready.

CHAPTER FIVE

Cassandra

As I hurried away from that awful man's office, I couldn't help but be a little confused as to what exactly had happened! I was on my way to the kitchen, I needed a bath before dinner tonight and was going to have to persuade one of the servants to help me, with buckets of water and so on.

Five months, I had lived here for nearly five months, it had felt like home, I knew the staff, I loved the children, I had made friends with a couple of the young educated women in the village. In short, I was content, not happy; but after my father messing up so badly, it had been utterly perfect for me to come and hide away here, Aunt Celia had finally, I thought, done something right! And the children, goodness me the children, in those five short months I had grown to adore and love them. Right from day one we had hit it off, initially they had been frosty, and I could see in both of them that they had set themselves the task of disliking me, however it had been the piano and my promises to teach them both which had so easily thawed them.

Now it could be said the three of us were inseparable, eating our meals together except when they dined a few times a week with their father. Their father that awful man I had just met, who it seemed to me for his own sport had been intent on embarrassing me, my discomfort must have been so obvious to him. It most certainly hadn't stopped him, quite to the contrary, the more my discomfort had grown, the more his handsome features had been contorted. Feeding off my sense of unease, he seemed to turn from a young looking handsome man into an older rather dark brooding man, for whom I could admit the sense of attraction was more than I had ever known before.

The knowledge that, had he stepped any closer he would have seen the hairs standing on end on my arms, and perhaps even heard my heart hammering in my chest so loudly I could barely hear him. It was both unnerving and exciting, and exciting was something I had long learned to live without. A young governess in a huge house in the middle of the bleak Dartmoor Moors, soon realised her life would be without excitement, so of course my heart was still hammering as I raced about thinking about which dress I would be wearing. My hand flew up to my mouth as I stopped stock still, for a moment as I realised I had been thinking, working out which one of my fine gowns, and I had only a few, was the lowest cut, and how I could best push up my breasts, wanting it would seem to impress my employer.

About an hour later as I finally sunk into a warm bath, having persuaded both Sarah one of the kitchen maids, and the cook who needed her to be peeling vegetables to help me, and having really hauled up more pails of hot water myself than the young girl, I was utterly disgusted at myself and had resolved to wear my gown with the highest neck possible. Not only that, I now intended to also wear a shawl about my shoulders, so no unnecessary flesh would be on show. It was obviously the fresh air, and the thought of dining with people over the age of ten years that had caused my mind to behave in such a manner.

The water was warm and the bath salts I had used smelled of lavender, I wriggled about a little relaxing and letting my mind wander. Having ensured when Sarah was finished to lock my bedroom door, I let myself relax totally, my fingertips brushing over my flesh in a pleasing manner, I opened my eyes briefly and cast an appraising glance over my body. He had been right, my breasts were on the larger side, round and soft, with large nipples, both of which now seemed to be standing proud out of the steamy bath water. My belly and hips were rounded and the triangle of dark hair between my legs, being wet now, revealed the folds of my sex, the plump lips were parted slightly with curls of dark hair obscuring my view, I was of course aware of my own body, each time I washed or bathed I ensured I was clean and during those monthly times, it was impossible not to be aware of my body, and of the blood that came from me.

As I wriggled about, fingertips grazing very lightly still over my skin, I realised I had never actually touched myself or explored, and after all it was my body. I hadn't ever known a man and now my life had taken this unexpected turn, to the wilderness of the moors, I doubted I ever would. A governess hardly ever found a husband, stuck somewhere in the middle between servant and the family she served. Therefore my body would go untouched and unloved, there was a strange sense of grief, as my fingers now moved to between my legs, I gasped softly as I rubbed, gently at first just exploring, but then as the feelings and sensations grew with more fervour my legs opening wider. One finger now making its way deeper, parting my lips even further as I slipped a finger inside myself. I moaned, shocked at how good it felt, more shocked at the events of the afternoon, which had seemingly been innocent had had such an effect on me that I was now locked in my bedroom abusing myself, but these thoughts didn't stop me.

What stopped me was a sudden tut tutting sound, I instantly froze and my eyes, which had been very firmly shut, flew open just as my legs flew shut. Seeing him sat there on my bed watching me with a highly amused look on his face, I was utterly struck dumb. I wanted to scream, I wanted to scream at him, scream at him to get out of my room, but I was unable to do anything but stare in horror as he stood up silently, and turned to go, walking towards the door it wasn't until he reached the exit that he turned and spoke.

"An excellent little morsel my dear, thank you so much. I had come to apologise for making you so uncomfortable earlier, not getting a reply to my knocking, and afraid you may have come to harm I let myself in, and what a treat when I did, I struggled not to come over there and help you out", walking out of the door now, I heard him say,

"See you at dinner, eight of clock sharp and yes, I want to see those breasts heaving confined in a dress, just as I have seen them now, free from restraint".

I covered my face with my hands and sobbed, how could I ever face him again, I would have to pack my bags now, and leave straight away, find some way of getting to the station, and get the next train back to London. But how could I, it was miles to the station and young Jarvis would never agree to taking me there at this time of day, with no notice. And the children, the children, how could I just leave them like that, I was stuck, I would have to stay, but I couldn't possibly go to dinner. I would feign illness, although if you could be ill from shame and embarrassment, then right now, I certainly was. No, no, no, I would have to go to dinner, go to dinner, wear the right kind of dress for him, one that would show my cleavage, and pull in my waist. I would avoid him, he would be able to see from a distance that I was there, and that I had done as he had asked. If I could just get through tonight, then all would be ok, we could go back to our paths never crossing, and if I was to ever receive another dinner invitation, I would, or course, turn it down.

I was shocked, shocked at myself, shocked at my actions and shocked that a man such as he would let themselves into the bedroom of a young single woman. Of course I was also shocked and kicking myself because as I had been touching myself, feeling my fingers on my body, he had been in my head, he had been there, it was his face and his hands I had been thinking about. I had imagined his lips on my skin, I had felt my excitement grow, but then the shame and humiliation of seeing him there had been almost unbearable. I would never be able to look at him again, let alone speak with him. From his vantage point at the end of my bed, he would have been able to see everything, and I know as my arousal had grown, I had pushed myself out of the water, my legs had spilt open wide, and my fingers slippery from being inside myself had been moving rapidly faster and faster, and all of this he had seen. I shuddered as I mouthed the words "no, no, no" to myself. But as much as 'no, no, no' seemed apt, I still had a dinner to get ready for, and with no one to help me dress, or do my hair. It was going to take some time.

I had been right, getting dressed had taken far longer than it should have done. I was so pleased the children had dined early, their father having requested their presence. He wouldn't have eaten with them, but after the events of the day, I had little doubt that he wanted to talk to the children about me. To find out if I was as terribly unsuitable as today's events had surely painted me as. I found myself sighing heavily more times than I could count, as I slowly got myself ready for the evening.

I choose a gown I had worn only once before, and after the glances and tuts had never worn again. When I had chosen it, it had been the deep mossy green colour of the bodice, matched with a beautiful cream skirt, adorned with embroidery in the same green as the bodice which had captured my attention, I truly hadn't noticed how low cut it was, both at the front and back. It had lain in my wardrobe unloved, and never worn again, and had I not needed it's hems in which to hide my jewellery, then it would have, no doubt, remained when I had left for Dartmoor. I couldn't help but admire my own reflection, I had some emeralds; earrings, and a rather impressive necklace set with pearls and an emerald the size of the end of my little finger, but it wouldn't do for a governess to go to dinner in such jewellery, and it certainly wouldn't do for anyone to know of my gem nest egg. So instead I satisfied myself with a small gold cross, and earrings my father had given me, set with tiny emerald chips, they were pretty and appropriate.

Glancing at myself in the full length mirror on my wardrobe, I groaned as my breasts seemed almost ready to burst from the bodice, I had put on a few pounds eating with the children, I invariably ate the same food as them, and the nursery food puddings, custards and cakes were showing!

With no more time to change, I resolved to not look in any mirrors, go down to dinner, eat as little as possible so I could still breathe in this bodice, make small talk and retire as early as manners would allow. Then try, as hard as I possibly could to avoid the Master of the house, and go back to my boring safe life as a respectable governess, with the hope that the horrors of today would eventually be consigned to a distant memory.

CHAPTER SIX

Thorpe

I chuckled loudly to myself as I made my way to the West Wing of the house, I had bid the children an affectionate goodnight, and wished them both a safe and enjoyable visit with their Aunt, my sister and having listened to them both play the piano and sat in sufferance while they repeated everything they had learnt today. I felt I was back on top of fatherhood for at least another few days.

Of course, it was their governess who was currently occupying my thoughts, I had hoped to sneak up on her, had planned on flustering her a little more, so she would blush even redder when I saw her this evening but I had little idea exactly what I was going to walk in on. I had genuinely knocked on the door, without much force granted, but I had waited a few moments, and tapped again I had assumed she was sleeping, and so let myself in, no one but me (and of course Giles) knew that virtually all the doors outside of the West Wing, and my own rooms all opened with the same key! What I came across was a delight I have rarely seen, I was in two minds whether to just let her finish and creep out, or do as I did and not let the girl have her moment of pleasure.

Her body was far more round and plump than I had expected, of course I liked that a man needs a woman with something to cling too, and flesh needs to wobble just enough! What is the use in a spank, a slap or even a thwack with a riding crop if it doesn't when seeking out its victim cause a little wobble with just enough quiver to see the fruits of your labour.

I didn't think she was practised, she seemed almost to be exploring. I couldn't believe it was the first time she had pleasured herself but from an eye as practised as mine that is how it appeared. I smiled knowing I had presided over countless first times, from young maids caught out and assuming they were in love, to a spinster in her sixties. She, I had found such a relishing challenge that I had fucked her more than a few times, the last and most memorable being in the stables after a hunt when we were both covered in fox blood, smelling of horses and sweat. Using a bridle, I had rammed the bit in her mouth, bent her over a bale of straw and fucked her until she begged me to let her cum. I acquiesced only, when after turning her over and pulling her skirts around her shoulders she had shown me exactly how she fucked herself with her fingers, at 61 and never married she was unsurprisingly skilled at it. Growing hard at the thought of it, I wondered what had happened to her, she came to one of our gatherings where she had commandeered a footman to use her all night. The very last time I saw her, she was clinging onto a bed post, with a banana stuck in her bottom while the footman fucked her. He was, if I recall, a jolly decent footman, but the next day he had gone, as had she, both I assumed off to enjoy the carnal pleasures of the decadence and debauchery I had awakened in them both.

Reaching the West Wing I smiled, I always liked to be the first one here, it was pleasing for me to look around the rooms making sure all was perfect and ready, and this was exactly what I did. The doors were already unlocked, as the trusted servants were now making busy. A few of them would be let off their duties for the evening, as they joined us after dinner, making up the numbers, some submissive and some scarily dominant. There was nothing more delightful than watching a housemaid, who normally scuttled about the place, trussing up a Earl and leading him about the place, a riding crop in hand should he decide to misbehave. Two of the grooms, who were long standing members of our little 'team' were standing about, both drinking a tankard of ale, obviously just bathed and shaved, wearing clean clothes for the occasion, they both just nodded at me. On these days, in this place formality was forgotten, we were three men, who later would all possible fuck and use the same woman, while she screamed and writhed in pleasure loving every second, begging for more. I smiled at their scrubbed appearances both of them looking just a little bit pink around the edges, it was one of the few rules we had, everyone must be clean, clean bodies, clean clothes and filthy minds!

Walking first through the dining room, I paused for a moment, the under butler Jarvis was there checking the place setting, I spoke to him briefly instructing him where Cassandra, our young governess was to sit. I wanted her in a place I could see her, but where she couldn't in return, watch me all evening, I wanted to be able to talk to her, without her feeling she was near enough to begin a conversation.

Continuing my walk and leaving the dining room, I ventured into the rooms which, over the past five years, I had decorated and tweaked until they were perfect. There was one vast saloon, the floor covered in the deepest pile carpet. The maids had been cleaning for hours until it was spotless, furnished with large over stuffed sofas and chaise lounges, huge throw cushions covered in the softest fur and velvet were strewn about, and the whole room was lit by masses of candles hung on sconces on the walls. A vast fire was lit in the massive grate, with the shutters drawn, the room was already dark enough for the flames to be dancing on the walls. Walls which were adorned with art collected from around the world, beautiful huge erotic paintings and tiny ancient etchings and carvings. This room was stunning empty, it would be even more stunning in a few hours' time when full of naked bodies with the sound of moaning, whimpering, begging and groaning filling the air.

Leading from the main saloon were a series of smaller rooms, a couple along the same lines as the main salon, opulent, comfortable and erotic, but there were two rooms decked out as dungeons; bare stone walls with metal rings hammered into them, there were wooden crosses, and one of the rooms sported a cage hanging from the ceiling, in which two or even three people could be placed. Whenever I went into the room with the cage it never failed to illicit a smile, two men from the village had been employed to add metal supports to the ceiling, to ensure it would hold the weight of the cage plus a few very willing captives. They were utterly perplexed as to why they were strengthening a ceiling in this room, and in fact the other items which had already been placed in the room had only served to add to their confusion, and that, I mused, was one of the very best things about being born into my position. No one would question me, as long as I didn't take a shot gun, and go about willy nilly shouting at the inhabitants of the village, I was pretty much free to do as I liked. No one would really dare to voice a word of disapproval.

It had taken me a few years to get this wing exactly as I wanted, it was a celebration of the debauched, the fallen and those for whom a sensory experience was all. It was my greatest achievement, and throughout the select world I inhabited, it was famous as the place to be seen. The invite everyone wanted, was the once a month weekend where as many as fifty people would gather to indulge in all things carnal. The weekend's started off tame enough, it always took a few full glasses of wine to loosen up the tongues, the corsets and the britches, but within a few hours, these beautiful spotless rooms would be alive with the sound of sex, pure unbridled passion and sex. There were no barriers, age or class meant nothing once the doors closed. A place where each person was acutely aware of why they were there and what they wanted, seeking out the perfect companion with whom to indulge.

I poured myself a small brandy from a tray in the main saloon, and sat down by the fire, eagerly awaiting my guests and the evening to start.

CHAPTER SEVEN

Cassandra

Making my way down to dinner, I was shocked to see no one around, I had expected from the invitation, there to be lot of guests, but the house seemed to be more deserted than usual. I sighed, suddenly feeling rather ridiculous in my low cut gown, my hair elegantly and time consumingly pinned up. It was just as I contemplated running back upstairs to my room, that I saw Giles, he nodded and beckoned for me to follow him. I did as bid although I was somewhat confused. We walked through the house, seemingly for an age into parts I had never ventured into. Looking out of the windows I worked out we were heading for the West Wing, which I had been led to believe was unused, and had been for many years, turning to Giles I asked.

"We are not eating in the dining room tonight? I was not told any more about this evening other than some guests were coming, and I should attend." Giles appeared quiet for a small age, finally he spoke, not turning around but continuing that small walk, his gait long and almost languid.

"No, you are right Miss, dinner is not being served in the dining room, and I can only assume if the Master didn't tell you who your dining partners were, he didn't want you to know." With those words he seemed to hasten his walk, long legs striding with more purpose, and I felt myself almost stumbling along to catch up with him. I was so intent on keeping up with the man that I didn't question him again. I think I was also well aware that he wasn't going to tell me anymore, he knew exactly who he worked for and there was no way he would be risking his employer's displeasure.

After what seemed like a walk of almost miles, we had moved throughout the entire house and had arrived at what appeared to be the entrance to another house, huge oak doors loomed up in front of me, each one was ornately carved. Looking closer, I blinked slightly as I saw the images, all of which appeared to be naked men and women in the kinds of positions, which could only be described in one word as "carnal". Giles saw me looking and smirked slightly as he opened the doors, with a small flourish.

"Enjoy your evening Miss" he said as he ushered me through the doors, he moved backwards and back out into the main house with the most surprising speed, I shuddered as the doors slammed behind me.

Pulling my shoulders up straight, and walking as tall as I could, I walked with what I hoped was the confidence I didn't feel. There were at least twenty people in this most impressive and beautiful of rooms. It was so large, the dining table which could seat at least fifty people was down one side of the room, whilst the other side was taken up with a huge fireplace, and many sofas, chaise lounges and great big huge velvet cushions strewn about the floor. The floor was carpeted with the deepest, softest carpet I had ever seen. I was unable not to notice that the images on the doors, which had shocked me so, were apparently tame compared to the artwork and sculptures which adorned the walls and tables. It would appear someone, and I assumed that person was my employer had a huge interest in the erotic and exotic! I realised I had been standing for some minutes utterly mute, in the middle of the room, just staring about me. It was only now that I started to take some notice of what was going on around me. The people who filled this room, the noise of their chatter and laughter although loud, I noted it wasn't annoying or even too much, it was a noise full of fun and laughter and I strangely found myself looking around, wanting to join in!

Taking a deep breath, I started to make my way over to a group of men and women nearest to me. They I am sure would have seen my look of confusion and fear and would, I hoped take some pity on me, maybe allow me to blend in with them and perhaps even join in the gaiety and conversation. As I approached a little closer I was shocked to see that two of the people in the chattering group were most definitely staff in the house. There was young Fredericks, a footman, a jolly good looking chap, who I knew all the maids giggled over and held a torch for. Unfortunately, it was rumoured that Fredericks was never going to be reciprocating any of those torches, for he rather preferred his own kind. Apparently when a young Earl had been staying for a few days for the hunt, he had requested Fredericks act as his valet, Fredericks had been hardly seen again until the Earl had left, whereupon Fredericks re-appeared looking rather too pleased with himself. The other member of staff was a girl I had seen a few times, but was never quite sure who, or what she did, and it appeared no one else ever was either. She had been the personal maid of the Master's late wife, and she just seemed to be allowed to flit about doing very little, with no one brave enough to ask why; but here she was, wearing a gown that made mine look almost nuns habit like!

Seeing them both standing there holding drinks, laughing and joking with a group of obvious well bred gentry I was perplexed. I saw Fredericks hand was firmly clasped in the hand of another young man, who was much taller and darker than Fredericks. Their hands were grasped tightly and they were standing close to each other. In the next moment, I saw Fredericks glance up grinning almost impishly, as he did the taller man, who looked to be in his late twenties chuckled and leaned down to kiss the footman passionately. I swallowed hard, in utter shock, looking around me absolutely expecting the room to fall into total silence and the two men be removed rather forcefully from the room. But instead, not a word or murmur was uttered, instead the conversation continued on unabated, and in fact the other people in the huddle I had been heading for were now laughing raucously about what, I decided, I really didn't want to know.

It was only now that I really started to look about the room, and at my surroundings. The small huddles of people were made up of men and women of course, but looking at them now closer, I could see from the clothing, the demeanour and even the stance, that in the room were many of different classes. This appeared not to matter, everyone was drinking, laughing, chattering and the closer I looked I could see holding hands, stroking backs, fondling buttocks even. There appeared more than just Fredericks, and who I now supposed to be that young Earl behaving in the unutterable manner. In the opposite corner, I noticed there were two women, I hadn't realised at my first glance, because one of the women was wearing a well-fitting evening suit, complete with a gold chain and watch. She was a thickset woman, her dark hair pulled back into a bun at the nape of her neck, her hands were covered in large chunky gold rings, the sort I assume a man of a certain class might usually be seen wearing. Her ensemble was immaculate, right down to the shiny black shoes I could see peeking out of the trousers. The woman hanging onto her arm looked like a tiny little bird, shiny black hair, unpinned and flowing down her back in long tresses, she was wearing a red gown, which from the front appeared very respectable, a high lace collar seemed to clutch at her neck, and when she moved, I could just glimpse the shimmer of gold, a choker style necklace I assumed; it was only when the slightly built young woman turned about that I could see the whole of the back of her dress was cut away, so deeply I could see the crease of her buttocks as she moved about. Her movements were graceful and I could hear from my short distance away her sing song voice as she giggled and conversed with the suit wearing woman and the others in her party. As she moved even more, I saw the golden shimmer again, this time I could follow it down. It appeared the woman was wearing some kind of chain attached to a choker and following it down I could finally see that the end of the chain was attached to one of the suit wearing woman's huge chunky rings. The giggling and laughing of the attached woman was growing louder and louder and I could see a little annoyance on the face of the other woman, just as I was about to turn away, I heard the suit wearer growl and say one word, her companion without another word, dropped gracefully to her knees. She quickly shuffled about until she almost seemed to wrap herself about the trouser clad rather chunky legs of suit wearer. Looking up, with an adoring look on her face, the woman, who was now on her knees in the middle of the room, appeared far more happy, without a hint of the shame or embarrassment one might assume you might feel if you were put into such a position.

A male voice suddenly boomed across the room...

"Sabine, it's not even 10pm and you are already enjoying yourself far too much I see".

The masculine woman, who of course was Sabine, looked up and chuckled, reaching down to pat the woman at her feet on the head and speaking in what I though was a German accent she hollered back, without a thought for any form of manners or decorum.

"Ya, well she is happiest there and so are the rest of us, it's so much quieter!".

I was dumbstruck, I was now standing alone in the middle of the room, and had been doing so for some ten minutes or more. No one had approached me, or I think even glanced in my direction, my only thoughts now were how did I get out of here. Could I simply turn around and head out of the doors, pull them open myself and leave the room drawing as little attention to myself as possible. I snorted a little under my breath, that didn't seem a hard proposition at this point, no one had approached me, no drink had been thrust into my hand and it almost felt as though people were not meeting my gaze or my nervous smile that must have so obviously said 'help', on purpose.

I resolved this was what I was going to do, leaving was the only option; I had absolutely no idea what was going on, but it wasn't anything I wanted to be a part of. As I turned on my heels, I heard a loud squeal of delight, and not six feet from where I was standing, a young woman who had only a few moments ago, I was sure, been standing quietly talking with a couple of older very respectable looking gentlemen, was now with the same two men, but I wasn't sure if either of them now deserved the title of gentlemen. The young woman had been bent over a chair, and I witnessed one of the men, holding both her hands down onto the seat of the chair, rendering her unable to move. Not that she seemed to mind, instead she continued to laugh and started to wriggle about. The other man was standing behind her, I felt myself absolutely rooted to the spot, unable to turn and run away, and absolutely unable to stop watching.

The world seemed to be going in slow motion, as I watched this second man, who must have been sixty had he been a day, start to lift up the woman's skirts while she just continued to wriggle about. As he started to pull the petticoats up, they kept falling from his hands, there were so many, in frustration he reached up and with one swift movement untied the ribbons holding the skirt in place, and ripped it down and off the women, she quickly stepped out of the skirts, the man kicked them to one side. I noted how the woman's demeanour was now changing, I saw how she kept looking up to the other man, her smile still in place but added to this was a look of anticipation. It was then I saw that the man was no longer holding the woman's hands, instead he had reached into her corset, and pulled from it her breasts, she wasn't a weighty girl, but rather she was well rounded, and that included the breasts which were currently grasped none too gently by the man standing in front of her. I knew by now, that the colour had drained from my face. I had no idea what was going on, but had figured out that no one was about to run over and stop them. I saw that others had stopped their conversations and were watching eagerly. Others had glanced over, but had not seen fit to stop what they were doing, they simply continued their conversations and laughter.

I pulled my eyes away from the woman's breasts, the nipples of which looked almost painfully hard. Her laughing had stopped as her nipples were being pinched with some force, causing her instead to gasp, also offering up the odd low whimper. The man standing behind her had, by this time removed her underwear, which was laying on the floor the white lacy cotton bloomers seemingly almost shredded. So there she was, bent over a chair, her bottom on show for all to see. The man looked up and beckoned to one of the men serving. He quickly raced over, his tray laden with items which were most definitely not drinks or canapés, I spotted some leather straps, and items moulded out of wood in shapes I really didn't want to think about. I felt myself craning my neck to look at the tray, spotting what looked to be a horse's bridle I was instantly even more confused than just a few moment ago.

Turning my gaze back to the scene unfolding just a few feet from me, I could feel the heat on my checks, and my heart thumping hard and fast in my chest, I swallowed a few times, and willed myself to move, but I just couldn't, I was absolutely rooted to the spot. I forced myself to look around the room, and noticed that the antics were garnering a fair few spectators, but for every one person who was stopping to look, there was definitely at least another who wasn't remotely bothered, and continuing their conversations without even a second glance.

My eyes alighted upon the woman's very round, very naked bottom. Just then the man standing behind her brought his hand down upon her rump with a resounding thwack, she instantly whimpered and seemed to almost come to attention. As his hand fell again upon her bottom, just as hard as before, he leaned forward and kicked her legs wide open. She didn't fight, she didn't call out and she certainly didn't appear from her demeanour to mind, quite the opposite in fact.

The man standing at her head, had now stopped his rather rough treatment of her breasts and was now instead stroking the woman's hair and face. He looked up and wordlessly took from the tray the horse bit and what looked to be a very small bridle, leaning down to kiss her mouth softly, he held the bit and bridle in front of her face and smiled approvingly. She seemed obediently, and without a second thought, to open her mouth, at which moment the bit was slipped into her mouth and the man got on with the business of securing the bridle behind her head. He took also from the tray a large plume, the kind you might see when watching a royal parade in London. Whilst all of this was going on, I had out of the corner of my eye seen the taller of the two men was still quite rhythmically and firmly spanking the woman's now very reddened bottom. Once the bit, bridle and plume were in place, and his companion had finished untying the woman's corset, removing it completely and laying long flat leather straps which were attached to the bridle over her back, and down her front so they would I assumed, once attached, lay between her full breasts, he took from the tray a large phallic shaped piece of wood. Attached to the wood was what appeared to be a tail, it was made from long hair of some sort, it was black and shiny, and he spent a little time ensuring the hair was laying in the right direction, combing it through with his fingers.

I took a deep breath, I knew what was coming next, and I simply didn't know what to do. I had entered in the last hour what appeared to be a fantasy world, I couldn't quite believe it to be true, and yet at the same time, I knew within myself there were feelings and sensations I couldn't quite place. My heart was beating a little fast, I had found myself licking my lips as I had been watching, and most worrying there was a warmness between my legs which was far from unpleasant.

Blinking, and now biting my bottom lip, I knew I wasn't going anywhere, I was going to find out whatever was playing out, regardless of the consequences, I needed to know what was happening.

The woman was now completely naked, and I realised with a small start I had never seen another woman naked, in fact I had hardly ever seen myself naked. I had certainly never studied myself, never stood in front a mirror and really looked, this afternoon in the bath had been the only time in all of my 23 years that I had really touched myself, explored my own body a little; and yet here now in front of me was a woman not much older than myself, completely naked at the mercy of two men in a room full of people and she wasn't frightened or aghast, quite the contrary, she was now wriggling about. She was unable to speak because of the bit, which was very firmly ensconced in her mouth, but this didn't stop her low whimpering and almost excited guttural moaning now and again as she looked about. The second man, the one who had placed the bit and bridle on her, was holding onto a small leather harness, keeping her in place, but he was also gently stroking her face.

Finally, after what seemed like a huge wait, during which time, I had realised I was actually hold my breath, the man holding the large wooden penis (I had, by this time, admitted to myself it was a penis)he dipped it in what appeared to be a large bowl of oil, he leaned over, placing one hand on the small of the woman's back, he pressed the tip of the wooden phallus onto the lips of her intimate area. She instantly pushed her bottom in the air, opened her legs a little wider, and seemed to then push back onto it. The man held it firmly, allowing her a few moments of pointless pushing her bottom back, before he in one swift action pushed the entire wooden implement into her vagina, it was large, at least 2 inches wide, and about 7 ins long I thought from where I was standing, but it slid inside her easily, the oil obviously helping. The woman gasped loudly and wriggled her bottom, at that the man, whose hands were still gripped tightly onto to the end that was poking out from her, to which the large tail was attached spoke sharply, the first time I realised, any of the three had spoken.

"Enough girl, stay still now". The woman immediately ceased her wriggling and stayed stock still, which allowed the man to quickly and deftly take the ends of the straps which were dangling over her back, and hanging down her front, attaching them to hooks which were obviously poking out from somewhere under the large tail, this meant the bridle and bit in her mouth, were now attached to the tail and the wooden penis which was buried deep inside her.

Both men's job now obviously done, they moved a few steps back, and allowed the woman to now stand up. She did so slowly, turning about to face them both, they both nodded and the one who had brandished the bit and bridle raised a finger in the air, and made a twirling gesture, at which the woman slowly started to turn around, stopping when she had turned away from them completely. Although I knew what they had done, it didn't stop me being surprised, or from gasping a little when I saw her naked round bottom with what appeared to be a tail poking out from between her cheeks. Her stance had changed a little, she was standing almost on her toes, with her bottom pushed upwards, her shoulders were back and her breasts were pushed out. Unable to speak due to the bit in her mouth, her eyes told the rest of the room, and her two male companions, exactly how much she was loving what was happening to her, she seemed to blossom in the objectification.

Happy with what they saw, one of the men reached forward and picked up the leather strap with a loop, which he placed round his wrist, then all three of them walked away, the men leaning in to speak at times into the woman's ear, what they said, of course, I have no clue.

Not one of the threesome had even glanced in my direction, and yet I felt as though I had been through something with them, I found myself incredibly, wanting to run after them, as they moved about the very large room, stopping now and again briefly to speak to people, the men were obviously showing off their possession, and the woman was enjoying her brief moment in the spotlight they had all created.

Of course, I didn't run after them, instead I paused for a moment, trying to bring my head back into some kind of focus, I found myself actually chuckling to myself as I looked down at the dress I had been so worried about wearing, it was certainly looking about the room again, one of the most demure here.

I wanted to have time to take stock of what had happened, I found myself not wanting to leave, there was something about the atmosphere, it was all of course way beyond my sphere of understanding. However I was not stupid, and I knew what was happening was unusual and perhaps even wrong. The room had a smell of the dark about it, a feeling I just couldn't explain. The people who filled it with their presence, their laughter and their chatter, were a mix I had never seen before. I had already spotted members of the house staff amongst the 'guests', and the closer I looked, the more I saw, even spotting Jarvis, the sullen youthful under butler with whom I had made my first journey to Dartmoor. But they were ordinary, ordinary in the fact that there was young, middle-aged and old, there was thin, slender, chubby and fat, there was beautiful, pretty, handsome, attractive, plain and even a bit of ugly; and there was of course very obviously a huge mix of class, status and money. I knew, on any given day, that the people who were currently holding animated conversations, flirting and in some cases just outright groping at each other, would in the normal course of events, not even give each other the time of day.

So just what was it that was gluing them together?

Having made the decision not to leave, I was suddenly rather pleased. It seemed like I was invisible, I resolved then to find a quiet corner, with a good view, take a seat, do some thinking and some watching. Spying a waiter who this time, although having forgotten his shirt, did at least have a tray laden with large glasses of wine. Wordlessly, I walked over, smiled, took in his rather chiselled chest and well-muscled stomach, and grabbed myself a glass. Then I did exactly what I had decided, I had spied a few large sofas and comfy chairs set to the back of the room, I headed for an empty one and threw myself down on it, at which point I also took a very large mouthful of my wine, settled back in the chair and tried to make sense of what was going on.

My first thoughts centred on myself, although my life thus far, had been rather sheltered, I was the child of musicians, and so I had spent time around all kinds of people, theatres and concert halls. Places that were well known for having their fair share of interesting characters! But what was happening here was a whole new thing to me. Even though my life had undoubtedly been a sheltered one up to this point; I was finding myself shocked but not disgusted, I knew enough about my body to know what I was feeling was arousal. The woman on her knees, and then woman who turned for all intents and purposes into a pony, , appeared to love every second. I didn't think it was jealously, there was nothing on all of god's green earth that would have enticed me to behave in the same fashion as either woman. However I admitted to myself there was a sense of almost envy, I couldn't understand what was making them behave like that, and yet the electric charge in the room was undeniable.

It was only then that my thoughts turned to Lord Pembroath, the Master of the house, Lord of the Manor and obviously the architect behind everything happening here and now. A wry smile appeared on my lips, at least now I understood why this afternoon's bathing antics would have been taken a pinch of salt! I looked about the room for him, I realised this was the first time I had given him a second thought. It would appear I didn't have to look far, as at that moment, I saw him, striding towards me, a smug amused look on his face.

CHAPTER EIGHT

Thorpe

From the moment, she had walked into the room I had been watching, and it wasn't until that very few last minutes that she had disappointed me. I had thoroughly enjoyed all the planning, I of course wanted to orchestrate everything, ensuring I was fully in control when I swooped, I needed her exactly right.

Sabine had of course been more than happy to help, her knowing look had told me just how predictable for me the plan was, but I didn't care, the sport was far too much fun. Word had quickly gone about the room that when Jarvis showed a young lady in, she was to be treated, almost as though she wasn't there, I most certainly didn't want her to feel comfortable, or be able to slip away into a dark corner, find a friendly group of folks on the peripheral and relax. Nope I wanted her to feel exposed, surprised and shocked.

The icing on the cake had to be the delightful trio, two mildly homosexual Lords and their pony girl! All three adored each other, the girl having been rescued by the two men from a brothel, where she had been since she was very young. They had been visiting, she had spent the evening with them, and from that moment on, the three were never separated. Despite threats and Lords Hervington and Barratt having to pay considerable sums of money to 'buy Lizzie out', they now all seemed so very happy. To keep the veil of respectability Lizzie was employed apparently as a companion to

Lord Hervington's senile sister, but I doubt she had ever met the old girl. I knew from conversation that all three of them shared one large room and one very large bed. Lizzie was very often their pony girl, it would seem that was a particular liking of Barratt, which the other two had been more than happy to oblige, and which now all three loved. But as often as they played, they were also the three very best friends. Lizzie could now read, she played chess, she loved to play the piano (rather badly, but wanting to indulge her, the two men could never bring themselves to tell her, instead guests were instructed beforehand to ensure the applause was rapturous).

With the two Lords both in their sixties, and Lizzie just in her mid-twenties, I know one of the men, once he had retired and scandal wouldn't be quite so terrible, planned on marrying her, they had big plans for a wedding of three, after the legal formalities of just two. All of this would mean that when the time came Lizzie would be well taken care of, something both men put considerable thought into. In fact just in case something went terribly wrong, before they all got married, Lizzie was in fact now a rather rich young lady in her own right, having a bank account and property in her name. She could of course leave tomorrow and live her life without her two Lords, but she wouldn't dream of it, for however much they loved and adored her, she loved and adored them straight back!

I smiled bringing myself back to reality, I had absolutely enjoyed, the scene watching the delicious young Lizzie stripped down to her plump delightful pale naked body, before becoming the pony girl, complete with a tail, which was of course attached to a well-oiled, large dildo. I was becoming mildly aroused as I recalled the scene, and Cassandra's face as she watched. My thoughts wandered for a moment and I smiled knowing that Lizzie was of course being paraded about now, with that huge phallus inside her, lucky little wench I laughed to myself.

But despite Cassandra's initial shock and outrage, at the moving tableau, she hadn't run away as I had planned, or even better swooned and needed smelling salts. Indeed she had seemed very interested in what was unfolding less than six feet away from her. From my vantage point, just out of view, apparently loitering behind a column, I had seen her initially when she entered the room appear almost in awe of what she saw. Her face then betrayed itself when she spotted a few of the staff, mixing amongst those who would normally be considered their betters, she was unable to hide her surprise, but also I saw there the pricklings of fear, as she was beginning at that point to realise all was not as it seemed. I hadn't asked young Fredericks and his beau to be as affectionate as they had been, however it had played out perfectly, their kiss timed exactly at the moment she was about to take a deep breath and ask to join them. The kiss had been enough to put her off, and as she had turned there was Sabine, with her pretty little submissive Nadia, who although very obedient, and happy when her Mistress pulled a little rank on her, give her a chance and the girl could and would talk the hind legs off a donkey. I doubted I would be able to spend more than an hour in her company without Sabine's calming presence, without tying Nadia to that donkey whose hind legs were almost missing, and sending them off!

Up to that point, it was all going perfectly, if I strained my eyes just a little I could just about make out a pulse at the base of her throat, which was quickening it seemed as every second ticked past. But the girl it seems is made of stronger stuff, or perhaps I have just assumed she is as innocent as she looks, when in fact it might all be an act, to ensure her employment. No, after meeting her, and her awful Aunt, whose name I couldn't quite recall, I knew she was as she said she was, a young respectable girl, who due to no fault of her own, had been left in dire circumstances. It had of course been obvious that the girl's aunt had been desperate to get her off her hands, with the minimum of fuss and, of course, assuring her own reputation remained as unstained as possible. I recalled that the conversation had been extremely brief, the Aunt had been boring, bland and fat, and I was running late for an evening to be spent in a delightful house of ill repute. I had asked her to write to me, which she had done, it had of course only been this afternoon that I had actually read the letter.

But none of this explained how or why after witnessing all she had, she was now sitting looking rather comfortable, with a large glass of wine in her hand, for all intents and purposes appearing to be readying herself to write an essay on what she had seen, rather than run away screaming, which had been my plan. However, I was sure that despite the outward appearance of calm, she was nonetheless like a goose or duck, on the mill pond, not a feather ruffled on the top, but underneath, she was paddling like crazy.

I loved a challenge, and this new governess was going to be that, I was rather taken by her looks, her eyes gave away so much, whilst her lips I had witnessed were bitten and chewed, a giveaway of course to the real feelings that were going on.   And, I had, of course, having seen her naked, a good idea of how good that flesh would feel under my always temporary; firm, strict, but reassuring ownership.

By the time I was striding across the room towards her, her bottom planted on a comfy chair whilst she sipped wine surveying the room, I felt as though my plans had gone awry, this was certainly not how I had planned it.

She looked up just as I had almost reached her side, I could see from her face she was relieved to see me, yet incredibly anxious, her employer had not only witnessed her naked, whilst she played with herself, but then an invitation to dinner was rapidly becoming something she didn't understand. I could instantly see that I was a little bit of an oasis, but at the same time I was also poisoned, she needed me, yet she really didn't want to need me, I was the enemy who might be her salvation. She stood when I reached her side, and I smiled briefly and paused before speaking.

"Ahhh Cassandra, I am pleased you managed to make it to my little gathering, and I am even more pleased to note you have poured yourself into the perfect dress as instructed, I have been watching you a little, if one forgets you are a governess, you really are a rather tasty little morsel".

I saw a blush rising on her cheeks and smiled once again, she obviously saw my small smile as I then saw a rather pink tongue briefly run over her teeth, her shoulders were pulled back and in front of my very eyes, her blush faded, it would seem, almost as fast as it arrived. She didn't say a word initially and I just stood watching her, it was a little like watching a clock, when one has removed the back, and you can watch the movement, the cogs whirling around and the tick tock, tick tock, I think perhaps I even heard a little bit of tick tock. When she finally spoke, her voice was just a little bit strained, I could very much tell how hard she was working to not just crumble and need those smelling salts.

"My Lord, good evening. I haven't seen you since I came down to dinner, and to be honest, I was beginning to wonder if Jarvis hadn't just taken me to another house, with the hope I assume that they might keep me"? I nodded biding my time a little, I couldn't help but admit to myself I rather liked her, she was full of verve and just a bit of attitude.

"Well now you have realised you are in the right place, what do you think, my little gathering is a lot of fun is it not? I had a feeling the very first time I saw you that these evenings may appeal to you, and by the looks of it, I wasn't far wrong". She smiled a little, looking actually rather tired, as if the effort to appear nonchalant was taking its toll upon her.

"I haven't quite decided what this evening is, so I think it's rather early to decide whether or not it's my thing, however you will be more than well aware that I am not a woman who has been very exposed to such things, but I am guessing for you that is part of the sport? Tell me, was my entire employment a set-up? If so, I do so feel for the children, their needs put behind the sport of their father". I snorted, genuinely surprised, and more than a little taken aback.

"I can assure you Cassandra that my agreement to employ you had more to do with just how annoying your Aunt was, and my desire to be rid of her company, so I could find the company of some far more entertaining whores, and as for sport, I merely invited you to dinner, you are free to leave at any time, but you are very welcome indeed to stay and enjoy what is on offer".

She didn't say anything for a while, her face very quickly setting to an almost bland and mundane look. It seemed an age before she finally spoke again, so long in fact I had been ready to almost walk away, leaving her to her ruminations.

"Oh, thank you, I was planning on staying, I can't promise I will enjoy and am certain I won't be taking part, if indeed participation is expected! But if a keen gatherer of knowledge is welcome, then I would be happy to stay. So please do tell me, what is this, we are in your house and yet, it feels almost as though we are in a totally separate house. I can see from you and all the other guests, that they are all extremely relaxed and happy, I am the only new girl. But I am certainly not the first girl you have welcomed here am I?"

Snorting again for a second time, a habit I decided I must there and then knock on the head, I was suddenly aware just how attractive she was. So determined to stay in control and appear cool, the only tell-tale sign of any inner turmoil was her pulse at the base of her neck, I could see her silky soft, warm, milky pale skin and pulse hammering away. I shrugged nonchalantly.

"I invited you didn't I? Nothing whatsoever is expected from you, please do simply enjoy, and as for what this is, this is simply friends enjoying themselves. Like minded friends, people who have gone from acquaintance to friend in the main due to a shared loved of the carnal! There are no rules, and no class barriers, whatever is enjoyed, is simply enjoyed. My only word of advice to you is to not put any barriers up as to what you will and won't do, there are many people who would give their right arms for an invite to one of these evenings. You it would seem have circumvented all of them! Oh and of course, I would assume it goes without saying, although I will say it, when you leave and those doors clang shut behind you, what has happened, hasn't happened or been witnessed stays behind those large wooden doors. You will NOT breathe a word to anyone, this way of life and our merry little band of friends and lovers is too precious. I hope that is understood? Your job, reputation and ability to get on in life is all very dependent upon your understanding of that point".

I was being harsh, and I knew it, my last few words had been spoken with a stony edge to my voice, but this was the important stuff, our way of life must be preserved, and although she was right that she was not the first woman I had introduced into the inner circle, she was certainly the only one coming in having absolutely no clue what was happening. It was a gamble, but one I felt was worth the risk, she was hardly likely to ruin herself, and she knew without a doubt the kind of power a man, such as myself, in my position could weld.

She didn't say a word; she merely looked at me and nodded, and then took a step back, gave me a half smile and stood looking around her. She obviously planned on saying nothing more. I was so used to women vying for my attention, that I wasn't sure what to say next, making an effort wasn't on my agenda, and even worse, I was fairly certain she wasn't doing it on purpose, there wasn't a game plan, she was just simply being herself.

I took a deep breath and smiled, hopefully without ending up looking like a benign uncle.

"So, would you care to look around, meet a few people? You could end up enjoying it, dinner will be a delicious affair and I have made sure to seat you with some interesting people, but we have a while before dinner and if you can bear to take my arm, we can walk and talk."

With another short nod, she took hold of my arm, pausing to pop her now empty glass of wine down on a side table.

CHAPTER NINE

Thorpe

It was surprisingly nice to have her this close, despite being in her presence for a decent while, it wasn't until she was clinging to me, that I realised how tall she was. Normally I liked women who were a little more diminutive, but Cassandra reached easily to my shoulders, she was just a few inches shorter than me, and as I turned my head to speak to her, she looked me straight in the eye. I could smell her hair, and see the intricate braiding she had obviously taken the time to do herself. I wondered briefly, had she known that this was the not a respectable dinner with a few local landowners, I wondered if she would have made such an effort. She turned her head from me, looking around the room and I leaned forward slightly so my lips and nose almost brushed her silky tresses. I inhaled deeply smelling the scent of flowers she was wearing, but also I caught the smell of her sweat. I wagered had I reached my hand up the back of her neck would be damp, her hair slightly moist, the events of this evening would of course be working their slow magic, I was a little impressed at how she was managing to keep her cool, and also a little turned on knowing she was squirming inside, and that I was responsible.

As we started to walk, I could feel her relaxing, and I felt almost happy for her, there was a little part of me that really did want to make it all ok, keep a hold of her all evening, have her sit with me, keep her safe and comfortable. Though really what was the point in that, I didn't want her comfortable, I wanted her squirming and just a little bit hot and bothered!

We made a beeline for Sabine and Nadia, Sabine had taken pity on poor Nadia's knees, and allowed her to stand, she had however kept a hold of the chain, attached to the fine golden collar Nadia was wearing. Nadia was obviously under orders to keep quiet, as when we approached she stepped behind Sabine, and placed her cheek on Sabine's shoulder smiling demurely. Sabine grinned broadly as I sauntered up, reaching up to clap me on the shoulder, with far more force that most men I knew. Her voice was always a surprise for although she seemed unable to speak without force her voice was feminine and gentle, with a thick German accent, her English was however perfect. Sabine and Nadia were both German, but had lived in London for some 15 years now, travelling to my gatherings at least eight times a year, they were one of the old guard, those for whom an invitation was always open. They had been part of the scene since we started gathering at my home, and I loved them both dearly. As however annoying Nadia was, she was also incredibly clever and a talented artist, she painted the most beautiful portraits, in fact two of Nadia's works adorned the walls of this room, and another.

"Ahhhh Thorpe, there you are, we were beginning to suspect you had scuttled off already with a few girls and had abandoned us all for the night, only to reappear tomorrow with your dick almost hanging off"

At those last words, Nadia's gentle laughter could be heard and Sabine joined in reaching her hand round to grasp Nadia's hand as they laughed together.

"Very droll Sabine, very droll" I said, as I rolled my eyes. Turning my attention briefly to Nadia I smiled.

"I see slut that your Mistress has you on a short leash already, I trust you are going to behave yourself tonight." Nadia, who hadn't stopped the low chuckling since Sabine's comment, looked up and grinned at me.

"Of you know me Master, I am never anything but perfectly behaved, unless of course my Mistress really wants me to be a little bit naughty". I nodded, and didn't speak further to her, turning to Cassandra, whose hand was of course still gripped about my arm.

"Cassandra, meet Sabine and Nadia, two of my oldest and most definitely dearest friends, they are both German, but we don't hold that against them".

Cassandra, gave both women a wide smile, but she didn't remove her hand from my arm, or in fact her body away from mine, she was standing really closer than one would think was correct in polite, company, but of course this wasn't polite company was it, perhaps she needed the comfort or perhaps she just liked it, I was happy either way. Her voice was bright and confident as she spoke.

"It's a pleasure to meet you both, Nadia your dress is so pretty, from the front one thinks how demure and respectable and then you turn around and goodness me, one thinks other things entirely". She laughed nervously as she spoke her last few words, almost as though her confidence had let her down at the very first minute. Nadia didn't speak, she just grinned in a most friendly of fashion to Cassandra and let Sabine do the talking.

"Ahh yes my dear, my girl does look a delight doesn't she, she wears it well the demure and the depraved, and yes, we are pleased to meet you, not often Thorpe here makes quite such a fuss about a woman, I trust you are going to be worth it."

I shot Sabine a look that made it very clear she should now shut up, and to her credit, she immediately did. I looked over to Cassandra, and saw that she was hopefully a little too engrossed in looking around and had possibly not totally taken in what Sabine was actually suggesting. I quickly introduced Cassandra to the rest of the group, a widow who had attended with her husband, a rather important Judge, who had always spent most of these weekends, on his knees with a gag of one sort or another shoved in his mouth, whilst his wife beat his bottom with a seemingly never ending selection of floggers and other items not specifically designed for this purpose. This was the first time I had seen Isabelle here without him, and I embraced her briefly she smiled, introducing me to the two young men accompanying her, both were attached I could see to her, and each other via a fine chain and a rope affair which disappeared into their dress trousers, I laughed, knowing damn well she had those boys literally by the short and curlies.

And finally a couple who I had not yet met myself, they were married and friends of Sabine and Nadia, she had asked whether they could come and of course I had acquiesced trusting her judgement. Sabine made the introductions.

He was a wealthy landowner, apparently very fair and hands on with his farm and tenants, and she was a delightful young woman, they had three children, two boys I learned very quickly as she gabbled away telling me proudly and a little girl still no more than one year old. They were obviously very much in what people tell me is love. Having never experienced the emotion for a woman myself I couldn't understand but the way his arm was round her waist, and how she hung on his words told me enough. She wore a low cut, but not scandalous dress, and round her neck was of course a collar, but unlike so many here tonight, this was not a discrete golden jewelled choker affair, this was a full leather collar, it was wider at the back serving to keep her neck totally straight, with a large loop through which was a chain and leather loop which he held onto. Seeing me staring he smiled and said.

"It's a nice reminder, she has a choker for everyday wear but when she wears that both of us remember exactly why".

I nodded again, feeling a little inexplicably jealous, I whisked Cassandra off before anymore could be said, dinner would be served soon, and I was beginning to regret my decision to keep her sat away from me. She was incredibly composed, but very quiet, not making conversation, merely answering my questions and smiling and nodding when introduced to people.

Moving around the room, I greeted an assortment of people, including some women I fully intended to indulge in later, all of them were well acquainted with my likes and desires and all came back for more.

I groaned inwardly as I saw Lady Sybil approaching, a huge smile upon her undeniably beautiful face, she paused in front of us, a waft of musk and vanilla swept over us, and I couldn't help but grin. My god the woman was sex, and did she know it, she wasn't submissive or dominant towards anybody, instead she was incredibly sensual and passionate, with an incredible appetite for sex, she enjoyed men and woman in equal measures. We had shared a very long friendship, one of respect and lust. I know she had hoped that I would give in one day and marry her, it would make her life so much simpler and easier. At the age of 29 her family had now given up hope of her ever finding a husband, and her reputation was ever so slightly tarnished, she had made a few bad decisions in the heat of the moment which she had come to regret. Her problem was finding a husband who would allow her to continue to be the beautiful butterfly she was, it was unthinkable for a man to cage her, I was sure she would wilt like a summer flower if someone tried. Perhaps a very much older man might suit her, she would look perfect on his arm in the right social circles, but continue on her life, in a quieter fashion.

She leaned forward to kiss me passionately and unashamedly on the lips, her tongue flicking out briefly, as if to taste me.

"Thorpe, Thorpe my darling man, I hadn't seen you all evening and I was starting to get slightly concerned I was going to have to make do with the fish eggs, whilst the caviar had gone missing."
As she spoke warm hands wrapped around my body, and shiny decadent red lips brushed my neck, she nuzzled in and I felt one hand cup my left buttock before letting go again.

Not really ready for her overwhelming personality, I peeled her off as gently as I could, and kissed her cheek.

"Hello Sybil, you are exuberant as ever, I have been looking forward to seeing you, and later I fully intend to show you how much, but right now of course duty calls, I have to be the host. Now smile sweetly and meet Cassandra, she is actually my children's governess, but she has a certain something which drew me in and incited an invitation for our monthly fun".

Turning my attention back to Cassandra, who hadn't herself moved at all, but instead, was looking with something approaching disdain at Sybil.

"Cassandra meet Sybil, a very dear friend of mine, she is someone who could tell you a few stories, and whet your appetite for our world". Cassandra smiled a tight little grin over to Sybil and reached out her gloved hand. Which Sybil took with her usual enthusiasm, pressing it to her face grinning.

"Cassandra what a gorgeous name, but I think Cassie is lovely don't you? Cassie suits you, and a governess, my goodness I am not sure I could do that. I mean Thorpe's little horrors are a delight, but they are after all still children, in about ten years' time they will become so much more acceptable. So, if I had a hat, which I don't, I would have taken it off to you".

She laughed a little at her own words, and I amazingly watched as Cassandra seemed to thaw before my very eyes, joining in the laughter, and not pulling her hand away. even as Sybil pulled at the fingers of her glove and removed it in one swift motion. She took Cassandra's hand in both of hers, bringing Cassandra's fingertips to her mouth and kissing them, looking up and speaking again.

"Hmmm Cassie, yes it definitely suits you". Without a hint of a blush or the suggestion she was embarrassed, Cassandra's spoke;

"How lovely to meet you, no one has called me Cassie since my mother, and she was the most wonderful woman, being called Cassie only brings back happy memories. Oh and I adore being a governess, the children are a pleasure and they love music almost as much as I do. I am afraid you will have to excuse my greenness, an invitation to this evening was extended to me, promising no more than dinner, so you can, I am sure imagine my surprise when I realised it was dinner and a little more".

I sighed inwardly, and I suspect a little outwardly, I knew how Sybil would chastise me later, and there was a danger such chastisement would have a detrimental effect upon whatever we were doing.

Tut tutting at me at the same time as she spoke, Sybil grinned.

"Oh now Thorpe, you really are very bad, inviting poor Cassie without telling her what to expect, and just look at the girl, as cool as a cucumber, not at all the quivering wreck I suspect you were hoping for".

Without referring back to me again at all, Sybil took Cassandra's other arm, and dragged her off, they paused only to grab two glasses of wine from a tray, and then continued promenading around the room, pausing every now and again to stop and chat to another guest. I was absolutely bloody fuming, I couldn't quite believe that all my cleverly laid plans had gone quite so awry. Well bugger it, and bugger Sybil, and Cassandra, I hope they both enjoy their evening together, because that was it, I was done. I mused briefly on having Jarvis come and remove Cassandra, tell her that one of the children was awake and calling for her, but decided that Sybil's wrath at me doing that would just not be worth it.

Looking up at the clock, I was relieved to see it was dinner time, and Jarvis was hovering with his usual total lack of anything approaching a personality near to the gong, ready and willing to thump it with the hammer held in his left hand, Jarvis had been to every single one of our gatherings and it had been made clear to him on many occasions that if he wished to join in he was very welcome, but never did he, he just shuffled about, cleared up and of course bonged the gong, which he did right that moment as soon as I nodded.

CHAPTER TEN

Thorpe

Dinner was its usual delicious affair, and I had purposely seated myself surrounded by the prettiest, most nubile and of course most sexually available women.

I watched Cassandra a little, Sybil had swapped seats and moved about so she was now not sitting anywhere near me, but instead next to Cassandra and the two women seemed to be getting on far too well. There was laughter, whispering and of course both women were engaging with all those surrounding them which included Poppy, who was Sybil's fairly constant companion these days. Poppy was an ex-prostitute who Sybil had taken from the streets, almost totally fallen in love with and now kept so she didn't have to work on the streets anymore. When I looked at Poppy I always smiled, Sybil in men placed so much upon looks, however vile a person you were, if you had a well-muscled torso and a big cock she was happy, add a pair of sparkling eyes, and some full lips, and she was in ecstasy. But it would seem in a woman looks were less important to Sybil, Poppy looked exactly like what she was, a woman who had spent too many years on the streets, living the life of a prostitute and she bore the scars of this life, both physical and I would assume mental very well. Poppy was someone I had got to know, at the same time as Sybil had and whilst Sybil had without a doubt fallen in love, I had gained a friend and someone I respected immensely. I realised with not a small amount of irony, she was someone I would not wish to cross.

I shrugged and turned to Lucy Harper who was, I knew, as pleased as punch to be sitting next to me, we had exchanged a few pleasantries. I now reached under the table and found first of all her hand, after a few moments of holding that, I moved my hand onto her thigh, and started to pull up the voluminous skirts she was wearing, she reached down under the table and in a manner far more practised than me, hiked her skirts up above her knees and took my hand which was at that point full of petticoats and skirts and placed it upon a now easily accessible bare thigh. I squeezed a little, looked over to the girl and smiled briefly, before my hand then continued its journey upwards.

My mind was thankfully taken away from all thoughts of Cassandra and my so called friend Sybil who had whisked her away from my grasp. Lucy's thigh was pleasantly warm and smooth, and my hand wended its way without any sense of urgency over her flesh. As I reached the prize I was searching for, I felt Lucy tense a little, and shift her bottom slightly up and forward so her hips were rounded, leaning up to meet my hand, just when I thought her legs must be as wide open as they could be, I felt her pull them apart even wider, making my journey even easier. Finally my fingers slid over her sex, I could feel from just that initial touch that she was aroused, her lips felt puffy under my fingertips, and the thick tufts of hair around those lips was moist, I wasn't one for a very hairy woman. In fact it was since I had mentioned it, that Sybil had taken a cut throat razor down there and was now most of the time smooth, soft and hairless, she reported that everything felt so much nicer and more sensitive. I knew she had, after a few too close shaves roped in the young butler she employed for the size of his cock rather than his abilities as a butler to undertake the task for her. I myself if I was ever to spend more than a passing dalliance with a woman generally launched upon their short and curlies with a razor, and all had reported how much they enjoyed both the shaving and the sensations afterwards. But, as Lucy was someone I had never before laid my fingers on she was as nature intended it, and as my fingers delved further into her soft, warm and wet flesh I could tell she had a jolly decent thatch down there. I resolved if there was time sometime over the weekend, I would get her laid out on a table with her legs strapped up and open, and I would remove every last sign of it.

Feeling her wriggling about and seeing her gasping just ever so slightly, as she attempted to continue to eat her meal and converse with those around her. This amused me greatly, there was not a month that went by, when two, three or more people unable to wait would either get rather involved at the dining table, and sometimes even scamper off to other rooms. In fact as I looked down I could see at least four people who had availed themselves of their dining companion's mouth.

I shifted my chair very slightly, giving me just a little more arm length, so now I really did have her needy tight little cunt at my disposal. She had had no children, and at just 20 years old, I knew she wasn't very experienced. She was a fairly new addition to our group, having been brought in a few months ago by her employer, for whom she worked as a lady's maid. Mrs Isabelle Weston was a woman who had been attending regularly with her husband. On first glance they both appeared to be a very respectable middle-aged couple, in fact, he was currently sat at the table, only eating when she nodded and ready at any moment to do exactly as she bid. I knew from their attendance, that he needed a certain type of dominance to enjoy himself, and his wife, loving him enough had over the years developed so she was able to become aroused as he did. They had both seen something in Lucy and had introduced her to the set. She was pretty, flirty and loved attention, she was what I would describe as fuck meat. She had no particular kink, she just enjoyed men's attention and loved sex. There were a good few of the same type of women in our group, they fulfilled a much needed role of being readily available. There were of course, men who fulfilled exactly the same role within the group and were as valued and needed as women like Lucy.

I looked over and smiled at Lucy, who was now fairly unable to disguise her delight and arousal. She grinned back at me, and closed her eyes briefly as my fingers which I knew were now soaking wet delved as deep as they could inside her. I slipped a second finger in as I pulled out, and held both fingers apart as much as I could, curling one finger up whilst inside her to stroke that slightly rougher patch inside her. She then started to murmur and had a little whimper, as I knew she would, it was therefore obvious to all around where my hand was. Of course no one really cared what it was we were up to, they were all too busy themselves drinking, eating, relaxing and making new connections.

I looked over and saw Sybil and Cassandra watching, they had been deep in conversation just a few moments ago, but now it seemed they were suddenly more interested in what I was doing. I glanced towards Sybil who flicked her head just a tiny bit in Cassandra's direction and then shook her head slowly. I knew what she was saying, after speaking to Cassandra, she had decided we were a perfect match, and was now warning me off, 'performing' in front of her as I would doubtless send her off running back to her bed chamber and her hot water bottle. I just shrugged in my friend's direction and turned my attention quickly back to Lucy, who was still wriggling about, my fingers were so practised that they had continued despite my mind briefly wandering.

Lucy was now holding onto the bottom of the thick damask table cloth, with so much force I thought she might pull it and the entire contents of the table into her lap. Never one to make anything easy, I grinned as I swiftly pulled my fingers out of her wet hole and pushing my chair back with my heels as I did. I leaned over, grabbed the back of her chair and shoved her back just enough so that I could then reach and slide my hands up her thighs, pulling those voluminous skirts ever upwards as I then pulled her onto my lap her wet pussy was pressed against my still very well buttoned up trousers, putting my hands on her shoulders. I pushed her downwards, my hands then wrapping about her hips I thrust them forward so her pussy pressed against the thick material of my clothing, but I knew she could feel my rock solid hard cock pushing up through my trousers, leaning forward I whispered in her ear.

"Well unbutton me, there is a good girl, how can I fuck that lovely wet pussy of yours whilst I am still confined", she didn't need telling twice. She reached her nimble, and rather more practised than I was expecting fingers down to my groin where she very quickly and efficiently freed my manhood from its confines. With one hand on the small of her back I leaned back and relaxed letting her work away. Picking up my wine glass, I took a large mouthful just as slightly cool, very soft hands finally wrapped themselves around my now fully erect cock, which had just most satisfyingly sprung from its clothing confines, straight into those soft hands. Putting the wine glass down,

I shifted my backside just slightly so as to push my crotch upwards, Lucy glanced down and smiled. She really was very pretty, a wide friendly mouth framed with full lips, and large bright green eyes giving her an open engaging look which I, at this moment, found incredibly endearing. So much so that I reached up and grabbing her around the back of the neck, I pulled her face to mine crushing my lips against hers, she greedily and happily returned my kiss, her tongue making its way into my mouth, before I had a chance to even think about moving mine. She kissed, it would seem like she did everything with a life loving gusto; pulling back from the kiss, I growled softly and bit her bottom lip before removing her hands from my shaft and grinning moving her again upwards so she was almost standing, ready to sink herself down on my waiting very hard pole. Rather suddenly she moved out of the way, and leaning down she again kissed me but more softly this time. Without a word she reached down between her full breasts and removed a small package, which she appeared to be unravelling, it took me a moment to see she had a sheath in her hand, and it looked to be a decent quality one, she leaned down and whispered.

"I always use 'em, my Mistress says I must, she doesn't want me down with the syphilis, or even worse with child, so she buys 'em for me". I shrugged and nodded, acquiescing and allowing her to place it over my shaft. Looking down watching, she continued grinning whispering.

"Don't worry, it's a new one".

I have used them myself in the past when in slightly less than respectable whore houses. So I knew the key was to get the damn thing on as quickly as possible and start the copulating, too much delay and the excitement was gone, and with that rubber covering your cock it was hard to get it back again, get it quickly up inside a warm and wet cunt, the sheath warmed up and so did you. So the very moment, she had managed to slide it over the head of my cock, I removed her hands, placing them around my neck, I grunted and shoved her down in one swift hard movement onto my erection, and of course this forced the rest of the sheath onto my cock. Lucy whimpered loudly as I entered her, my hands moving to rest under her skirts on her hips I leaned forward and spoke quietly into her ear.

"Make me wear one of these darn things girl, you are going to have to ride me really hard, I can't feel a damn thing" with that I reached up and after untying the pale pink ribbon which held together the bodice of her dress, I pulled it apart, her breasts deliciously spilled out onto my hands and I grabbed both of them none too gently. Her nipples were already hard, smiling feeling her wince as I pinched them both roughly, before my hands then cupped them; her breasts were full and felt warm and heavy in my hands. She closed her eyes just as I leaned down and grabbing her breasts harder this time I pulled them upwards so I could close my mouth over each of her very large very hard nipples, biting softly as first, and then harder as I heard her gasp and whimper, she made as if to pull away, but my hands clamped around those soft gorgeous mounds ensured she stayed exactly where she was.

In response to my attention to her breasts, she started to move faster, she had until that moment been fairly slowly riding my cock, using her legs she was able to push herself upwards so I almost left her body, and then she would slowly slide down again, her pussy lips stretching, to accommodate me, but my attention and insistent biting, was having its desired effect, and she now started to fuck, hips rounding as she rode like a professional, flinging her head back. I let go of her breasts watching as they started to bounce with each thrust, I grunted a little myself, even though the sheath was not ideal, her movements were so agile and energetic that the rubber covering was wrinkling and moving almost exciting me more. I glanced about me and saw that the noisier Lucy had become, the more attention we were garnering from our fellow diners. So much so in fact that Colonel Winters who was always present, but being a voyeur never did much more than find himself a comfy seat and watch, so although after dinner he was rarely acknowledged, he was so charming, friendly and interesting, he always was welcome. He had moved himself back a little from his seat and was obviously watching and masturbating, his hands had freed his penis from its confines and I could see that his female companion was offering to assist him, and he rather uncharacteristically had allowed her to. Just as Lucy had started to speed up, I could see him relinquishing his cock to a rather voluptuous woman, sitting next to him, her chubby bejewelled hands disappearing under the table. I licked my lips and grinned, lucky sod, I loved a well-padded woman to fuck, so superbly and luxuriously well padded, I always rather felt it was like fucking in First Class.

Rather than make me lose my concentration, all this drifting away from the lovely woman currently bouncing on my shaft only served to heighten my enjoyment as I turned back to Lucy, her eyes met mine and she smiled in-between needy murmurs and whimpers. I reached up and we kissed again, tongues dancing, I could taste the salt from the small sheen of sweat on her face, I shifted her ever so slightly forward, so my cock was totally straight going inside her, I placed two fingers on her clit, which was swollen and poking out from its little hood, I pulled away from the kiss and whispered so only she could hear.

"Not long now Lucy, let me feel you come while I fuck you, you move at the speed you want, and press my fingers harder if you need, there's a good girl." She didn't speak, but I could tell from her actions she had heard me, I felt her urgency grow, she brought her knees up, and hooked her legs about the chair, planting her feet firmly down on the legs so she could ride me ever quicker and faster, she didn't move my fingers and so I let my now sodden hand move in time with her movements. She pounded my cock as hard as she could, I took my other hand, and wrapped it around the back of her neck, pulling her face downwards towards mine, I wanted to hear the little grunts and whimpers she was now making, we locked eyes and I nodded encouragingly to her, just as she thrust her hips forward in a rocking motion, so that now, as she lifted herself up, and then slammed her body back down onto my cock, she also thrust her body forwards. This was enough to send us both to the edge, and I caught my breath, and steadied myself for just a moment, managing to hold off my climax just long enough for her to reach the end of her race. I knew she was coming; my cock was being squeezed even through that awful sheath by the most delightful powerful contractions, which seemed to go on for ever as her whole body tensed for a few moments, her whimpers in her final few thrusts turned from gentle to almost primal. Able myself to finally let go, I flung my head back and lifted my hips off from the chair as I powerfully thrust myself deeply into Lucy, her body was shaking, and I knew having already come just a few moments prior, that I was riding my climax into the tail end of hers, our eyes were still locked as I almost bucked off the chair finally coming, two more long hard thrusts, with my hands on both her shoulders holding her, so I was inside as deep as possible, and I was instantly spent.

We were both panting and grinning at each other, as Lucy lifted herself up and off my rapidly softening pole, leaning down between my legs, she grabbed the sheath and pulled it upwards and off in one movement, rolling it up, she placed it inside a handkerchief she had pulled from somewhere about her person. I reached up and kissed her softly, she smiled returned the kiss and then climbed off my lap. She gave a rather interesting little shake of her hips, almost I thought to ensure everything was in the right place, she turned to me, whilst retying the ribbon of her bodice, still smiling as she spoke.

"Well, that is the earliest I have enjoyed myself of an evening, I don't think I have touched my dinner, I wasn't very hungry before, now I'm famished". I laughed loudly and nodded, as we both with some veracity tucked into the plates of food that were still laid in front of us, grabbing my wine glass, I held it up to her.

"I will drink to you Lucy, I didn't realise what a nice little mover you are, quirky little find for your employers I would have thought", she had her face currently stuffed with roast chicken, and her chin was covered in grease, her fingers grasped in one hand the leg of chicken she was eating, whilst the other held a fork which was laden with potatoes. I realised she had moved on, one of her needs had been sated, and she was therefore onto the next physical need, so when she just nodded and said something with her mouth full, which I couldn't decipher, I merely leaned over and kissed her exposed shoulder, before turning to my right to speak with Raj.

Raj had been a friend since we were at boarding school together, seemingly eons ago, there had been three of us, myself, Prince Rajmata Vishwanah, known by his friends as Raj and Simon who was now the Earl of Thatchingham. We had become firm friends, mainly due to the fact that we were the only three in our dorm who utterly refused the advances of the older boys for whom we had to fag. They having themselves been buggered senseless in their first years as boarders, felt it was only their right to continue to do this once they were the older boys, with their own fags to abuse. However, I was fairly big for my age and was handy with my fists, Raj simply refused and threatened that he would tell his father, who as a member of the

Indian royal family would ensure all of the boys would be sent to prison (all rot of course but he was so sincere with his lies), and Simon, well Simon hid. He was at school, a rather small and weedy boy, but he was also exceptionally intelligent, and knew he would have ended up fagging for his entire school career. So with the common bond of keeping our bottoms safe, we forged a friendship which has lasted until this very day. Both men were part of the founders of the Carnal Set, and Raj being a dominant like myself, often brought with him women he had chosen and found with me in mind. Simon, I knew, was far more passive, he was married to a fabulously horsy rather manly woman called Elizabeth and she ran the house, and their relationship. I knew she had to approve all the men Simon wanted to have sex with, and she would very often watch and direct, because, despite Simon's excellent hiding habits at school, which had saved him, he was without doubt as homosexual as they come. His marriage to Elizabeth was borne out of love and understanding in equal measures, she was far more interested in the female sex, as he was the male, so between them they made the perfect team. Best friends and occasional lovers, had meant over ten years of happy marriage they had two handsome, if rather horsy looking sons.

Seeing I was finished with Lucy, Raj slapped me on the arm.

"Thorpe you old goat, we haven't even been served dessert, and there you are balls deep in a woman, I prefer not to mix my pleasures too much, the food you always serve is generally too good to miss out on". I saw Lucy, who despite her outward appearance of just stuffing her face had obviously been listening frowned at the balls deep comment and turn away from us so as to speak to her employers, who were seated just a little way down on the table from us, they had of course been watching our antics carefully. Not having any idea of the effect his words had had, he just continued.

"I have brought a couple of lovelies with me this month, both are Indian, my wife found them for me, twins would you believe it. Twins Thorpe, I don't think we have ever had twins before have we brother"? Raj and I very often would threesome or foursome together, although both of us were strictly into women only, we found that together our dominant traits really did complement each other. Raj although he had the ability to be far crueller than me, was often also tender and gentle, wanting his subs to adore and worship him. His own wife Bibi was a gorgeous and delightful creature, delicate as a flower, Raj utterly adored her, she was currently pregnant with their first child and so was absent but had obviously organised a couple of approved girls, to play with her husband. Bibi had been brought up to be naturally submissive to her husband, and her love for him and his for her, meant that although Raj played and enjoyed many women, he always came back to his Bibi, and he was fastidious about not bringing anything infectious home. When Bibi came along to our carnal set weekends, Raj allowed her always to choose who they played with, it was the one bit of control she was permitted, and she never made a mistake, always finding a woman or a man, or both who would complement her and her husband's enjoyment. I grinned at Raj.

"Twins eh Raj, that's a new one, I don't think we have had twins at our gatherings before. I shall definitely be interested in meeting them! I did have grand plans for a girl I invited, my governess believe it or not, well when I say my governess, I of course mean the children's governess, she has been here months, but can you believe I only noticed her today. This morning in fact, and well she is intriguing that is for sure, but that darn woman Sybil has taken her under her wing. I can see her and Poppy clucking over her like a pair of old mother hens, I mean really Raj, am I that foreboding that a girl would need the protection of that pair...hmmm well"?

I saw Raj peering over and finding Sybil and Poppy, and then of course Cassandra siting between them both, all three were deep in conversation and you could see the odd peal of laughter coming from them. They were chatting also to their dining companions, and of course it being Cassandra's first evening the vultures were circling, she was a prize indeed and there would be men, and women queuing up to spend some time introducing her to our world.

However, I wasn't too worried about someone stealing Cassandra from beneath my nose, if there was one thing Sybil was good at, it was keeping vultures at bay. She may be happy to whip Cassandra away from me, thinking it was a terribly fun sport to do so, however she wouldn't allow just anyone to leap on her, I knew however annoying, she was keeping her safe for me.

After Raj had spent a little time observing he turned to me and grinned.

"Now, she is a good looking woman my brother, but she is not a fling kind of girl, she will be wanting a husband that one! So the question is, are you hoping to persuade her that an evening or two with you is worth it, or are you now looking for a wife, and one slightly more suited than that awful woman you were married to?" My initial reaction to his words was to guffaw slightly, however as I looked over and saw Cassandra talking to Poppy, it was only now I could see how beautiful she was. Although I had seen her a few times, this evening and earlier in the bath I had seen plenty of her delectable body, all of my thoughts thus far had been centred around getting my hands upon her unspoiled flesh. I had seen her in abstract, full breasts, round hips, eyes which seemed far too knowing framed by shockingly dark lashes, and that full rosy mouth, it was only as I looked over now that I was able to put it all together and view her for what she was, a beautiful young woman, unspoiled and intelligent.

I felt myself frowning, this was not at all what I been after, and Raj could not be further from the truth, I was seeking, as always nothing more than pleasure, it could be fleeting, it could, as in the case of Sybil be reoccurring, but it was also no more than that. I did not want nor need a wife, or a mistress. The thought of someone having a say or trying to curtail my life in any way simply was not going to happen. It must have taken me a few moments to process these thoughts, because when I turned to answer Raj, he was sat with a very expectant look on his face, his eyebrows were raised and I knew he found it all very amusing.

"My old friend, you know me far better than to think I would ever be looking for a wife, I was just rather taken with the way she conducts herself, and deduced it would be so much fun to break all that down and have her quivering in my arms. It's sport brother, sport – you as much as anyone know that, as long as she enjoys herself it's all harmless now isn't it? So, let's not hear that M word uttered from your mouth again this evening". Raj simply nodded, continued to grin somewhat inanely and turned about in his chair to address the footman who had just arrived at our table. The man, whose name I think was Robert, bent down and whispered discretely in Raj's ear, smiling he stood up, slapping Robert on the arm.

"Excellent, excellent", he said, slapping Robert again on the back as the man walked away to continue his duties, Raj turned back to me.

"My twins have arrived, so I shall briefly sojourn and find the dear girls, make sure they are happy and well taken care of. I hope we can meet up later, and enjoy them together, of course I can't promise by then we won't all be the best of friends and well acquainted with each other", and with those words, and a low chuckle, he was off as ever, pleased as punch with himself.

"Lucky sod", I said as he wandered off, not to anyone in particular, more to the room in general. Raj really was a lucky sod, born to immense wealth in India, his parents having been rather clever had moved his entire family to London, just before British rule of India would have quite curtailed their lifestyles. Seen as refined and exotic, with the money to prove it, they were an instant hit in society, and had remained as thus ever since. Raj had travelled briefly to India to bring back Bibi, who brought with her an enormous dowry, it had been an arranged marriage of course, but one that suited both Raj and Bibi immensely. They fell in love within days of meeting, and Bibi's sweet nature, coupled with a surprisingly open mind had meant that she embraced Raj's extra marital activities, becoming part of them, rather than a lonely woman at home night after night.

As the tables were being cleared of the previous course, and the final offering of cheese and grapes were being laid out, I realised I hadn't really managed to eat anything at all. Grabbing a plate I greedily filled it up with cheese, bread and fruit, sitting back with another large glass of wine, I ate at some speed, watching the people about me. However, once my eyes landed on Cassandra, that is exactly where they stayed.

CHAPTER ELEVEN

Cassandra

I was surprisingly managing to pick my way through dinner; the odd delicious morsel was making its way to my mouth. Meeting Sybil and subsequently her lovely friend Poppy had been like a breath of fresh air, both women seemed so carefree and happy, neither were worried about what anyone else was doing, unless of course, it took their interest or fancy, at which point they were more than happy to get involved.

I had guessed that was what had happened when Sybil saw me with the Lord Pembroath, I had piqued her interest, and of course little did she know at that point, that she was in fact saving my life! That was rather over dramatic, but my resolve had most certainly been wavering. As my employer had shown me around and introduced me to people, there had been part of me wanting to just collapse onto him and avail myself of smelling salts which I was sure more than a few of the women here had tucked away. But I just wasn't the fainting or hysterical type. I had the ability I knew to appear calm and in control, just when I was feeling anything but inside.

It really was the worst possible display of manners, the lack of respect he had shown by bringing me here this evening. How on earth did he think I would react? Perhaps he had heard my parents were both musicians, and had assumed that I would be used to such things, that my upbringing must have occurred within a harem. If he had really believed this, I found it incredible that he would employ me to be the guiding light and example for his children. This, therefore left the alternative, which was that he simply didn't care how I was feeling, or how I would react. His words warning me off telling anyone had made it perfectly clear that he feels absolutely untouchable. I feared I was perhaps just here for the sport of it; and if that was the case, there was no way I was going to give him what he wanted. Inside I may be slowly fainting away from shock, but on the outside I would, I steeled myself appear cool, calm and collected.

So when Sybil had appeared and been so terribly friendly, it had been with a light heart and a thankful smile that I had allowed her to whisk me away. I totally ignored the slight pang of something I couldn't quite describe as I left Lord Pembroath standing for a moment alone, our eyes met for just a second, and my heart banged in a way I had never experienced before. Luckily Sybil's constant chatter was a perfect foil for these feelings which I quickly rammed to the back of my head. Sybil introduced me to Poppy, her friend who, as the evening wore on, I understood to be slightly more than just a friend. It was true, I was ashamed almost to admit to myself that I had had no idea before this evening that such things actually happened between two women, I had heard of course that some men were unable to control their primal urges with each other and indulged in what were described as illegal and vile practices, but two women actually sounded really quite nice. Of course I was rather naive about everything that happened between a man and a woman in the bedroom, and so I guessed I was as uninformed about two women.

But nonetheless Poppy seemed, despite her outward appearance, which included a rather nasty scar given to her, I was told by an angry man not wishing to pay for what he had used, and a voice obviously not schooled in anyway, she was kind, generous and seemed too sweet a nature to have lived the life that Sybil alluded she had done before they met.

Once seated for dinner, I availed myself of yet another rather large glass of wine, and looked about me. Since I had been with Sybil, the rest of my dining companions had become far friendlier, I was inundated with people wishing to talk to me, and find out who I was.

Apparently there were not new people every month, and I was something of a first time novelty.

Dinner was a delicious affair with every kind of cold cut and meat you could think of, teamed with potatoes which were boiled, mashed or roasted and big platters of salads and vegetables. The footmen serving the meal kept up a continual round of drinks topped up. I understood from Sybil that for the staff who served at these gatherings, as they were specially chosen and their discretion was absolutely needed, their remuneration was very simply, that for every two months they served at the table and looked after the guests, the third month they attended as guests themselves. This of course explained the staff members who I had seen earlier. Poppy explained, and I agreed that having people from every different class and walk of life meant that the Carnal Set (which is what I was told this monthly gathering was called) was unique, with no barriers as to who was invited, apart from the fact that no one was paid to attend. I found myself feeling almost calm, despite my initial shock and my lack of understanding, once people started to talk to me, I realised these were some of the nicest people I had ever met. Had I perhaps been a little more religious than I actually was, I may have had a harder job accepting what was happening around me, but as it was, religion had always been something I paid lip service to. It all seemed rather farfetched, neither of my parents had been regular church goers, as musicians Sundays was often the only day they were not either performing or practising. As far as I could make out, everyone here was here because they wanted to be.

I had been mulling all this over in my mind whilst half listening to Sybil and Poppy telling me in hushed tones all about the other diners, when I looked up and saw Lord Pembroath. He was sitting at the head of the very long table, which of course was his right and privilege, him being the host and all, sat next to him was a rather pretty young woman, she didn't look to me to be of very well breeding. Her manners when the food had come around left little to be desired, and her elbows, arms and hands were splayed about the table rather indiscriminately. But it seemed my employer didn't mind this at all. Sybil was explaining to me, how he, Lord Pembroath that is, always sat a different young woman next to him, that way none of them would get any ideas it was ever any more than it was. This said, amongst the women it was seen as a coo, and this young lady, named Lucy, was obviously enjoying her moment at the head.

My attention was then taken by the rather dashing and handsome young man opposite me, Sybil had introduced him as Captain something or other – there were so many new names and faces I just couldn't keep up. His smile though was engaging and I instantly felt guilty that I had no clue as to his name, because his voice and demeanour were just as pleasant.

"Cassie, isn't it? Or should I call you Cassandra, both are terribly pretty names", he said without his eyes leaving my face.

"Oh, oh, oh", I replied feeling ridiculously flustered.

"Cassie is just fine; I am rather enjoying being called that old nickname". He nodded briefly before continuing.

"So tell me dear Cassie, with this being your first visit to our happy little gathering, what brings you? Are you married, if so who to, and is he or she here? I do hope not, you look like someone, one might want to get to know better. What is your kink Cassie, whatever it might be, do not fear there will be someone here who will be a perfect match, if only for the night, I must confess, I am rather hoping we both enjoy the same kind of things though"?

I had of course been listening intently to his words, not wanting to appear as green as I really was, I had been hoping for something a little more simple, a conversation about the weather say, or even the meal, but nope it would seem I really was surrounded by people for whom the sexual was the every day, I smiled and shrugged, deciding that honesty really had to be best policy I said to him.

"Well, your enquiry is very interesting, but I am not sure I have a kink, or actually even know what one is, I am a governess you see, in fact I am the governess here, for Lord Pembroath's children. I hadn't met him until today, he invited me to dinner, and it wasn't until I arrived here, and came through those rather large and imposing doors, that I realised it really was more than just dinner." I paused for just a moment as the young man's mouth had fallen open and was looking like he was almost gasping for breath, he leaned over and unable to actually reach my hand across the wide table, he just stretched his fingers out, and laid his arm on the table in an almost plaintive manner.

I looked across to Poppy, who I had just heard chuckling lightly, she caught my eye and winked, before addressing the man.

"Now, now, Rupert, Cassie here is finding the whole experience rather enjoyable, she doesn't need a shoulder to cry on, you think my Sybil would let anything awry happen"? The man, who of course I now knew was called Rupert, grinned and I straight away knew that his apparent sympathy had been somewhat over stated. I felt Poppy squeeze my hand as she carried on almost berating Rupert.

"So if Cassie decides she likes us enough to want to join us, then I am sure you will be one of the first to know, but until then, please assume she is under the undeniably fierce protection of Sybil". With that she winked and grinned and Rupert nodded just a little bit ruefully.

"Well Cassie", he said turning his attention back to me.

"I am rather pleased to meet you, and I do hope you are not so shocked that you never come back. I for myself, am one of the more mundane of those who attend, I just enjoy people, women or men its all the same to me, I like the intimacy that can only be found when bodily fluids are exchanged". I found myself smiling and almost laughing, had that sentence been said to me, about two hours ago, I think it is safe to say I would have probably needed some smelling salts, but as it was his words sounded almost sensible, which meant I was able to speak in a somewhat calm and what I hoped was friendly tone.

"Thank you so much, I have to say that despite my obvious greenness, I am rather enjoying meeting everyone"; and it was with those words that I heard a noise from the end of the table, and suddenly found myself not enjoying the evening anywhere near as much.

CHAPTER TWELVE

Cassandra

I saw that both Sybil and Poppy's eyes were fixed upon the end of the table, where I knew Lord Pembroath was sitting. At last glance I had seen him chatting to the pretty young woman, who looked a year or so younger than me, but was obviously far more confident than me. I could see she was almost bursting with what I assumed to be pride at the fact she was sat at the head of the table with the handsome host as her dining companion. I had decided not to glance over to him, I was still not sure as to his motives for bringing me here tonight, but I having almost certainly decided there was something of the hint of it being for the sport of it. If that really was the case, then I had no intention whatsoever of doing anything to make it easier for him to enjoy his sport. But the fact that so many of my fellow diner's faces were now glancing upwards towards that end of the table meant my own curiosity got the better of me, and the moment I looked, I wished I hadn't.

From what I could gather, my eyes were arriving on the scene after Lord Pembroath, and his young lady friend had already been enjoying each other's company for a while, I could see his hands on her breasts, the nipples of which even from this distance I could see were hard and as his fingers were pinching them, extremely hard I thought, I could see her simultaneously flinching and whimpering, all of which made him be even rougher. I swallowed hard, unsure partly of what I was watching, but also, there were unexplained feelings of not quite jealousy and not quite hurt, I just felt irked, shocked and a

76

little like crying.

I took a deep breath and turned to Sybil, who had turned slightly in my direction, with an almost sympathetic look playing over her rather beautiful face.

"Sybil", I whispered.

"Is this normal? Is it part of a show or a performance, does he always do this"? At those words Sybil didn't exactly laugh, but I could see my words had caused some mirth, but as soon as she turned totally to face me, and seen the look on my face, her own face dropped to one of a solemnness as she grabbed my hand and spoke softly.

"No, no, no dear, not every time, Thorpe is just doing what Thorpe does, he likes women, and when sat next to a young wench like that who will have been fluttering her eyelashes and flirting with him from the very moment she realised where she was sitting, he simply can't resist. This is what happens at these evenings, myself I am a little more reserved, and tend to wait and choose my partners carefully, I prefer a little privacy you see. I will happily indulge with men, women or both at the same time, but I like some comfort and I dislike the thought that others are watching and enjoying. Thorpe, well Thorpe has something of the exhibitionist about him and sometimes can't help himself, but I suspect it also has something to do with you. The way he looked at you earlier, there was just the hint of something approaching true attraction and interest, and our boy Thorpe, well he can't handle that. He is utterly convinced he will never fall in the L word, or be as he sees it, tethered by or to another woman. So without realising it, this little show is him telling you just that".

I know I looked utterly confused, and as she continued speaking, Sybil was now stroking my hand ever so lightly.

"Don't worry Cassie dear, for Thorpe a fleshpot like that one there, whose name I believe is Lucy is just that, someone to enjoy and then move on. But well if you are curious keep watching, I suspect you won't ever have seen a man and a women fucking before, it might just whet your appetite". With that she laughed softly but good naturedly. I didn't say a word but I also didn't let go of Sybil's hand. I watched from my seat at the table, partly interested, partly horrified, and partly I knew aroused as Lord Pembroath seemingly without any effort on his part plucked the woman from her seat and with her skirts raised high enough so that the rest of the viewing table caught flashes of her round fleshy bottom, he thrust her somewhat unceremoniously down on his lap. Her breasts were still revealed, and his hands didn't stop their grabbing, and almost kneading of them. I saw him whispering to her; saw her face flushed and smiling, watched as he crushed his lips to hers in a manner which seemed almost violent. There was then what felt to be a short break in proceedings as she leaned down and I assumed unlaced his clothing, I nor anyone but him or her could actually see what she pulled from his britches, but from the look on his face and the low grunt that he emitted, I gathered it was his manhood. I had never actually seen a grown man's penis, I knew what lay there between their legs, but it was a sketchy knowledge. Something which since my employment as a governess and the almost total erasing of my marriage prospects, I had assumed was going to stay sketchy. However I felt myself grinning wryly to myself as I realised that my invitation to this evening, with this interesting group of people meant my education, if not my personal experience was going to be dramatically improved.

The sound of the woman whimpering brought me out of my thoughts and sent my eyes straight back down the end of the table; where I could see that the both of them were now lost in what they were doing. It was as if no one else existed, I could see Lord Pembroath's face, and hear both of them making noises akin to what I assumed animals sounded like. The volume in the room had gone down slowly in increments as more and more people had looked up from their conversations and taken an interest in what was happening. It was at that point that as I glanced about the room, I noticed a man, who must have been well into his sixties, sporting a rather impressive moustache and military medals. He was seated next to a woman, about twenty years younger than him, and at least five stones heavier than everyone else in the room, she wore an amazing gown of emerald green, and her chubby fingers were adorned with jewels and rings. Her cleavage was an amazing sight and I could not quite believe her corset was managing to do the job it clearly was doing, of keeping her huge bosoms aloft. She was smiling at the moustached gentleman who very obviously had his breeches unlaced and I could just see the tops of his hands, as he watched the pair at the end of the table, touching himself, the woman whispered in his ear and without much of a smile, he nodded and relinquished his penis to her hands which were now almost greedily groping under the table. I couldn't help but smile, as all could then be seen was the glimmer of the jewels on the rings as her hands now moved at some speed under the table, which in turn caused that impressive cleavage to jiggle and bounce about much like how one would imagine a jelly on a horse and cart hurtling across a bumpy field would look. The man whose penis was currently in her obviously vice like grip was now torn between his view of those amazing bouncing breasts and the show being put on by the host and his current companion at the head of the vast dining table.

The couple at the end of the table won out for the man, just as they did for me, and I found my gaze returning back to them. I was watching with a combination of interest, horror, amazement and I was surprised to note just a pang or two of jealously. She was now riding him, how you might a fine hunter, her back was stretched out and her breasts when he released from his grip were bouncing to the rhythm of her actions. Every now and again, they would seem to pause, to almost lose their momentum as they kissed deeply. I saw him again speak to her, and his hands were then lost under her voluminous skirts, at his words, whatever they might be, she sped up and I could see that she was riding him now as fast as she dared. Her feet must have been planted on the floor and I could tell she was using them to lever herself up and steady herself as she moved down again. All of a sudden, she seemed for just a second to freeze, and then her hips thrust forward violently as she almost fell upon him, her whole body was quivering for just a moment as she moaned and whimpered even louder than she had been doing. He seemed to take this as some kind of cue, because his spare hand clamped onto her hips and he began bucking his hips upwards, it was just a few seconds before her whimpers and moans were joined by his low grunts. I saw them both then slow down, until their movements were bare shadows of what they had been a few moments earlier. He leaned up and kissed her softly, and for a short while they stared into each other's eyes, their breathing ragged and laboured.

My own heart was beating far faster than it should have been, and I could hear the loud timbre in my ears as I sat back, no longer looking, I had seen him lift her off him and she had almost immediately set into the plate of food set in front of her, whilst he had turned to the man at his side and they had begun conversing. Poppy turned to me and smiled.

"You ok lovely?" She asked, I nodded and attempted to look as nonchalant as possible.

"Oh, oh, yes, thank you I am fine, all of this is rather new to me. I have it would seem, lived a very sheltered life". Poppy nodded as she listened to me, pausing for just a moment before she spoke again.

"Yes, yes I am sure you have Cassie love, but no more than most women with your upbringing, you must not be fooled into thinking that whilst you were sleeping all of your peers and contemporaries have been behaving the way we do here, we are now and almost certainly always will be on the edge of society, disapproved off and secret. If you decide you like us, and this way of life, you also become someone on the edge of good society".

Sybil who had been listening to Poppy, also smiled and said.
"Yes, Poppy is right however what you must not forget is that in our world, society and people are the most friendliest you will find. I always think a bit of mainstream gossip and marginalisation is more than worth the warmth, friendship and love of those with whom we share this common interest. But you Cassie, you are not here as most, who already know what they want and like, you are here because your employer has taken a fancy to you. If you decide this isn't for you, I hope you won't judge us too harshly, I always hope there is room in this world for many different types of people. We aim to make the world an interesting, rather than perennially dull place".

I sat listening and despite everything, despite the shock, and the surprise at what I had seen this evening, when I answered Sybil it was completely truthfully.

"I can't promise that I will become part of this, I can't even promise that I will ever really understand it, but what I can promise is that I will never think badly of anyone who does. My world has become so very small since I came to work here. I have never lived a crazily cosmopolitan life, but before my father died I was happy in my social circle, it is not until you see another social circle of people that you realise loneliness has crept up on you. I adore being a governess to the children but meeting new people, however strange the circumstances are, is wonderful". As I said these final few words, I realised I was staring over to Lord Pembroath, who himself was appearing to just stare into space.

Both Sybil and Poppy grinned and simultaneously took my hands, starting to talk almost at the same time, but it Poppy who deferred and let Sybil have her say first.

"Cassie dear, I hope Poppy and I have found a new friend tonight, regardless as you say of whether or not you decide you are carnal enough for our set. Talking of which, after dinner which is of course ending soon, is when the real fun for many starts, but you should know, not everyone indulges every month, and for some just the atmosphere is more than enough. So don't you worry, if you want to stay after dinner, if all you want to do is wander about, or find a comfy seat somewhere and enjoy a drink, then no one will bother you at all. Poppy and I will be around all evening and will happily spend our time with you, we have no firm plans, and goodness me we have both pressed enough naked flesh against naked flesh to last a lifetime". As she was speaking Poppy was nodding, agreeing with her every word.

I took a moment to think, really I would have loved to have the company of these two women all evening, however as I had now decided that this really had to be a learning experience for me. I also admitted quietly to myself that I knew with the two ladies as my personal guards I would not speak to, or perhaps even see Lord Pembroath again this evening. Despite witnessing his earlier behaviour, I wanted to see him again this evening and perhaps even spend a little time with him. I had to be brave, so my answer however reluctant, was also resolute.

"Thank you both so much, I too hope I have made two new friends here tonight, you have made me feel so very welcome. But I wouldn't dream of holding you both back from your enjoyment of your evening, I shall spend some time exploring, I think I have now gathered my wits about me enough to not need any smelling salts, and to also be able to resist any advances."

Poppy and Sybil both smiled and like many of the diners rose from their seats, and both leaned over and kissed me, Poppy whispering.

"We will be about anytime you need us sweet Cassie", and with that they were off, holding hands, and looking all for all the world like a couple of school girls, as their heads came close together and I heard them laughing and giggling together.

CHAPTER THIRTEEN

Cassandra

The vast dining table was slowly emptying, I received many smiles, nods and hellos as people walked past me, I was struck with how relaxed everyone seemed as they wandered away. Some were making their way into the main part of the large hall we were all currently inhabiting, and some heading off through one of the four doors which led off the hall.

Before I knew it, the table was empty and I was the only one left sitting looking I suspected a little forlorn, gathered around were footmen and the maids who had been serving all waiting to begin clearing the table, a task I knew they would not begin until I moved. So it was somewhat reluctantly that I did exactly that, rising slowly and grasping my wine glass as if for comfort. I turned and headed back into the main hall area, where the fire had been stoked so it was a blazing furnace of heat. Darkness had fallen in the time since we had sat down for dinner, and I saw that seemingly hundreds of candles had been lit in two huge chandeliers hanging from the ceiling, in sconces on the walls, and set upon every table and surface were candelabras. The rest of the house was well equipped with gas lamps, and upon moving in I had been taken on a tour by a very proud housekeeper, showing me every darn lamp and explaining how the Master had spent unthinkable sums having the main house lit by gas lamps. However it would seem he had not done the same here, instead he was spending the entire yearly budget on candles for a

small village in one night. I could instantly see why, the room was vast, but with the fire blazing, all the candles lit and the sumptuous furniture and fittings, I doubted I had seen a more comfortable or inviting space in all my life. Add to this some of the most interesting people you could meet and I was suddenly overwhelmed again. This world it seemed was beyond my sophistication or understanding.

I took a large gulp of wine from my rapidly emptying glass, and decided to take one of the four doors and see what I could find. With the glass still grasped tightly in my hands I made my way to the nearest door, pausing for a moment or two as I walked past. I saw Rupert, who I had met earlier, he had teamed up with a woman who although was at least twice his age, was utterly stunning. I could see Rupert was slowly stripping her and she was standing stock still allowing him to, it was almost as though he was worshipping her. She had her eyes closed and he was reverentially removing her clothing, his fingers had just finished unlacing her gown, which was a deep dark purple, embellished with black lace and feathers. He removed the dress carefully, and I saw her nod almost unperceivably, at which sign Rupert stood behind her and started placing soft kisses over her collar bone, the woman was incredibly slender, her skin in the candlelight appeared almost luminescent, her neck was stretched out, and curly dark hair was spilling out from the messy bun on top of her head. She licked her lips and still without opening her eyes, murmured in what I assumed was approval and delight, as Rupert's lips skimmed their way over her skin stopping when he came to stand in front of her. At this point he reached up, and started to unlace the woman's corset, her slender frame seemed almost willowy and I could see small breasts currently pushed together and upwards by the corset which was swiftly being removed.

Rupert looked up and saw me standing there very obviously staring, but instead of chiding me, he instead just grinned, leaned forward and poking his tongue out licked his way down from her neck to the small dip between those tiny breasts. I saw the woman shiver and wriggle just the merest amount, Rupert looked up again and winked at me as at that moment he had finally finished unlacing her corset and he quickly pulled it away, placing it carefully down next to her dress which was laying crumpled on the floor.

She was now stood wearing nothing but some very expensive

looking bloomers, Rupert turned his attention away totally from me, still standing in front of her he cupped her breasts in both his hands before squeezing gently and leaning forward to kiss her lips softly. At first she didn't move, her eyes were still firmly shut, but as his hands moved down from her breasts to run over her hips and down under the silk of her bloomers, she murmured again and this time as he kissed her, she met his lips and they stood together. His hands now on her hips, slowly moving down removing the bloomers, their kissing was incredibly sensual, her hands hadn't moved, and lay down by her side as it appeared both put all their energies into the kiss. I was rooted to the spot, and despite telling myself I should be moving, was unable to do so just yet. Rupert opened his hands, and the bunches of silken cloth in his grasp fell to the floor. The woman stepped to the side, she was now completely naked, whilst Rupert was fully clothed. It was at that point that she opened her eyes and I saw in the candlelight large luminous dark eyes fixing their gaze with Rupert's, and I knew at that moment that for the two of them, no one else existed, I wasn't really there at all. I started to move away, feeling inexplicably sad, I looked back as I heard a soft gasp and saw his hand disappear between her legs, I didn't stop, feeling for the first time this evening as though I was intruding, it didn't matter that the two of them had started and it would seem were continuing their love making in a room full of people.

I finally walked out into a small ante room, furnished with more soft chairs, erotic art and a blazing fire in the grate. I noticed this was where the staff working, had stored the drinks for the evening. A small fashioned wine cellar could be seen through an open door, and I could make out footmen sitting with their feet up whilst a couple of others refilled carafes of wine. When they saw me looking, one of the men jumped up and came out of the room with a smile upon his face and a carafe of wine in his hand, he started to fill the wine glass I suddenly realised I still had grasped against my belly.

"Yes Miss, can we help you, were you looking for a refill? You don't need to come out here; there are plenty of footmen with trays wandering all the rooms". I nodded and allowed him to fill the glass, before turning and smiling as I answered him.

"Oh no, thank you though, I am simply exploring, I haven't been here before you see". It was his turn to grin and nod as he spoke.

"Oh yes Miss, we know you're the governess ain't you, we were surprised to see you here tonight, but pleasantly so of course, my name is Ruthers, Will Ruthers. Next month is my weekend to indulge, I hope you might be here again enjoying an evening of pleasure, and I would hope you might find some time to enjoy some of that pleasure with me Miss. I can assure you I know how to treat a beautiful well-bred woman like ya'self". It was at those final few words that I heard stifled laughter coming from the cellar, the other men had obviously been listening to Ruthers. I felt myself blushing from head to foot, and not really know what to say, I took a large sip of the wine, which far too predictably, went down the wrong way leaving me stood there coughing and spluttering over Ruthers. He quickly took the opportunity to move a little closer so he could pat me on my back, something I didn't really need of course, I could still hear snickering coming from the cellar, and I was now at the point of just wishing the earth would open up and eat me up. It was just at that moment that I heard a low male voice calling out impatiently.

"Ruthers, get yourself back to work now man, I am not beyond throwing anyone who abuses my trust and their plum job, out on their backside in the middle of the night". Despite my choking, I almost found myself laughing, Ruthers who had up to that moment appeared relaxed and almost languid in his movements suddenly stood about three inches taller, immediately moved back from me and stood at a respectable distance. He then incredibly, executed a quick bow before walking backwards away from me back into the small cellar from where he had appeared.

It seemed that the surprise not only had an effect on Ruthers, but also myself, as I appeared to not be coughing or choking anymore, however I knew I felt hot and bothered, and was sure I was still blushed on every bit of visible skin, and in fact on every bit that wasn't. Of course, I knew exactly who that voice belonged to, and my tummy did an inexplicable flip as I prepared to turn around and greet him. When I finally did there he was, apparently well recovered from his earlier exertions, smiling that wry, almost teasing smile of his. I could see two rows of perfectly straight white teeth, and for just a moment my eyes took in his mouth, lips with a deep cleft on the upper he slowly stopped smiling, and I saw for just a second his tongue rub over those perfect teeth. He had a little stubble I noticed just below his bottom lip, he was clean shaven, and recently clean shaven at that, but his valet, or perhaps he had missed just the merest hint directly below his bottom lip. His chin was also clefted, not as deeply as his lips, but just enough so that his chin appeared to me, in that lost moment to be utterly perfect.

I realised he was almost certainly waiting for me to look up, or to say something, but I was lost in my reverie, my eyes were now darting along his jaw bone, which was strong and perfectly set, I was, just as he cleared his throat, staring at two small dark moles I had spotted on his neck just below the perfect jawline. Finally, after the throat clearing continued I looked up and met his gaze. Now I had finally forced myself to look at his entire face, rather than just the abstract perfect parts which made up his face, I could see he was highly amused. This was only confirmed when he started talking.

"Cassandra, Cassandra, or should I call you Cassie? You seemed more than happy for Sybil to do just that". I nodded my head a little too enthusiastically at the mention of Sybil's name.

"Oh yes Sir, Cassie is just fine and you have such lovely friends, Sybil and Poppy were so kind to me, you are lucky to have such kind and dear friends". He didn't seem to agree with me as I saw him briefly suck his teeth and bite the inside of his mouth before he spoke again.

"Well yes, aren't they a delight, I am pleased you seem to have enjoyed yourself so much this evening. And, its Thorpe, my name is Thorpe I think that in this most relaxed of settings that first names for all are more than appropriate, and mine is Thorpe, and you are now Cassie it would seem. I do have to be honest, I think I prefer Cassandra".

I swallowed hard, willing the blush to depart, and my breathing to return to some kind of normality. I wondered briefly just how long I would get to spend with him this time. Now I knew what happened at these gatherings, I would imagine that my innocence and absolute resolute decision not to join in.....just yet, would render me a most boring of companion, but it was with a hopefully light friendly voice that I answered him.

"I will do my best to remember, it's rather hard to suddenly stop seeing someone as your employer, Lord Pembroath, and turn them into Thorpe, the man stood in front of me. But I confess I am grateful to you for your invitation, I adore my life with your children, however it is very safe to say, that since moving here my invitations to social gatherings have been somewhat totally and utterly missing therefore the chance to meet such interesting people has been very gratefully received".

I could see a look of faint surprise on his face, as he took my arm, and led me away from the servants who were no doubt still listening to our conversation; it had only been recently, since entering the grey area of governess that I had realised just how involved with a household the staff were and how much the servants knew. Half closed doors, vents, grates and just open flapping jaws not noticing an almost invisible housemaid meant that the servants oftentimes knew more of what was happening in a house than the inhabitants did. I was therefore rather grateful to be led away from those open ears, I leaned slightly closer to him as we walked, in the manner of someone making sure they can hear a confidence, despite the fact the small hallway was almost totally silent. The only noises being the hushed tones of the serving staff, and the odd person trotting up and down heading to one of the doors that led off to, at this point, I didn't know where.

As he started to speak, he seemed not to mind my almost conspiratorial stance, and certainly he didn't lean away from me. I couldn't help for just a moment before he spoke to feel rather warm, comfortable and intimate with him. He smelled musky, of a scent I couldn't identify and when he started to speak, I could smell wine and cigars on his breath. I found that the tummy flipping was back, and my skin was starting to feel hot again, so when his hand moved from holding my elbow in a respectable fashion, to being placed on the small of my back in a manner that was certainly not respectable I caught my breath, but did absolutely nothing to move away from him. However I couldn't help but smile and only just manage to not laugh.

"I am then rather glad I invited you Cassie, and even though my dearest friend Sybil saw it fit to steal you away from me, I am rather pleased I have found you again, and if you will allow me, perhaps we can continue what we started earlier and finish our tour"? He paused then, but seeing me smiling and most definitely almost laughing he looked at me quizzically.

"Have I said something to amuse you"? He asked with just the merest hint of annoyance. I paused for just a moment, which gave me just enough time to weigh up my options, I quickly decided that honest was going to serve me best in this situation and turned to him, looking up as I did.

"When you placed your hand on the small of my back, my initial reaction was surprise and the thought of respectability ran through my head, my look of amusement, and obviously trying not to laugh was when I realised how ridiculous that was. I have witnessed tonight so much, so as to make a hand in the small of my back not only respectable, but tame and harmless". He immediately joined in my mirth, and laughed, using the hand which was the centre of our conversation to pull me slightly closer to him, an action I couldn't help but welcome and love.

"Well then Cassie", he stopped then again, and frowned.

"No, damn it, Cassandra, you are Cassandra, Cassie is very pretty and nice, but you are Cassandra, let the others call you Cassie, I shall keep Cassandra....so Cassandra I shall not be worried about keeping my hand there then, I am rather surprised at your reaction to this evening, perhaps I slightly underestimated you. I was expecting a quivering wreck needing smelling salts, instead you seem to be actually enjoying yourself and interested in our hidden world". With those last few words, I felt his fingertips dance over my back, which was still covered in corset and dress, but regardless the touch felt warm and my skin seemed just a little bit more alive.

Whilst speaking we had been stationary, but now he pushed me just a little bit, into a walk and we made our way towards one of the doors. Just as he leaned over to open the door, I stilled and turned my head up to him as I spoke.

"I would, of course, love to continue what we started earlier, but I hope you understand I am not really ready, and not really sure if I shall ever be, to join in. I have found myself intrigued by what I have seen, and very interested. Friendly welcoming people and an atmosphere I have never felt before have all combined to make this one of the most interesting evenings I have ever had. I do hope therefore my company will not be too tiresome for you. After watching you at dinner, I have the feeling you are normally in the centre of activities, indulging in everything you possibly can".

He didn't say anything for a moment, but smiled removing his hand from the door and turning his gaze downwards, his whole body also turned and almost pressed against mine, which of course had the reaction he must have known it would, I felt myself relaxing a little so as to almost, but not quite, melt into him.

I realised and knew he was playing me a little like one might with a puppy, but I couldn't make myself mind. I tried to conjure up the images of him rutting with that woman earlier to give me a little strength to gather myself and pull away, but it was useless, despite seeing that, and despite his actions, I was currently almost helpless to do little more than blush and attempt to stand as straight and upright as I possibly could.

It was almost a whole minute I was sure, before he spoke again, his green eyes I noticed during this time were flecked with bronze, and the lashes surrounding them were full, but not long, which meant they framed his eyes, making them appear larger. He smiled then and as he did, the skin around his eyes wrinkled into tiny crow's feet and the desire to reach up my fingertips and trace over those tiny wrinkles was almost unstoppable. But, well brought up woman that I was, I did stop and by the time he spoke, I had gathered my thoughts and body enough to actually listen. I was glad I did listen, his words and the gentle low tone he used felt like they were a salve to my worries.

"There is Cassandra, a time and a place for everything, and you are correct most months in fact, all months until this one, I would by now have ensured my card was full and I would be enjoying all that there was to offer, but you my little governess are a surprise and one I think it is worth sacrificing some of that lust for. I can think of little more I would enjoy right now than showing you around this little kingdom I have created. If you love it, and want more then that is brilliant, however if decide after this evening to scurry back to your scholastic life with no more excitement than a child's piano recital on the horizon then that my girl is just fine as well, so come on, less dragging these heels and more discovering".

I grinned and nodded rather happily, and with a little trepidation headed through the now open door.

CHAPTER FOURTEEN

Thorpe

After watching Cassandra from my vantage point at the end of the table, I couldn't help but be impressed by her; I had earlier, whilst simultaneously fucking Lucy, seen Rupert Smythe having a chat with her. Never one of my favourite people Rupert, he had been brought in by Lady Suzanne Conrad, and had consistently worked his way through every woman over forty, not only in our circle, but beyond, into London society. He was well known as someone who simply moved from woman to woman, charming her, bedding her and then gently fleecing her for as long as possible, before moving onto his next. I had for some time thought he was the kind of leech we really didn't want at our gatherings, until Lady Conrad, who was herself a slightly older, intelligent, beautiful and incredibly wealthy woman who I trusted implicitly, and who was part of the founding members of our set, explained to me that most, if not absolutely all of the women knew exactly what Rupert was about. They controlled him and others like him, to the point of almost deciding to whom they would be going to next, this meant that widows who at a time in their lives when sex was an enjoyable pastime, without the worry of falling with child, who had no intention to sacrificing themselves to marriage again could enjoy young men such as Rupert whilst keeping themselves clean from disease and scandal. Once I understood this, I left Rupert and his ilk alone, he was of a good family I knew, but his father had lost all of their money and with no profession after leaving the Army, and no marriage, Rupert was almost the male version of what Cassandra was, without of course the ability to become governess, or a lady's companion. I was rather surprised to see him conversing with Cassandra, and wondered if it was their shared circumstance, because at such a young age, with no money Cassandra was most definitely not part of his shoal. My annoyance had most definitely surprised me, even though I had been balls deep in Lucy at the time, I had managed to feel a shudder of irritation that Rupert be talking to her.

It had though been whilst the table had been clearing, and I had been wolfing down cheese and bread that I had really been able to watch her. I saw Sybil and Poppy very obviously offer to stay with her, their protective wings were open, but she turned them down, wanting it seemed to forge her own way. Cassandra was undoubtedly beautiful, but she was also unspoiled and I knew that was what had initially drawn me to her. It had been the motive for my invitation to her to attend, which had so far proven to be entirely fruitless, however I had a feeling that actually Cassandra was going to prove to be so much more interesting than simply another virgin to deflower.

Just as it became clear, it was going to become only myself and her left at the table, I decided that right at this moment, I wanted to just observe her for a while, I wasn't sure what she was going to do. It may be that she was actually going to find her way to the large wooden door which separated us all from the real world, and scurry back to her bed chamber however, I had a feeling this was absolutely the last thing she was going to do. I quickly rose and not making eye contact I made my way to stand near to the large fireplace, it was impossible to stand too close, the fire burning in the grate was incredibly hot, continually stoked and fed by a footman for whom the only task of the night was keep the fire blazing, and candles burning in every candlestick, candelabra, sconce or chandelier. It sounded like an easy job, but it really wasn't, there being literally hundreds of candles scattered around!

The hall and all the other rooms were in the main kept very well lit. I was therefore able to stand, and make small talk with those around me and still keep an eye on Cassandra, who was now as predicted, alone at the table. At first glance she appeared quite happy and even a little confident, sat there sipping wine her shoulders pulled back, and her stance relaxed, but as I continued to watch, I could see a few cracks appear in her demeanour, her eyes were darting about a little too much and her hands were grasped just a little too tightly about her wineglass. The servants were now hovering, making it clear they would like to begin the task of removing the aftermath of dinner. I could, of course, with just a snap of my fingers and a few words in the right ear have them move back and leave her to her thoughts without any pressure to move, but I really didn't want to do that. A little pressure whilst she made her mind up as to her next move, wasn't going to do any harm at all, and in fact may even make things a little more interesting.

So, after being brought a brandy, I continued to simply watch and wait, and I didn't have to wait very long at all. The look on her face suddenly changed, I saw a resolute look pass over it for just a moment, she arose, the wine glass which it seemed she was now using as a shield against who knew what, was grasped to her belly. She looked around the hall, and in contrast to earlier when everyone had been asked to not notice, I saw that that arrangement had been swiftly quashed by Sybil, and Cassandra's slightly shy glances as she looked about were met with welcoming smiles, and a fair few hungry looks. She didn't speak to anyone though and after, I assumed, picking a door at random she headed off purposefully in that direction.

At that moment, I looked up and saw Raj coming my way, on each arm was a stunning young woman – as promised the identical twins. Each one was dressed elaborately in a sari, both were bejewelled with dark skinned bellies showing, and each woman was ravishing. The light in the room, which was of course just firelight and candlelight made them both appear to be almost alight themselves, light bounced and glittered off jewels in their noses, from which fine chains ran with the tiniest of bells hanging from them, the chains ended upon large hanging golden earrings, which also were adorned with the tiny bells. I could see golden bangles running up their arms, and each had a large golden armlet in the shape of a snake on their left upper arm. As they walked nearer to me, I could see their hair was wound in intricate plaits, into which was woven glittering gossamer thin golden chains, as they approached, despite the low hum of the room around me I could hear the tinkling of bells, looking down I could see both the women's feet were bare, and painted in the most intricate of henna tattoos, around their ankles were more tiny bells, and it was these that were emitting the low tinkling, in time with their footsteps. I had seen of course on many occasions Raj's wife Bibi, when she was just as beautifully dressed and decked out, but I had to admit that these twins were a cut above.

The look on Raj's face of course said it all, he was beyond pleased with himself, and as the three of them walked they garnered attention from those they passed. Upon reaching me, Raj smiled and held his arms open in an expansive gesture, he paused for a moment before speaking.

"Well my brother, did I not tell you the most beautiful women in the room tonight would be at our beck and call, are they not perfection"? I laughed, how could I not. But more strangely I felt myself slightly irked, I didn't say anything, but my immediate thought was that actually despite the stunning delights of these two Indian women, there was another woman here tonight who would actually in my opinion take the mantle for the most beautiful creature. I shook myself slightly as I realised my thoughts were somewhat akin to those of a sixteen year old boy. I grinned at the women and took each one's hand in turn, speaking to them both as I did so.

"You are most welcome here, I think it is very safe to say you are adding an exoticness to the proceedings which has rarely been seen...", I leaned in then as I continued speaking.

"Of course however delightful you are right now fully clothed and perfectly groomed, the real test will come when you are both naked, with just a sheen of sweat glistening over what I am assuming is delicious smooth skin. Raj will of course take perfect care of you both, but I have it in my mind to sample at least one of you tonight". With that I moved back and nodded to Raj, who was still grinning like a fat man at a banquet.

The twins, who I knew could speak perfect English said nothing, simply smiling and nodding their heads towards me, I could see in both of them the look women get when they are sexually confident , and well aware of their allure, it was something I enjoyed wiping off their faces, normally with a spanking paddle across fine plump buttocks.

Turning to Raj again I grinned as I spoke, beginning already to stride away.

"Enjoy yourself my brother, but keep a little back for me won't you, they look delicious". He didn't say anything but still grinning, he and the twins moved towards one of the doors, which I knew was going to lead them to one of the dungeon style rooms, a slightly more tame one than the other on offer, but still Raj was a man who knew exactly what he liked.

However much I liked, and did in fact love like a brother Raj, there were times over the years I could have happily strangled the man. Bibi was his second marriage, and was probably totally invalid as although the word separation and even divorce had been bandied about no one had yet to see any evidence of it. His first marriage had also been arranged, but that time Raj didn't meet her before the wedding, the size of her dowry had seduced both him and his family into accepting the marriage with very little forethought, and then all were surprised when she turned out to not only look like a potato, but to have the personality also of a potato. She was a thoroughly unpleasant woman, for whom her marriage had rather obviously been a way to get away from an overbearing mother and make a new life in England. The marriage had lasted less than a year, and I knew it to be unconsummated. She and her had parted rather amicably, she had taken her sizable dowry, and gone off to live somewhere quietly and rather happily by the sea, eschewing as much as she could of her Indian upbringing, and dressing like a well brought up British spinster.

There was sudden talk of a divorce, and I knew that Bibi's family had no idea of the first marriage, or their new son-in-law's quite possible lack of ability to be married to their daughter. But Raj had fallen in love with Bibi almost at first sight and she with him nearly as quick and nothing as trivial as a legally binding marriage would have kept them apart. Bibi was lucky to have a family with immense wealth, which meant that should Raj die tomorrow and his first wife demand his estate, Bibi, and the as yet unborn child would be more than well cared for. But for some reason all of this irked me a little, Raj's upbringing although exile was still in the manner of a Prince and his attitude was one of privilege by right.

As I watched them walk away, I realised I had lost Cassandra, in Raj making his grand entrance, she had managed to slip away. It took me some time looking around the huge room to realise she wasn't there, and so it was through one the doors she had gone. There was a slight danger she had chosen those large wooden doors leading the way back to the main house and the safety of her own room. I was however fairly certain this was not the route she had taken. I was beginning to think of her incredibly in the same terms one might a female heroine in one of those awful cheap books women nowadays seem to enjoy reading, and as such I now felt as though she had managed to give me the slip.

Brushing aside all of those who tried to engage me in conversation or chatter, I headed off purposefully, asking the revellers nearest to the doors, if she had been seen heading through them. It was not until I reached that awful man Rupert, who was at that very moment being sucked by a woman, who naked and with her back to me, I just couldn't identify. His irritation at me speaking to him during such a moment was obvious – but dammit this was my house and my hospitality he could have his dick sucked as soon as I had the information I needed. He nodded his head at my enquiry and wordlessly pointed at the door behind him. I didn't acknowledge the man any further, and strode away through the door.

Straight away I spotted her, it would seem my heroine was getting herself in a little bit of bother with some overconfident servants. I grinned to myself, as I decided that heroine or not, she definitely now needed a hero to rescue her.

From my vantage point I could see just how flustered she was, her earlier calm countenance appeared to have diminished a little. I waited just a while longer, and it was not until she started coughing and spluttering on some wine which had obviously gone down the wrong way that I decided I really should take some action. Rather than move, I simply shouted at the errant footman, and managed to stifle the grin that found its way to my face as the man almost jumped ten foot in the air, and rather quickly went about his sanctioned business, rather than trying to charm Cassandra, a task he was currently miserably failing to do anyway.

As I sauntered over to her, I noted that she was blushing down her neck and all the way down to the swell of her breasts. She did however appear to be grateful and pleased to see me, and I felt myself feel a little protective towards her. I had demanded her presence, perhaps yes with less than honourable intentions, but now the girl was here and had shown herself to be so absolutely not what I had expected, but in fact, to be so much more and I knew I would not be letting her out of my sight again anytime soon.

She continued to surprise me, by being not only grateful to see me, but most definitely pleased, her demeanour had changed. I had seen her watching me when I was using Lucy, and so I had expected her to be very cool towards me. Not wishing to be too close, however it would appear that witnessing that act had in fact warmed her up a little, and so when she stood a little too close, and then welcomed my hand on her back, I was rather heartened, instantly forgetting those gorgeous twins, and everything I had planned for them. Raj was just going to have to cope without me, something I knew he would be more than able to do.

I was therefore rather pleased with myself, that after we had exchanged what I could only describe as some playful exchanges, I opened the door and introduced Cassandra to our world.

CHAPTER FIFTEEN

Thorpe

My hand felt comfortable, resting where it did, just in the small of her back. She was wearing many layers and so I couldn't in any way feel flesh, or even her form; but where my hand rested, I knew was just where the soft curve of her buttocks would begin and my fingers traced that as yet only imagined flesh. Having her close was surprisingly comfortable and yet rather arousing at the same time. Of course, I had a ulterior motive, as I so often did, I wanted her close and near to me, when I opened the door, I knew she would be shocked and surprised and I wanted to not only comfort her, but ensure I enjoyed every bit of it.

I pushed Cassandra into the room first, and followed her in, I had decided to simply throw Cassandra in at the deep end and so had escorted her straight into one of the dungeon rooms, and it had already been put to good use.

The room was not huge, but at the same time, it was large enough to accommodate about ten people happily even with the plethora of ropes, chains and various equipment dotted about the place. I had resisted the urge to make it really appear as if it was a dungeon! Instead in keeping with the rest of the wing, this room was opulent looking. I had kept the walls bare and stone so the rings and fixings could be attached, but under foot was thick red carpet, the two flogging horses were both upholstered in thick red velvet, and every cuff in the room was padded with the same thick red cloth. There was a fire blazing in the grate, and in the corner was a table set with every form of refreshment any man, or woman who had exhausted themselves disciplining their companion could possibly wish for. Right next to this, was a smaller table covered in candles, playing with these candles was something that was relatively new to us, and nothing I saw as particularly exciting, however there were some women who seemed to relish it. I had seen both men and women covered in hot wax, apparently loving every minute of it, also on this table was an impressive array of dildos both glass and wooden. There were even a few on long poles, which I had been known to use, there was something delightful about a woman cuffed to a cross, her legs splayed open wide, with a large well lubricated dildo inside her, with just enough pressure so she looks like she is balancing on the stick. The furnishings and set-up of the room meant that it seemed almost at odds with itself, the setting in some ways respectable, but then a glance to the left or right would reveal its true use.

A large rack was bolted to one of the walls, and upon that rack were many paddles, canes and even some whips. The rules of the room, and in fact for everything we did was simple – everyone consented, and the moment anyone uttered the word agreed to mean they were not having fun, everything stopped.

I felt Cassandra take a deep intake of breath, as she stood close to me, I pulled her just a little closer, so my arm now snaked around her waist and rested on her hips, I leaned down and whispered in her ear, creating a confidence between just the two of us.

"What do you think Cassandra? This is perhaps for many the real reason they travel all the way out to the middle of Dartmoor every month, there are two rooms like this, each slightly different. Of course some come simply for sensual pleasures, or just a raw fuck and whilst they are fabulous, this my dear Cassandra is the heart of us".

I could almost feel her listening, sense her quickened heartbeat and all of a sudden, I realised just how much I hoped and prayed to my non-existent god that she was excited and curious rather than disgusted and abhorred. She looked up to me and smiled a little weakly, I could see the colour had drained from her face, she too was whispering as she spoke, although her voice was stuttering very slightly, in a so far very uncharacteristic show of emotion.

"I, I, I don't really understand, these people are forced to do this? I, well I, I didn't think, well I didn't realise, I don't think I understand", and with that she looked up to with eyes full suddenly of tears and it came to me that of course her countenance and deportment this whole evening had taken its toll upon her, and perhaps this was the final straw. Feeling even more protective towards her, I led her to the corner of the room, where a chaise longue was placed, for exactly the purpose we were going use it for, to watch. I motioned and she obediently, sat herself down on the seat, I sat next to her and was unable to not pull her towards me, and again wrap my arm around her waist. She turned her head towards me and again smiled, and I knew despite the impropriety of my actions, compared to what she was viewing around her it was nothing and she welcomed the comfort and security. I found myself, instead of mocking, teasing or in any way belittling her being as reassuring as I could. I now knew how much I wanted this woman, and I knew she was too intelligent and too independent to fall for the bombastic approach. With one arm tightly around her, and the other hand grasping one of hers, I pulled us both back into what I hoped what was a comfortable position and said.

"Just watch Cassandra, just watch, all I will tell you is that everyone here, is here because they want to be, and because this makes them feel alive and vibrant, and fulfils in them, a deep need. I promise nothing will happen to you, and I won't go anywhere, you are quite safe, so watch and hopefully enjoy". She didn't speak, but I did feel her body relax slightly against mine as she took advantage of the security and closeness of my embrace.

CHAPTER SIXTEEN

Cassandra

Just as I thought I had accepted what was happening, and even though I still didn't really understand, I had felt relaxed and welcome. Being close to Thorpe, as I was now to call him, had seemed almost perfect. Then all of a sudden, after walking through one door, I felt transported to a place so alien to me that I felt my entire being recoil in shock. Had I not had the strong arms of Thorpe around me, I knew I would have fallen to the ground. I was therefore incredibly grateful when he led to a seat, and we sat down together. I allowed him to keep me close, needing the comfort he offered. After he reassured me, I did exactly as I bid me and I sat back and watched my mind as open as I could possibly force it to be.

There were only another five people in the room, two women, and three men, there were none I recognised, one of the women I knew had nodded to me at the dinner table, and I was sure I had seen each of them, but they appeared as strangers to me.

One couple, a man and a woman were at the end of the room, he was standing watching the woman strip, I heard him barking out each item of clothing to remove, and she did so quickly, folding the clothing and placing it down on the floor next to them. I saw he had in his hand a collar, it looked like something you might place upon a dog, it was black leather with small studs adorning it, attached to the collar was a long strap of leather, with a loop at the end. I saw then that the woman was eyeing the collar with a look of desire on her face, she looked up at the man, and smiled, he however didn't break into a smile, but simply pointed to the floor and said.

"Come on my girl, you know better than this", at which words she seemed to just fold and gracefully fall down to her knees so she was knelt at his feet, she shuffled forward a little so she was directly in front of him, her knees just touching the ends of his boots. It was only at this point, I realised how her nakedness was the least of my thoughts at this moment, I had become in such a short time almost accustomed to seeing such things. What was causing the breath to stall in my throat was her actions towards him, and the fact he seemingly expected such things. I saw him nodding more approvingly, at her actions, as she now knelt up and leaned forward laying her head on his thigh.

I turned my head slightly to Thorpe, who was still sat very close to me, and he smiled almost gently at me, I couldn't help but admit to myself how wonderful this closeness felt. Just at that moment, he beckoned over the one footman in the room, who had been standing next to the table full of drinks, his eyes had also been fixed upon, and roving over the naked woman. But he now, knowing exactly what side his bread was buttered upon, rushed to Thorpe's side who quietly requested two brandies, the man nodded and turned away, fetching the drinks just as quickly as he had arrived. When Thorpe passed the drink to me with a small wink, I took it gratefully, and immediately took a sip. I knew my head was slightly muzzy already, from the copious amounts of wine I had consumed at dinner, however it was not enough for me to worry about my conduct, and the brandy certainly did its job very quickly, calming and soothing my nerves. Enough in fact, so I was able to relax a little more into the sofa and turn my head back to watch the couple.

We were close enough to them for me to see the look on her face it was one which, even my lack of experience and knowledge of lust could tell was simply pure need. She had started to rub her face against his thigh, her soft skin pressing against the thick material of his clothing, she was whimpering ever so slightly, and her hands now came up to curl about both his legs. She then moved a little, tilting her head upwards so as to look up to him, reaching her hands up and over her head in a imploring fashion. I noted only then for just a moment, the sheer beauty of this tableau, the man was probably in his late 30's, he had closely cropped dark hair, and a short beard. He was well built, and well dressed, having removed his jacket he was standing in his shirt sleeves, which he had rolled up to his elbows making him almost look like a farmhand about to start work. His voice when he had briefly spoken had been well educated, without a true hint of accent. The woman had of course not spoken, and naked as she was it was impossible to even hint at who she might be. I had been in such shock when I had entered the room, I confess I had no clue what the dress the woman had been wearing might have been like. Now however she was naked, and her long blonde hair, which I assumed at some point had been pinned up, cascaded over her shoulders. Her skin was creamy white, and in the candlelight appeared almost to be made from porcelain. I could see she was about the same age as her male companion, and was very pretty. Her body showed some signs of age - you might say her belly was round and her thighs a little thick, whilst her bottom as she knelt up was dimpled and well sized. However none of these possible imperfections detracted from how beautiful the couple looked. Just as my eyes were roving over her body again, he took the collar and held it out in front of her, she immediately stopped moving and knelt back down to her knees, placing her hands demurely on her thighs. The man leaned down and I could see a look of incredible tenderness pass between them, before he spoke again, this time addressing her in a softer but no less commanding tone.

"You know the rules my girl, if you want it, you must beg for it, and beg for it well." At those words I saw the woman swallow hard and look around the room, her eyes resting on those watching; myself and Thorpe, and then the footman who released from his serving was now back to standing by the drinks table with his eyes fixed upon her. The three others in the room were also half-watching, however they were more interested it was safe to say, in what they were doing and as yet my eyes hadn't been brave enough to venture that way.

The man saw her looking, and saw the look on her face, and pulled the collar back and away, himself taking a couple of steps back from her, so she was immediately and suddenly stranded in the middle of the room. As he spoke I could hear his sense of annoyance straight away, as did she, seeming to almost shrink away from his words.

"What? You are saying you have actually noticed anyone else in this room, are your eyes not only for your owner? If your Master can see nothing and no one beyond the property which is knelt before him, why would that property decide others in the room mean she is excused from behaving in the way she knows pleases me"?

The words obviously and straight away had the effect they were supposed to, because she let out a small cry and crawled back towards him, her head low in what I assumed was supplication. Amazingly, I felt myself leaning forward and my heart quicken. The brandy in my hand was now perfectly warm and I sipped it slowly, all the while allowing Thorpe's arm to remain around me and his hand to wrap about mine, fingers grasped tightly. I felt warmness between my legs which I tried to ignore, crossing and uncrossing my legs under my many skirts. Thorpe of course could see all of this and when I turned again briefly to look at him, he dropped my hand and leaned up to tuck a stray hair behind my ear, allowing his little finger to then trace down my neck before, he grabbed my hand again and softly stroked my fingers with his, when he spoke his voice was low, almost a whisper between just the two of us.

"You seem calmer so quickly Cassandra, almost enjoying what you are seeing – it's quite perfect isn't it, it does make me feel jealous. He knows his girl very well, they are married you see, have been for many years, have three children. He is a doctor, very well respected in his community but here they can be just what they need to be". I choose to still say nothing, I feared in some ridiculous way that I may say the wrong thing, perhaps anger him, and in my innocence I was desperate for him not to leave my side, his body was so close I could feel his heart beating, it was so wonderful, that I never wanted the moment to end, but yes he was right, as I glanced back over, there was something perfect about them. I nodded again, but this time I managed a genuine smile as well, as we both turned back to watch.

By the time both mine and Thorpe's eyes had trained themselves back upon the couple she had moved a little forward, her arms in the air, and it was then finally that we heard her speak.

"Please Master, your collar, please collar me, I want to feel and know I am owned, the leather round my neck, put there by you reminds me I am nothing but property. I may be loved, cherished and desired property, but I am simply that, please my Master put your collar on me, and use me, let me know how I may please you". As she fell silent, she allowed her arms to fall down to her side, and her head to drop slightly.

I was suddenly aware how relieved I was that her words seemed to have had the desired effect, as the man then bridged the gap between them and leaning down he pulled her head up, so he could kiss her softly upon her lips, before he placed the now open collar about her neck buckling it, and then taking a small padlock from his pocket, he attached that to the ring of the collar, rendering it secure for anyone else but him to remove it. He carefully placed the tiny lock back into his pocket and smiled down approvingly at his wife.

"Good", he said

"Now you are appropriately attired, let's see what this room has to offer us. Now stand my girl, and go fetch a blindfold and a spanking paddle, I think your bottom is looking far too pale, let's give it a little colour heh".

She nodded, as she spoke quickly,

"Yes Master", she arose as elegantly as she sunk down to her knees just that short time ago. It would seem she knew exactly where she was going, and without any hesitation on her part, she paused at the rack nailed to the wall, and grabbed from it, what I assumed was a spanking paddle. Made from wood, it looked a little like a rather flat and short cricket bat, before I could stop myself, I had gasped and placed my hand over my mouth, I instantly felt warm breath on my neck and then heard Thorpe's voice.

"Don't tell me you are giving up now Cassandra, its only just starting to get interesting", I swallowed hard and whispered back.

"I don't know why you have brought me here Thorpe, or what you are expecting from me, but I will, I believe at some point thank you". I was aware how honest I was being, and of course totally aware that I was in some ways laying myself as open and bare to Thorpe, as the woman naked and kneeling currently handing over a spanking paddle, with the obvious hope it will soon be used on her bottom. Thorpe said nothing, but I felt his grip on me tighten ever so slightly, which did nothing but please me, and cause those tummy flips to continue.

My eyes were drawn back to the room, the couple who had taken all of my attention so far had moved to the far end, where a contraption was set up, which I could see already was going to involve her bending over it, and being tied in. She was currently holding up her arms so her husband, although in these circumstances, she appeared to call him Master, could lock leather cuffs to her wrists, the cuffs were made from soft leather, and fastened around her wrist with a small buckle to which a tiny padlock was added. We were now too far away from them both to hear what was being said, but I could see he was constantly talking to her, and she listening, twice as he fastened the cuffs I saw him leaning down to kiss her with a tenderness I had never seen before. For her part the woman seemed to me to be younger, she was squirming about, excited and nervous, the calm steadying hand of her Master was obviously so very much needed.

For myself I was now at the point where I realised I had not stumbled upon some kind of dark cult where sacrifices were made each month, but instead, although I had still not totally figured it out, I was absolutely certain that everyone here was here because they desired it. I found myself watching now, a woman at least 15 years older than myself being strapped into a piece of apparatus which was without doubt a prequel to her bottom being pummelled with the wooden paddle currently grasped in her husband's hands. I realised with a start that I was feeling jealous, not for the nakedness of the woman, or her humiliation in front of strangers, I was jealous having never seen before such emotion or perfection between two people.

I made myself turn away from the couple, just as he started to spank her round plump bottom with the paddle, I could hear her whimpers and cries, but found myself incredibly, not wanting to intrude any further.

CHAPTER SEVENTEEN

Cassandra

There were three other people in the room, and they were most obviously an entirely different prospect, a young rather stunning black woman was attached by the same kind of cuffs I had just seen on the blonde woman, to a wooden cross. She was strapped by her ankles and her wrists, her feet were set on two small platforms which only just gave her purchase, and meant her feet and toes were stretched out, giving her the appearance of standing on tiptoes. She was of naked, a state I was becoming increasingly comfortable about, and her black skin was as smooth as satin, and just slightly shiny. I suddenly noticed that she was completely shaven, between her legs was completely smooth and hair free. Due to her position, strapped onto the cross, her legs were shoved wide apart, and this meant from the short distance I was away from them and although I could not see in detail, I could see plump lips which were parted and the pink, wet insides of her sex could be seen.

The two men with her I realised were twins, and in contrast to the woman's black skin were both pale to the point of being almost albino, both were stripped to the waist, revealing almost identical well-muscled torsos. They both had long blonde hair, which was held back from their faces by black ribbons, creating long low ponytails which ran down their backs.

As I fixed my gaze upon the three of them, one of the men I saw had in his hand what looked to be a leather thong, with a leather ball attached to it – I had no idea what it was, or what it was for. Up until this moment, the men had been talking in low voices to each other, the woman seemingly ignored apart from a hand upon each of her thighs. Now they sprang into action, and I could immediately see her start to squirm and wiggle. One of the men turned around and suddenly slapped her hard on her breasts, leaning forward then to grab a hold of both nipples, and I found myself wincing along with the woman as I watched. She whimpered and winced, crying out at what must have been a sudden pain. One of the twins, the one with the leather strapping in his hand reached up and placed his hand on her check. Speaking softly as he did.

"Quiet now slut, or will I have to use this"? As he spoke he was holding the leather strap and ball up to her and she immediately fell silent, but I could see her silence was going to be an impossible task, as the pulling and pinching of her nipples increased with the young blonde man, whilst his brother had been speaking. Swiftly moving to a small table set up next to the cross, to my shock and amazement, he grabbed two small clamps. I knew straight away what he was about to do with them and my eyes were instantly and rather horrifyingly glued to the woman's breasts. Thorpe being so close to me, must have sensed my heightened interest, because I felt his breath on my neck, just before he spoke again.

"There are some Cassandra, for whom what appears to be a considerable amount of pain is needed and desired, that young woman is one of those, and the twins are more than happy to dish it out. There are different levels for each, the two you see here are called submissives, they just happen in this instance to be women, and the men in the room are known as Dominants. I am a Dominant Cassandra, there is to me nothing more perfect that a submissive woman who is like putty in my hands. I can mould her to please me, and in the pleasing she is satisfied, but you must not think all of us wish to inflict, or suffer lots of levels of pain. A lot of pain does very little for me, I prefer a woman desperate to please".

All of Thorpe's words to me, felt like he was sharing a confidence and for the moment when he spoke, I felt privileged and almost special. Unfortunately, a by-product of what I was witnessing and the close, intense proximity of Thorpe had struck me rather dumb.

Despite every word he said striking a cord somewhere deep inside of me, so much so that I almost wanted to cling to the man and beg him to show me exactly what he meant, I was instead, silent. With wide eyes and a quickly beating heart, I tried to speak, but no words would come forth. The best I found myself able to do, was smile up at my employer hoping I didn't appear to be of a simple mind, and then turn my attention back to the three people. In my absence the woman had obviously been unable to remain quiet, the clamps were on her considerably large and round nipples and were pulling them down in an alarming manner, I saw her close her eyes and stretch upwards. She was unable now to actually make any more sounds than some muffled cries because the leather strap and ball were now showing exactly what they were designed for, having been strapped around her mouth, in the manner of a gag. It was tight around her head and meant her mouth was constantly open as the smooth ball was thrust inside, and held there by means of the leather straps. I wasn't sure as to the purpose of the gag, apart from to render her speechless.

As we were watching, one of men went to a large table near to where the drinks where set out and after a short time, he selected a large glass item in the shape of what I knew to be a male penis, it was I hoped larger than any real penis may be. I briefly mused upon what the glassblower's order sheet might have been to make such an implement. He was grinning broadly as he made his way back to the woman, who was now almost totally silent, the clamps on her nipples having been loosened just a small amount, and I could see that the other man was doing what I could only describe as playing with her. His hands were between her legs, and I could see fingers disappearing and then reappearing as he slid them inside her. Being strapped to the cross meant she was slightly higher than both men, however they were both well over six feet tall and she was very slender and petite, which meant that when the men stood in front of her, she was at their eye height, so as he leaned forward to whisper to her and bring his other hand up to tweak and fondle her breasts he was able to keep eye contact the entire time. This contact between the two of them seemed only to heighten the intimacy, he was whispering to her, and she was starting to whimper softly, the gag was however muffling the majority of any noise she was making. As his brother walked back over, and paused briefly to watch them, I allowed my eyes to wander down her body and fix finally upon her sex, and his fingers, the absence of any hair between her legs gave me a view and the ability to study something I had not seen before tonight. His fingers were quite obviously very wet, a wetness which was coming from her. Each time he pulled his fingers out of her, she thrust her hips forward and moaned I could see that her sex was puffy and swollen; the pinkness of her flesh there was in stark and complete contrast to the rest of her perfect smooth black skin.

At that moment the other brother must have decided it was time to up the stakes a little, as he approached the woman holding the glass phallus up in front of her, I could see there was a brief moment when something akin to fear washed over her face, which quickly turned to apprehension and anticipation.

He reached up and placed one hand behind the back of the woman's head, pulling it forward slightly, he then held up the glass object up to her face, I could see from her mouth was a long stream of drool, she was with the ball thrust in her mouth, unable to swallow and so her salvia was running down her chin, and onto her bare breasts. The man then moved the phallus to her mouth and rubbed it over her chin and her lips, I could hear him them speaking in a loud voice, I was immediately surprised to hear a broad northern accent.

"Come now slut, it's in your interests to make sure we get this good and wet.....ahh there, that's a good girl", he said as she leant forward slightly so as to ensure the vast glass penis in his hand was well wetted with her drool.

Pulling back from her, he then took a step back, as did his brother, then leant down to her feet, I could see him reaching behind the wooden cross obviously pulling out a peg or some such, which then enabled him to lift the small step upon which her feet were stood up. I felt myself craning my neck to get a better view, and then catching myself, I blushed briefly looking up to Thorpe, who was staring at me with an amused look on his face. I felt my blush deepen as I quickly turned around and continued watching. Both of the woman's feet had now been raised up by about a foot, with her arms strapped the way they were, this meant that her knees were now bent, and I could quickly see why they had done this, her legs were already wide apart, but now with her knees a little bent, there was perfect access to her sex, and I could see even from this distance that her thighs were shiny and wet and her lips were parted. I would guess she was now rather more uncomfortable, having to support her knees in that bent position would take some doing.

Both men now took a few steps back from her and almost as if appraising a job well done, they slapped each other briefly on the back and grinned. For myself, I was now torn between a feeling of horror and jealously, together with the fact that I knew that my own sex was probably as wet as the woman's on the cross was, and crossing and uncrossing my legs was doing little to alleviate the ache down there.

I turned my attention of course now back to the woman, she was wriggling about on the cross watching both men intently. The one who was holding a now very wet, but still very large glass dildo in his hand moved so he was standing just to the side of her, and I saw him start to rub it between her legs, I imagined it was cool, whilst her skin by now would be raging hot, he was slowly rubbing it up and along her lips, parting them easily with the smooth wet surface, she immediately shuddered, and moaned loudly, and I could only imagine how it felt, my own body was in a heightened state watching, and it was all I could do not to wriggle on the chair next to Thorpe.

He continued slowly rubbing it over her vagina, right up and almost to her belly, and then down again, his brother was now doing no more than watching, and I could see in him adjusting his clothing between his legs, and a very quick but studied glance revealed a large erection pushing against his clothes, which was obviously the cause of the readjustment every couple of minutes.

The woman was by now shaking a little and with each pass of the phallus, whimpering. His hands were grasping the end very tightly, and I see that leather thongs had been fed through holes in the bottom, and he had wrapped these about his hand, giving him a little purchase on what must have a been a very slippery and rather heavy item. Looking up to her he spoke again in the broadest of northern accents.

"Well slut, is that nice? Hmm is it? A good girl like you can do so much more though can't she? Let's see if this great big cock is going to fit inside that little tight cunt of yours shall we", with those words, and without looking up again, he pulled the dildo away from her for just a moment, and then with it now vertical he slowly, but without stopping pushed it inside of her, it was as he had said large, and I could see her eyes almost watering and her body stopping stock still as he did this. It was then that I realised the other brother's role in this scene, it was simply to ensure she was ok, I saw him watching her face intently, she was of course unable to speak and say whatever phrase or word Thorpe had intimated would mean they stopped, so instead I guessed he was watching her for any signs of distress beyond what was desired and planned.

It was very obvious she was not now in distress, whimpering and moaning loudly enough for it to be heard even with the gag shoved in her mouth. The dildo was being pushed in and out of her in what I guessed was the manner would happen if you were having sex. She had pushed her neck back and was loudly making her pleasure known, the man was using his other hand now to press and rub at that little sensitive nub, I was well aware how good this could feel, as despite my realisation earlier today in the bath at just how little I knew about my own body, there had been times when crossing my legs, and having a seam of my underwear pressed against that part of my body had given me unexpected and delightful sensations. I assumed he was doing exactly this to her now, and the combination of the glass phallus inside her and his fingers rubbing her were sending her off to her own world of pleasure, something it suddenly seemed both men did not want. The one whose job it was to watch her now moved forward and tightened again the clamps on her breasts so her nipples were painfully crushed by them, he also picked up from the floor next to the cross a small whip with leather straps. Moving behind her he started to rather gently at first, strike her bottom, which was not covered by the cross, its design rather cleverly ensuring that the crossover of wood happened where the small of her back was, thus leaving her bottom free and rather vulnerable. He paused for just a moment, and I could see him watching his brother, the dildo shoved inside her faster now, he then matched his striking of her round bottom with each deep thrust inside her.

I was by this point sitting nearer the edge of my seat, my eyes glued on the three of them; I knew my mouth was open slightly, caused by a mixture of surprise and excitement. Thorpe hadn't moved, his arm was still wrapped about my body, and I felt at some point the empty brandy glass being removed from my hand, and his hand then wrapping tightly about it. I heard his breath quicken a little next to me, I smiled assuming that this was also a newish experience for him, not used to being a bystander, just witnessing events.

I looked back to up to the cross, and could see that the woman was now trying to speak, obviously pleading, the lashes to her bottom had become increasingly severe, and the dildo was pushed inside right to its hilt, the only visible part of it was the leather thongs wrapped about his hand. Whilst he continued to ram the phallus inside, his other hand briefly moved from his place on her clitoris, reaching up and round the back of her head, expert fingers quickly moved to remove the gag, throwing it down on the floor at their feet. Immediately it was removed, I heard her take huge gulps of air, breathing now almost as if she had been slightly suffocating. This only lasted a few seconds, as soon as his hands had found their way down between her legs and found her clitoris, she again started to whimper and moan loudly. Then she started to speak, I realised with a start it was the first time I had heard her, she had been the centre of everything, and yet verbally silent until now. Her voice was surprisingly gentle, and had the lilt of someone not born in England, who had yet spent most of their life in the company of well-spoken Englishmen. She was it soon became apparent begging, what for, I was not I confess, very sure at all.

"Please Masters, please may I", she begged, her voice although gasping and ragged was clear.

"Please may I release, please Masters, please Masters, I can't hold it", she continued.

The twin who was still, lashing her rump but now very much softer, pausing every few strikes to rub her bottom, and then using his hand to spank her as hard he could then spoke.

"But why slut, tell us what you are and what you want, come on and then maybe you can". She let out a loud moan, and I could tell that each word was an exquisite torture, neither man was giving an inch and the rhythm of the movements was causing her to shudder and I guessed the begging was for her orgasm, something I had heard of, but had no knowledge of. She took a deep breath and it appeared as though she was only just managing to speak.

"I am a dirty little cum slut Masters, your dirty little slut, please, please may your dirty slut cum Masters, please", she pleaded, the desperation in her voice now so apparent that I found myself willing them to let her.

The men then exchanged glances and nodded to each other, before the one who had already been speaking continued.

"You may release slut, but make it quick, my brother's hand is no doubt getting tired fucking your needy little slit. If he stops your chance will be lost". She obviously needed no more encouragement, and before he had even finished speaking she relaxed her body briefly before thrusting her hips forward, as her whole body stiffened for a few seconds. I could see her toes stretch out as she murmured and whimpered incredibly quietly now, her whole body was shuddering and shaking a little, her eyes were closed and her tongue flicked out to run over her lips a few times, as soon as it started it seemed she was finished. I saw her relax, open her eyes and grin, no more than 20, or perhaps even 30 seconds had passed, and yet I saw a look of pure happiness on her face as she looked down at both men. They had judged exactly the right time to stop, each was holding their implements of either torture or pleasure, depending on how you looked at it! This time when she spoke, her voice was calmer, yet still quiet and respectful.

"Thank you Masters for letting this slut release, she is so very grateful". Neither man spoke; apart from to grunt a little, I could now see both were unbuttoning their trousers. They paused in this endeavour long enough to together reach up and unlock the cuffs, firstly on her wrists, and then around her ankles, so as to release her from the cross. She fell into their arms, at first collapsing a little, the exertion and being strapped in one place for a while taking its toll, however both men rather tenderly held her, reaching down to rub her ankles, and then her wrists, and in no time at all she was standing and wriggling about in their arms rather happily it seemed. Leaning up to kiss them both, her arms snaking about their bare torsos, as all three of them embraced, her wriggling suddenly started to become a little more sensual, and I suspected she had felt the bulge between one of the men's legs and had guessed what was happening next.

All of a sudden after a look passed between them, I could sense the atmosphere again changed, and they now moved back from her, one man clicking his fingers and pointing to the floor, where a large a pile of cushions was scattered. Without a word, she moved to the cushions, and dropped to her hands and knees, with her very round bottom in the air, her head up, she watched both men who now very quickly were loosening and pulling down their clothing. Almost simultaneously I saw two very large (not as large as the glass phallus!) erect penises spring out free from the confines of material, neither man bothered to remove their clothing completely and so there then followed an almost humorous few seconds as they made their way to woman, only able take smallish steps. She knew what was coming, and I could see her splitting her legs open a little wider and stretching up, opening her mouth in anticipation – it was then that I also realised what they were going to do, and I gulped, my free hand reaching up around my throat. I felt Thorpe lean in and quickly whisper.

"It's ok Cassandra, she will be just fine, she, can't believe her luck". I nodded my head, but didn't take my eyes from them, the twins had now reached her, and it would seem pot luck had decided which twin would get which end, one was positioned in front of her mouth, and without waiting for his brother he was unceremoniously shoving his whole erection in her mouth, she was instantly gagging and choking a little. He paused for a few seconds speaking to her in a low voice what I assumed were soothing words as he stroked her cheek a little before continuing again to use her mouth in the manner in which you would assume a man would normally use a woman's vagina, he was literally thrusting his penis in and out of her mouth.

For his part, the other twin was in fact doing exactly what you would assume a man would do, and after stroking her hips and her bottom, I could see him for a moment seeming to be concentrating intently, before with his hands parting her bottom cheeks as widely as possibly he entered her in one swift movement. Thrusting as deep as he could, his hands then moving to her hips, which he used to gain some purchase, his large hands hanging on, meaning his hips could thrust and fuck her with some considerable force. As had been the case earlier when she had been gagged her mouth was full and so the whimpers, moans and groans coming from her were muffled, this time by the presence of a penis being thrust in and out of her mouth, and if the gagging and choking sounds were anything to go by, down her throat. The twin who was using her mouth had moved his hands over her shoulders, and down her back and was rubbing and caressing her skin as he pumped his penis in and out of her mouth.

At the rear of her, I could see the other twin again parting her bottom cheeks and looking down intently transfixed watching his own penis moving in and out of her. At that moment, I happened to look up and to my almost amusement, I saw that the couple earlier, the one's Thorpe had said were married, were also engaged in almost the same act, and I wondered if all of this behaviour culminated in the very basic act of sex. In their case, she had her hands tightly cuffed behind her back, which meant that she was in a position with her bottom very high in the air, and her shoulders and face low to the ground, her husband was holding onto a bar bolted and protruding from the wall which meant he was able to fuck her with a surprising amount of speed and force something from the sounds emitting from her she was seeming to thoroughly enjoy.

There were others I saw filing into the room, each couple or in one case I noted foursome were starting whatever it was they each did, and wanted. I then realised suddenly that I had had enough, perhaps not enough for ever, but enough for tonight. I was tired, confused, rather shocked and a little scared, and despite the delight at having Thorpe so close and near, and seemingly happy to pay constant attention to me, I knew I needed to be alone. To think, to rest and decide what exactly tonight's revelations meant and what; if any impact they would have on my life.

I turned to Thorpe, and I knew immediately that he was ahead of me, knowing exactly what I was going to say, before I had managed to say it! However, I still managed to get my words out.

"Thorpe, had I a clue at the beginning of the night, what the evening would bring, I would not have left my room, but I am so glad I am here, and instead of slapping you around the face, as I should have perhaps done at the beginning of the evening, I am thanking you, thanking you for showing me a world I would have never known existed had I not seen this, and thank you for trusting me. But now I think I have seen enough, my head is absolutely spinning and I need quiet".

Thorpe smiled and nodded as he spoke.

"My dear Cassandra, I could see you starting to fade, and I understand why. It can't be easy faced with such things, when you had no idea they existed, or perhaps even more shockingly, were happening almost under your nose. You know my plans for you, and this evening were far from honourable, however you have exceeded my expectations, and shown yourself to a person worth a little more than simply a night of emotionless fucking, however much I know I would find that satisfying."

At those last few words, I found myself coughing, spluttering and finally losing the calm I had managed to keep such a strong grip on all evening. I crumpled against him and felt my eyes suddenly full of very silly and very pointless tears. He of course saw me and sprang into action, leaping up from his seat and giving me his arm, helping me to my feet, his arm still around my waist, as he spoke to me in a soft soothing tone.

"Cassandra, my Cassandra, come now, time for some quiet, sleep and perhaps reflection, you have been a delight, and I am very glad we have spent the night as we have, and not as I had first thought". I simply smiled as I allowed myself to be lead out of the room and back into the hallway. Thorpe, then with his arm about my waist, led me to the large wooden doors. I thought to myself, without rancour that I had passed through those doors just a few hours ago perhaps still an innocent as to the intimate ways of men and women, and now I was leaving, with my innocence removed entirely from my eyes.

On our way across the room, Thorpe had seen Jarvis and beckoned him over, not speaking, until all three of us were safely through the doors and back almost in the world of the normal. He turned first to me:

"Thank you Cassandra for your company this evening. Your company is something I surprise myself by wanting more, and I believe I am right that the children are spending the next fourteen days in London with their Aunt Elizabeth". I nodded furiously as I spoke, quickly answering him.

"Yes, yes that is right, I was not needed and so I have plans to turn the nursery into something a little more befitting of the children's ages, I can assure you I was not planning on being idle Sir". I found myself the very moment we had left the wing back into the mode of employee, something from Thorpe's face I saw he found irritating; his voice also sounded just a little annoyed.

"Come now Cassandra, surely this evening had taught you that is precisely the kind of thing I don't care about, my children love you, they are well mannered and becoming well educated, why would I care anymore than that about what you do with your time. My question relates to the fact that I will also be on the estate over the next two weeks, and wondered if perhaps you would care to take breakfast with me on occasion, and dinner even. An outing or two might also be in order, a picnic at the lake, a ride out across the moors? In short Cassandra, and although I wince a little as I say it, the kind of things that a man and woman would undertake should they wish to get to know each other a little better".

My tears, and apprehension were turning as his words spilled out into a rather excited and perhaps even skittish mood, and despite trying so very hard to stay calm and appear controlled on the outside, I failed miserably and looked up to him with a huge grin.

"Thorpe, I would love that, I would really love that, I will eat my breakfast in the dining room each morning, and hope you might find time to join me, and the other things you suggest, I will leave it for you, Thorpe to suggest when and where". With those words, and the absolute knowledge that I was gushing like I was perhaps thirteen years old promising I really would love a pony forever. I saw a look on Thorpe's face which could only be described as approval; he only uttered a few more words, before sending me on my way.

"Goodnight Cassandra".

I didn't stop smiling as I followed Jarvis back into the main part of the house, the walk to main staircase from which I could of course easily find my way back to my bedroom. I nodded my thanks to the rather tired looking Butler, and headed to my room, pausing to check on the children as I did, I was a little surprised they were sleeping so soundly, they were both so very excited about their trip to stay with Elizabeth. She was Thorpe's older sister, and despite an outward appearance of stone, she was a kindly woman, who after bringing up two sons herself now loved spending time with her young niece and nephew.

It was just past 3.30 am when I finally sunk into my bed. I hadn't bothered to even wash my face, simply stripping my clothes and leaving them where they fell, pulling a nightgown over my head, and sinking so very gratefully into my soft, clean bed. I had been expecting to toss and turn for some time, my being so very full of thoughts and questions, but my body's need to sleep took over and within a few minutes I was lost to a deep, dreamless sleep.

CHAPTER EIGHTEEN

Thorpe

I wasn't sure why my heart was beating so very fast, but it was, and it was beginning to annoy me. I had known and felt exactly when she had had enough, I was surprised however that she had so readily gone away to her bed, I guessed she really was feeling overwhelmed, tired and perhaps just a little emotional. I wondered if she realised I would not be there for breakfast this morning, it was already 3 am and the carnal set always indulged for two evenings, one day and of course two nights, there were no formal bedrooms for anyone, and already I could see dotted about the large hall, couples and larger groups, snuggled up and hunkered down sleeping. Many were naked or half-naked, a fair few having imbibed rather more wine than they had perhaps planned were snoring loudly. My well trained staff would wander around after about 3 am with blankets and extra pillows, making sure all were comfortable. In some of the other rooms, ones I had not ventured into so far this weekend, were large beds, big enough in a couple of cases for four people to sleep comfortably, there were also sofas, and chaise lounges, and enough soft places to lay your head down and sleep. During the day, no one really did a thing, some could sleep for most of it, others once they had arisen would eat, wash and dress in clean clothes and then spend an enjoyable few hours in conversation or simply relaxing. It was of course free for anyone who wished to, to continue having sex, or any other intimate pleasure they desired, but very few ever did, the night was our chosen time!

I looked about, half-heartedly thinking about finding a warm body to use to purge my frustration from spending an evening without touching Cassandra. I wondered briefly why I hadn't invited her back this evening, it wasn't that I didn't wish her company, but more that I didn't want to overload her, I was concerned she could just see too much and simply have enough. So I would continue my weekend without her, and it would do the girl no harm whatsoever to understand that although I would enjoy spending some more time with her, she was in no way a priority. I felt instantly better, and ignored the little nagging clock in my head which was slowly counting down the hours until all these people left my house, and I could spend some time alone with Cassandra.

Not having the energy to fuck anyone, or for that matter indulge in anything remotely carnal, I looked around the huge room, looking for a spot to lay my head, despite living here I had always slept amongst my guests, but for some reason tonight nowhere looked suitable. I could see as I glanced about more than a few welcoming smiles and even a couple of beaconing fingers making the invite to fuck and then sleep more than obvious. I shrugged and on a whim I strode away out of the hall, through the large wooden doors, almost running then to my rooms. My valet was nowhere to be seen, he would have taken the opportunity of an early night, and no doubt after more than a few ports he would be sound asleep.

I didn't bother to undress further than my boots, there was no fire in my room and I suddenly found myself shivering with cold. Grabbing a huge knitted woollen throw from a sofa where I would often read, I wrapped it about my shoulders. I sunk onto my bed, pulling the covers and the throw over myself, falling within a few minutes into a restless sleep full of images of women I had known over the years, none of them however were Cassandra, and in my dream I was searching and searching for something, pushing aside all the women, but never quite finding what I sought.

I awoke some five hours later, feeling in no way refreshed or rested, but knowing my guests would be wondering where I was.

However much I tried to instil a sense of freedom and the lack of any need to defer to a host, some of those who attended the gatherings seemed totally unable to function without regularly checking that the way they were behaving was correct.

With this in mind, I pulled the cord on the wall calling for my valet, he would be surprised, and probably sleeping off a heavy night drinking and playing cards however I just didn't have time to worry. He was nothing, if not capable and I knew he would muster the requisite energy to appear in double quick time.

I was right, less than five minutes had passed when Simmonds appeared, looking slightly less than his usual well turned out self, but nonetheless he was awake, and functioning. As soon as he saw I was actually in the room, wanting to be dressed and turned out looking less like the mess I was, he sprang into action, nipping back out of the door and barking a few gruff orders to who must have been a chamber maid lurking about. In less than fifteen minutes, a fire was dancing merrily in the grate warding off the chill in the air, I had a cup of tea in my hand and hot water was rapidly being ferried in by various members of the house staff to fill the bath I had demanded be filled as quickly as humanly possible.

"Did you not attend your dinner M'Lord"? asked Simmonds as he helped me undress, and then step into the steaming hot water, which as always smelt of some oils or another, sandalwood I had once been told.

"I attended, but for some reason felt the need for my own bed to sleep in, of course I totally forgot no fire would be burning, and simply wrapped myself up and fell asleep. Now be a good man and leave me for ten minutes, but no more, I have to get back to those who are mainly still sleeping off the night before". He simply nodded, and headed out of the door, glad I was sure for a few minutes to compose himself. Letting out a long sigh, I sunk back into the hot water, letting the scented oils do their job of relaxing me, my muscles I could feel were slowly un-knotting, and my whole body felt as though the tension was leaving me. I realised that ten minutes was never going to be enough, that I could have laid there for a good half an hour and still felt like more. However there were some duties as host that I could not shirk, nor in fact did I wish to. My thoughts just had enough time to drift slightly and of course they made their way to Cassandra, I wondered what she was doing right now, sleeping still if the wench had any sense. I suspected not, knowing she would have been at the breakfast table early, and perhaps was even still sat there. I felt a tiny pang of guilt, which I quickly dismissed, training was everything and being aware of her place would do her no harm. If she thought for a moment she was, or could become special then all manner of demands would be made, and behaviours expected, and I had absolutely no intention to allowing anything of that nature under my roof.

All too soon, although I was fairly certain it was longer than ten minutes, my man reappeared, looking a little more awake and less dishevelled, holding a large white bath towel in his hands. It was a little slowly and reluctantly, that I rose from the bath and allowed a large towel to be wrapped about me. We then together managed in a fairly short amount of time to get me dressed and looking as good as it was going to get when you were forty-two years of age and feeling as though you had been knocked over by a horse and cart.

Finally ready, I gave my valet the rest of the day off, strode quickly through the house, making myself not pause, or go near to the dining room, instead I took a longer route which meant I bypassed completely all of the rooms downstairs, which Cassandra might use.

Making my way through the doors again, and back into my sanctuary of debauchery, I sighed with relief, as for some reason, there had been a little fear that some of the magic of the place had worn off. I was so pleased to note that this was not the case at all, my whole body relaxed as I walked through the doors and noted with pleasure the groups of people dotted around who had now awoken. Most of them it looked like had freshened up and shaken off the night before, the second trench of staff were in situ, whilst last night's slept now, to be ready to take over and work all night again tonight. Breakfast was available most of the morning, and merged then into lunch, the two meals taken buffet style from two large sideboards set near to the dining table. A few people always ate here, but most were more comfortable scattered about the large hall on cushions with low tables. Sofas and comfortable chairs were full of chattering, laughing people virtually all of whom seemed to be eating and drinking. It was then I realised my own hunger, I strode towards the food, grabbing a plate and loading it up quickly with eggs, bacon, tomatoes and large slices of fresh bread.

With my plate of food in one hand and a cup of steaming tea in the other I made my way about the room. I was searching for Sybil and Poppy, however annoyed I had been with them the night before, we generally always ate breakfast together, and their company was familiar and un-taxing enough to be a welcoming prospect. I spotted Sybil first, and then Poppy, they were sat near to the large doors which led out to a veranda, which in the summer would be open and full of people, but now in March, were almost all shut, with just a beautiful view to admire.

Sybil and Poppy were chatting ten to the dozen to another woman, I wasn't able to see exactly who they were so engrossed in talking to, so I almost turned around and walked away. The thought of sitting with three women all of whom I knew were perfectly capable of talking at the same time and still somehow understand what each of them was saying, would give me a headache and make me want to tie each of them up on a cross with a gag, without any intention of fucking them! However just as I was starting to spin on my heels, that darn woman Sybil looked up, saw me and beckoned me over. I sighed and almost continued on my heel turn, intent on simply ignoring her, an action which would no doubt annoy her, but I was sure would in no way surprise her. Just at that moment the woman who was sitting with them turned her head and glanced over, and I saw to my surprise, and I admit slight excitement that it was Cassandra. I stopped in my tracks, this damn woman was somehow managing to turn each and every plan I made on its head. Now had I been a stronger man, I would have stuck to my resolve, and done exactly what I been intending to do, and go find someone else with whom to eat. However, the very moment she saw me, she grinned broadly, it was such a wide happy almost beguiling smile that I found I had no choice but to let my feet continue over to the three women.

"Good Morning ladies", I said as I joined them, collapsing down onto a large overstuffed armchair, as I did I glanced up at a clock on the wall, checking before I continued in what I hoped was a conversational, yet non-committal manner, I wasn't going to end up spending the entire day with her, I really bloody wasn't.

"Ahhh yes, it is still morning I see, so darn often its past midday before anything like breakfast can be consumed". I heard Sybil snorting, and Poppy almost giggling, I didn't look over at Cassandra, it was Sybil who spoke first.

"Morning Thorpe, I didn't see you anywhere early this morning, but on mine and Poppy's customary wander about your massive house to avail ourselves of one of your bedrooms, and take a bath we found Cassie. The poor girl had no idea that we would all still be here today, and so rather than have her eat breakfast all alone in that large old dining room of yours, we brought her back here with us, to sit, eat, drink tea and chatter whilst looking over the beautiful view". I nodded and sighed a little, I did however glance over to Cassandra, who was this morning dressed in a delicate, demure pale green day dress looking almost too pretty. Her hair was looser than I think she would have normally dared to wear it, wisps falling out from their pins, curling and framing her face. Rather than address her singularly, which for some reason I felt almost unable to do, I spoke to them all again, my voice as gruff as I could make it.

"Well yes, I slept in my own rooms last night, I just couldn't for some reason find any comfortable place last night. I am here now aren't I, rather than allowing myself the luxury of the sleep I needed, I dragged myself out of my bed and ensured I was here, some of our attendees seem to get so bloody jumpy when I am absent". With that said, I looked up waved to a footman to bring me coffee, I needed something to wake me up, and tea just wasn't doing the job.

The women also had full plates of food, obviously very recently obtained, and for a few minutes no words were heard as we all tucked in. There was nothing like a heavy night before to ensure a decent appetite the very next day, however of course my night before hadn't been really in any way heavy, I didn't let this stop me. I noticed Cassandra too was making easy work of a plate of poached eggs and bacon, eating slices of bread and butter with relish licking the butter from her fingers.

Poppy finished first, and setting her plate aside, she sat back and let out a small belch, which of course elicited gales of laughter from Sybil, a look of surprise from Cassandra, who quickly then broke out that huge grin seeing no one else was offended, and from me, an expected eyebrow raise, however I couldn't resist myself turning to Poppy, I said,

"Call that some wind Poppy, you are an amateur", and with those words I let out a huge belch, which actually was far louder than planned, so much so some of our fellow friends sat nearby looked up in somewhat surprise before laughing. Poppy bowed her head and laughed, still grinning as she spoke.

"Ahhh Thorpe, you are without a doubt a far better expeller of wind than myself, I am a mere child in your presence." She then sat back and grinned, patting her full stomach happily as she said.

"I am indeed a lucky lady, I have almost forgotten how hunger feels. For so many years I was never not hungry, always that aching gnawing feeling of never having enough to eat, but now look at the bounty that surrounds us, and I, well I get to partake, without guilt or fear of reproach", she paused then and smiled, looking over at Sybil who was listening. I could see with very slightly shiny eyes, Poppy reached over and took Sybil's hand as she continued briefly.

"Yes, yes a very lucky lady indeed I am, a very happy lucky lady".

It was then that Cassandra spoke, for the first time this morning, for she had been content thus far to sit and listen still munching away at her food.

"Yes Poppy, and there are so many without food in their bellies, I loved living in London before I came here, it was the only home I ever knew, but I never found the sight of the starving poor easy to comprehend, my upbringing was comfortable. I haven't before known the wealth of some here, but I was never hungry, my parents were musicians, my father was the conductor, Edward Somerfield, so we were always on the edge of good society. Those involved in the entertainment of others will never quite be accepted by all, despite all enjoying their evenings listening to them. My mother was a kind, beautiful woman, who although was never able to actually roll up her sleeves, and get stuck in practically helping in soup kitchens, such a notion being utterly alien to her, she did however send considerable sums to help one stay afloat. We would now and again visit, ostensibly to check her money was being spent wisely and on those that really needed it, but in reality it reminded both of us, just how very lucky we were and to never take the food in our bellies for granted".

With that she stopped, and blushed momentarily bright red, as if her words and the forcefulness of their delivery had surprised herself as much as it had the rest of us. Sybil, being Sybil of course leapt up and flung her arms around Cassandra's shoulders briefly kissing her cheek.

"Cassie dear you really are such a good find, so very interesting and with so much more to you, than one might assume. I do hope we really can stay firm friends, Poppy and I have loved your company, haven't we Poppy"? Poppy nodded and agreed with her darling Sybil, whilst I just sat back and held in the sigh that was brewing, women really were so terribly annoying for so much of the time. Of course Sybil's words were entirely correct, and Cassandra was the most delightful of creatures.

I closed my eyes and sat back, whilst the three of them continued with their banter and chatter, each had their tea cups filled and I could see it was going to be some time before any one of them would wish to move. Of course I could have simply stood up, made my excuses and left, however there was something rather nice, being so close to Cassandra, hearing her talk and make conversation. I felt I was getting to know her a little more simply by listening to her in a different environment, with other women discussing perhaps trivial matters in which she was knowledgeable and confident, I realised then what an intelligent and self-aware woman she was.

CHAPTER NINETEEN

Cassandra

I had awoken after a surprisingly restful night's sleep, my head was a little muzzy, but considering I usually would have drunk no more than a glass or two of wine with dinner, this was to be expected. For just a moment, as I lay in my warm and very comfortable bed the events of the previous night seemed to be fantasy. However, as I became more and more awake, everything came flooding back and I actually cried out, partly in surprise I guess at my own behaviour, and partly due to the sheer surprise of what had gone on, when examining it from a totally sober point of view.

Sitting up slowly, I pulled the velvet edged rope, telling the kitchen maids I was awake, someone would be along presently with a large basin of warm water, a cup of tea would follow, and the fire would be lit in my grate, all before my feet would have to hit the ground. Being a governess was a strange life; I was part of the staff and yet in so many ways treated like a member of the household. However I knew there was only so much I could expect, for instance, if there were guests or family staying, the chamber maids would be busy serving them, and I knew I had to wait until absolutely everybody else had been seen to. As a governess, this simply wasn't possible, so there were times, when I sorted myself out, this also had the added bonus of currying favour in the servants' hall. I became known as someone who knew her station and was without too many airs and graces, and so therefore most of the time I was treated very well.

After I had managed to haul myself out of bed, gratefully drunk the cup of very hot tea and washed away all of last night, I finally allowed my mind to wander a little. I tried to process exactly what I had seen, and perhaps most of all, trying to understand my reaction to it. I hadn't run away, I hadn't been horrified (well perhaps some of the time I had been), I didn't feel in any way ill towards any of the people I had met last night, and truth be told I was really very much hoping for the chance to spend a little more time with some of them. That train of thought brought me to exactly where I was trying to avoid going, Thorpe, Lord Pembroath, my employer, wealthy landowner with impeccable breeding who was quite frankly the most interesting and exciting man I had met for many years. I sighed to myself as I recalled last night, somehow despite watching him earlier in the night copulating with an unknown woman, I had found myself able to trust him, confide in him and allow him physically closer than I would have ever thought I could. My sigh had turned to a smile as I realised just how much I had wanted to be so close to him, and just how much I then enjoyed his company and that closeness. He was unlike any man I had ever known, and although I had not known many men, and none in the intimate sense, still Thorpe was different. Despite the fact his default seemed to be being rather rude to people, his gruffness and even the fact that he was instigator, host and enthusiastic member of a group of people who indulge in openly with each other in the kind of behaviour that most respectable people would not even knew existed, he was someone I desperately wanted to spend more time with. I realised that I just wanted to be in the same room as him! I am not stupid and by now I had realised that what I was feeling was intense attraction.

I suddenly remembered the breakfast invitation, cursing myself wondering how on earth I could have allowed it to slip my mind. I had been planning on a basic day dress, one of the few I wore in the classroom and nursery with the children, both of whom would be on a train by now. I had said goodbye the previous night, knowing that Bessie their old nurse who still took care of the practicalities of child rearing would have assured they were up, dressed, breakfasted and on the 7.00 am train

But all of a sudden, the thought of breakfast with Thorpe, and then the possibility of a day perhaps, maybe possibly doing something which would involve seeing him again, meant that a dress with slightly frayed sleeves, and un-removable ink stains was just not going to be good enough. Opening my wardrobe I grinned to myself, not having much choice was sometimes a good thing; I pulled out one of two good day dresses, neither of which I had had an opportunity to wear prior to today. Pale green with tiny green foliage embroidered on the bodice, with lace about the sleeves and hems, it was pretty and modest.

I rather hastily pinned my hair up, it was still slightly mussed up with ringlets from the night before, but this I reasoned, might appear more by design than the accident it was.

The dining room was set up for breakfast, but I noted with more than a little disappointment that there was just one place set. It was not at the head of the table, but set for me, down one of the sides. There was no newspaper, and I saw that nothing had been cooked, the kitchen were obviously waiting for me to call for breakfast.

I reluctantly sat down at the table, my appetite had completely gone. I thought perhaps I could or should wait a little while, but I knew the workings of a large house well enough to know that Lord Pembroath was not expected for breakfast. As it was only the governess who was, the fire was low, the table set with the minimum of items and the silver dishes where breakfast would have resided were cold and empty.

After about ten minutes of just sitting, staring into space, I resolved I wouldn't trouble the kitchen; instead I would head down there myself, have a large mug of tea from the pot always on the huge table and avail myself of some bread and jam. The staff would thank me for saving them a job, and I would enjoy the bustle and warmth of the kitchen. Yes, I nodded to myself that, was exactly what I was going to do.

It was just as I strode purposefully out of the dining room that I saw the very welcome sight of Sybil and Poppy, both looked tired, and a tiny bit dishevelled. Like me they were now dressed in more modest day dresses, having no maid to pin up their hair, it was rather messy which was giving them their slightly dishevelled look. I grinned broadly seeing them, and Sybil called out straight away.

"Cassie, Cassie dear, good morning, how fabulous to see you, Poppy and I were just commenting that we wondered where you were today, and if we might see you, and as if by magic there you are, in front of us, looking as fresh as a daisy".

My mood was immediately lifted, and I headed over to them both.

"Good morning Sybil, Poppy, what a lift to my morning and my mood, the house is so quiet. I couldn't face breakfasting in that dark room alone, so was just heading to find bread and jam in the kitchens". Sybil clapped her hands and grinned;

"Well then Cassie, you really must come and eat with us, we have not done more this morning either than requisition a bedroom for a bath. So come back to the West Wing with us, the breakfast buffet is always a treat". With those words and obviously not giving me the chance to object, she slipped her arm through mine, and the three of us turned and made our way through the house and back to the West Wing. After a moment or two of silence, I said.

"So there are still people in the West Wing, the gathering or party, I don't know what to call it, is still there"? Both women nodded, but this time it was Poppy who spoke.

"Yes, it's always a weekend and most, if not all stay for the whole weekend, Friday night and Saturday night. Everyone will be gone by 11 am at the latest tomorrow, off back to their lives for another three or so weeks, and then back again. Of course not everyone is able to make every month and actually if all those who do come, did come all on one weekend there would be more than the house could cope with. Somehow miraculously some might say every month, just about the right amount of people turn up. The founding members, that are Thorpe, Sybil, I and a few others you may have met, are nearly always present, but not definitively. Even Thorpe whose house this is, has the odd month when life takes over, and we all have to muddle on without him. He of course assumes it's chaos and he is irreplaceable as host, however we manage, somehow"!

I had been listening intently and found myself suddenly and inexplicably disappointed he hadn't told me, he had sent me off last night, seemingly warmly, with the promise and feeling that my growing affections had been in some way reciprocated. To suddenly learn that in fact, he obviously had grown tired with me and had hoped I wouldn't be around today, or in fact this evening was rather more upsetting than I was going to let anyone know about. I resolved in that very second to put him from my mind, to act in a friendly but distant way, and ensure there was no need for him to ever need to extricate himself from my company again. Realising I had stopped walking, and was standing still with Sybil's arm still through mine, I smiled at both women deciding I was jolly well going to go with them, I was very hungry and their company was so very welcoming. I smiled and turned to them both.

"Sorry I got lost in thought for just a second there, but let's get to that breakfast table, I fear it's my stomach rumbling that we can all hear". With that I made myself laugh and my feet move in the right direction. Of course I saw the look pass between Sybil and Poppy, and felt Sybil's hand squeeze my arm, but I knew both would not mention it. There was however a small amount of comfort to be had in the knowledge that Thorpe was in the bad books of the formidable Lady Sybil, somewhere I would most definitely not wish to be.

Breakfast was as extensive and delicious as the women had promised, and I very happily filled my plate with food, far more than I would normally, but I was going to be eating for comfort, despite telling myself how much I didn't care, I very obviously did.

Sitting back with a plate on my lap, surrounded by and propped up with huge velvet covered cushions I watched out over the terrace. The gardens, farms and then onto the moors which surrounded the estate was a stunning vista. One terrace door was slightly open which let in a much needed breath of cool crisp air, the odour in the room with so many people, and so much food and drink was becoming a little overwhelming.

I knew I was being quiet, and Poppy and Sybil were allowing me to be. They themselves were chattering ten to the dozen to each other, including me in the conversation, without expecting me to actually answer or take an active part. For this I was so grateful, I listened to them, my mood lightening with each minute, their stories of the goings on the previous night; who had paired with who, who had drunk too much, who surprised everyone by running around naked until 5 am and who decided he was in fact homosexual after everyone else had known for years was enough to shake the dour from me. I found myself laughing along with them, smiling at the jokes, and again part of me, a larger part I decided than last night wanted and wished I was part of it, because however welcome I was; however many smiles and 'good mornings' had been directed my way when I had been loading up; my breakfast plate, I really was an outsider. I was very much aware that for as long as I was employed at this house, each month this would be happening, and I wasn't a real part of it. I was being tolerated this month as a bystander, because they were kind people and because Thorpe their host had requested it, however I knew very well that one wouldn't be able to simply come along every month without any intention of becoming a true part of the gathering.

I had, for just a moment, phased out from Sybil and Poppy's conversation, but hearing Sybil brought me straight out of my thoughts and into the real world again.

"Ahhhh now, there he is, our genial host, the man looks fit to beat a horse, what a dark mood I can see brewing, well let's make it worse shall we". Without waiting for an answer from either myself or Poppy she started to smile and wave her hands about gesticulating for him to come over, and come over he did. I found myself unable for a time to say much, I had looked over and smiled unchecked when I had first seen him, unable to stop myself, but as soon as I felt a little in control of my feelings, I concentrated on my food and the view. Reminding myself over and over how annoyed I was with him.

Poppy and Sybil really were the most brilliant of foils, they continued in the manner I assumed they always did, which gave both myself and Thorpe the chance to sit quietly and not engage ourselves in too much conversation. I however felt compelled to speak when I heard Poppy talking so openly and honestly about being hungry, my outburst was as honest as Poppy's words, but I felt the surprise of both Sybil and Thorpe as I spoke and even worse, I felt the blush hot on my face, spreading down my neck.

I did my absolute best not to look up and over to Thorpe, who unlike myself and Poppy was sat on a large low armchair as was Sybil. I allowed myself to glance at him, and from somewhere within me I felt a desire and almost a need to crawl over to him, he was sat and I was on the floor, which I realised with a start excited me a little, I wanted to crawl over I realised and stay at his feet, wrap myself about his legs, place my head in his lap and look up. Hastily setting the now empty plate on the floor next to me, I took a deep breath and willed the thoughts to leave my head. They were not bidden or welcome, however instead of doing that I again looked over to him, my hand reaching up to my throat, as I tried to not allow myself to blush. He wasn't looking at me, instead he was staring out of the terrace doors, taking in the view just as I had done earlier, I wondered if one ever grew tired of such gazing at such countryside. As I watched him I decided not, my mind however was full of thoughts as far removed from the bleak moors as it was possible to be, that desire to be at his feet wasn't abating instead in my mind's eye I saw myself there, at his feet, the rest of the world had disappeared and it was just the two of us, my hands were laid on my thighs, my cheek was resting on his knees and my whole body was pressed against his legs. I swallowed hard and made the image disappear, forcing myself back to reality, trying to get back to the room and Sybil and Poppy, knowing their delightful insights would have me back with my feet on the ground within moments.

But instead of it being one of those ladies who shook me out of my daydreaming it was Thorpe himself, who seemed to be suddenly standing next to me, this did nothing to help my mind, his presence so close and near, him standing tall and straight next to me, whilst I sat at his feet on the ground.

I looked up and smiled as he spoke.

"Cassandra, you seemed to be enjoying the view as much as I myself do, would you care to leave these two unstoppable gossips to their chatter and take a walk with me outside? I will have Jarvis bring you a cape, so you don't freeze".

I swallowed hard and despite all my promises to myself perhaps just forty minutes earlier I agreed within seconds.

"Yes, thank you Thorpe, I would enjoy that my head is still a little muzzy from last night and so I think a walk will help clear it", I looked over unable to stop grinning, and looking at Sybil and Poppy I saw they were both themselves grinning. Thorpe turned away saying,

"I will fetch the cape, it will give you ladies a chance to squeal a little, I can see it almost bursting out of your pores", with that he strode away at some speed, over to seek out the butler no doubt, and the promised cape.

Thorpe was right, as Sybil and Poppy took no time in indulging in the squealing, Sybil grabbing my hand once again.

"Now Cassie dear, our Thorpe rather likes you, of that there can be no doubt and from the look on your face, the feeling is very mutual indeed", I said nothing, knowing I just simply had a silly look on my face, Sybil obviously wasn't needing any response from me, and just continued.

"The thing is my dear Thorpe likes conquests, and he likes women, he likes submissive women, he likes being in control, none of that is in itself a problem, the problem lies in the fact that he has never been a man to be satisfied with just one woman. He like me and so many others here enjoy many people, we have those we consider to be special, my beautiful Poppy here, I adore her, love her and enjoy every minute we have together, but neither one of us is satisfied with just that, but that is something we understand and accept in each other". I turned my head and saw Poppy was smiling and nodding, her outward appearance was one of being in absolute agreement with what Sybil said, however the look in her eyes told a whole other story and I suspected she lived as she did so as to be able to spend the time she did with her beloved Sybil.

I still didn't speak as it was obvious that Sybil still had things to say, and I was right, she spoke quieter this time leaning in creating an air of secrecy.

"Cassie, the thing about Thorpe is that I have, since I met him, believed that he has the capacity for the kind of all-consuming love that would be required should he be monogamous. I am convinced should the right woman arrive in his life that he would be able, and would want only her. I am not saying that is who you are my sweet girl, just that perhaps all is not lost and you should perhaps cautiously follow your heart". I smiled as I listened, trying to take her words in, I hadn't allowed my mind to wander very much further than the next few minutes, all of the thoughts I had had earlier been instantly erased, persuading myself he must have just forgotten to tell me about today. Taking a deep breath and choosing my words carefully

I turned to my new friend.

"Thank you Sybil, your words are a very sobering warning to me, however I have not thought beyond enjoying a walk, I can assure you I am not making any great plans. Regardless of anything else I will never forget I am a mere governess here because my family fell into such a position that I could not support myself. There are no happy endings for people like me, we fall between the cracks and make the most of what we get. I have met some wonderful people this weekend, and Thorpe is one of those, yes one of the most exciting, but still one of many. My greatest dilemma is going to be working out if I am able to take the steps that are needed to make my life as exciting again, or if each month I will be reading by the fire in my room enviously thinking about what is happening here". I saw my words and reaction had surprised both Sybil and Poppy, and they were sat almost open mouthed listening, as I spoke. I had by now risen to my feet, and saw Thorpe striding back, almost as fast as he had rushed off, my tummy and my heart did respective flips at the same time as I saw him. I knew instantly my words of just a few seconds ago had been utter rot. Thorpe was the reason I was here, and was going to become the reason why I was going to wish to come and be here over and over again.

Seeing me he smiled, it was an unguarded open smile and I saw it was just for me, he made eye contact and he really was just smiling at me. I sighed happily and again looked down to see those knowing looks passing between Sybil and Poppy, I ignored them, and grinned to them both as I went to meet him.

CHAPTER TWENTY

Cassandra

I smiled as Thorpe reached me and without saying a word he wrapped a large woollen cape about my shoulders, he himself was wearing a thick jacket, which he had obviously acquired at the same time.

"My late wife always used to keep some spare items, just in case guests came inadequately attired she really was the most awful of people but yet she was practical".

Neither of us spoke for a while as we made our way outside, the air was very cool and I could feel the remains of an early morning frost, the ground being just slightly crunchy underfoot. It was incredibly nice to be outside away from the cloying full house, the noise and atmosphere of all of the people whilst incredibly welcome, was also overwhelming. In a move which was entirely impulse based, had I stopped and thought about it, I would have never moved, I reached my arm out and slipped it through Thorpe's walking now as close to him as possible. I knew he approved, as I saw a small smile appear.

It was me who in the end broke the comfortable silence.

"Your late wife, she and you didn't get on? The children are such a wonderful delight it seems incredible that she could be as awful as you say she is". He snorted and laughed a little, a rather hollow laugh, but not a bad natured one.

"You are right, my children are a constant source of delight and pride to me, however they are as they are, due to the fact their mother died when both were very young, mercifully too young for either of them to remember that she had no interest in either of them, beyond pushing them out, and ensuring they were fed and alive, she wasn't at all bothered. When guests were in the house she would make a show of having them brought to her to say goodnight, but it was always so very obvious that they had very little idea of actually who she was".

I listened intently, I knew Thorpe had been previously married, and had a sense that she was not a woman who had been loved by all in the house, however I had no real details or idea of who she had been.

Thorpe continued talking as we walked, my feet and the bottom hem of my dress were slowly getting sodden as we now walked over the lawns, however there was nothing that could have persuaded me to mention this fact to him. There was always the risk that he would decide that we should cut our walk short and head back to the house, and that would have been far more terrible than a wet dress.

"Her death was met almost universally by a sense of a non-event, it wasn't that there was any hatred or even dislike just a sense of nothing. In life she had only ever been interested in her horses, and when death came, even they seemed not to notice." I waited a few seconds taking his words in and choosing my own very carefully.

"That is so very sad Thorpe, sad for you; the children never really knew their mother and you tell me that rather than being to their detriment is one of the factors that has determined them becoming such lovely children, what an unlovable woman she must have been. You didn't marry for love then"? As soon as the words left my lips I knew I had overstepped the mark, I frowned and quickly gabbled.

"I am sorry, please forgive me my inquisitive nature sometimes means I say more than I perhaps should". I looked up and saw he wasn't looking angry at all, instead he was grinning. He stopped, and took both my hands in his, my hands had become cold, and his were warm, he had up to just a few seconds ago been wearing thick leather gloves, these were now stuffed in the pockets of his jacket. He was facing me, smiling that smile again, the open one, the one that seemed to be only for me, I smiled back nervously, taking a step back, but still holding onto my hands he spoke in a tone more gentle than I had previously heard.

"Cassandra, you don't speak out of turn, I like your honesty, I like the way you speak sometimes rather obviously without thinking first and I like most of the time the things you say, so please don't trouble yourself that you are saying more than you should. For some reason I want to know what goes on in that head of yours, what makes you tick". I couldn't help but grin happily, my day was turning out better than I could have anticipated and before I could think or say another word, Thorpe bent down and placed the softest of kisses on my lips. It was for just a brief moment, and yet I felt as though I could possibly melt there and then into his arms, it felt as soon as his lips met my lips they had again left them. I closed my eyes for the briefest of seconds enjoying and indulging, flicking my tongue out wanting to taste him on my lips. When I opened my eyes again, I looked up, his face was close to mine and he was smiling. I had lost the power of speech, but was able to meet his gaze and return the smile. He reached up and ran a thumb down my face, and round my chin, I felt myself shiver as he did, pausing with his thumb on my chin, he again leant down and this time the kiss was a little longer, and just a tiny bit more insistent, for just a second or two our mouths moved together and I felt just the tip of his tongue in my mouth. This time when he pulled away, he took a small step backwards, I just sighed and my hand unconsciously flew up to my mouth running my fingers over my lips. I smiled, my first kisses, and what kisses they had been. He must have known that I had never been kissed, I had never before these last few days been so close to a man.

"Oh my Cassandra" he said

"What are you doing to me, I think you might be a witch, casting a spell over me, just as soon as I resolve to not get too close to you, there you are looking beautiful and unspoilt, and I find all I want to do is be near to you". At those words my heart was hammering so hard, I feared it might actually leap from my chest and end up a quivering beating mess on the grass at our feet. This however did not happen, and I somehow managed to summon the power of speech. Swallowing hard before I spoke, I looked up and spoke softly, daring to move forward breaching that small distance he had placed between us moments earlier when he broke the kiss.

"I am no witch", I said with a small chuckle,

"You know who I am, and I think you knew when you invited me last night, and since that very first conversation, and even though you walked in while I was bathing, and I have watched as you have had sex, I have wanted and desired to be close to you. I don't understand fully why, and I know it is a dangerous emotion to have, because you are a dangerous man Lord Pembroath, and dangerous men can sometimes take women like me, and turn us into something else. Then when that dangerous man no longer wants her, he leaves her almost as if she was desolate, she is forever changed and forever has lost the innocence that may have one day seen her enter a favourable state with another man, less dangerous or interesting, one far less beguiling or handsome, but one steady and worthy".

There was from Thorpe none of the anger I had been expecting, even as I had been saying the words, my heart had been screaming at me to stop, that I should just enjoy this for what it was for just a while longer. Why ruin it now, when the excitement was peaking, when my heart was hammering and my whole body just longed to be close to this man, but as is generally always the case with me, my head won and I just had to speak, I had to say it. I was not someone who could become what that young woman was last night, I knew this to be an absolute truth. I didn't judge her, or wish her ill in any way, but despite my enjoyment of the previous night and the hope that somehow I would be able to become part of that close knit group of people, I knew inside I was a woman for one man, and I needed a man who was for one woman.

Thorpe's face gave away little, he smiled almost softly as he spoke.

"You see Cassandra, this is one of the reasons I find you so interesting, you are my employee, you live here at my behest and I could with one word and a sweep of my hand have you removed from here, ruined with no chance of employment ever again", seeing the look of utter fear on my face he moved quickly to grab my hand and bring it to his lips kissing softly.

"No, no, no do not fear my sweet girl, that is something I would never do, but you are brave aren't you, so much braver than I had anticipated or even given any thought too. Everything I have shown you, you have seen for the reality of what it was, you have seen I know the beauty in every tableau, and in every relationship you have seen it as I see it. But you are a woman I know who would not be happy to share, or be shared, and that is something you know that in my world is rare. You may think 'but I am not of your world', but you are Cassandra, because I know that as you sat last night and watched those women you were jealous weren't you, your neck ached a little for a collar, your heart skipped a few beats at the thought of such a level of ownership and your body desired the submission, I am right aren't I"?

I paused, I had to, I needed to think, to assess and I realised be as absolutely honest as I possibly could. It took me some time to get my head straight, and Thorpe didn't push me or grow impatient, he simply waited, I realised he knew that I needed this time, that what he was asking me to admit to, to actually say out loud was vast in its implications. Before yesterday I had never seen, nor entertained such thoughts, I was a governess, and one who knew her place, enjoyed her life and accepted the implications and limitations placed upon her by society. But now here I was, stood in the cool crisp spring air, not quite sure what was I was being asked, or how to respond, this man was my employer, he was the owner and Lord of everything the eye could see, his family and breeding were impeccable, and he himself was self-confident, self-aware and the most exciting and frighteningly interesting man I had ever met, but was he actually offering me anything beyond a night full of what I had seen last night. It was then I realised what I wanted, and what I needed, and it was also then that I realised and knew that Lord Pembroath would not be able to give that to me. Finally, I thought I might have the right words to say.

"Oh but you are a clever man, and a man who has proven as much of a surprise to me as you claim I am to you. When I came to your home, it was to look after and educate your children. I took the position of governess accepting some inescapable facts, one of which was that as a governess I am rendered almost un-marriable, I have no dowry at all, I have no home of my own, I have nothing whatsoever to bring to a marriage and coupled with this no real ability to ever meet a man. A governess by the very fact she is working as a governess will be doing so because she has no chance, she may be well bred, well brought-up and well-educated but she is on the edge, somewhere between servant and the people she works for. She cannot look to the staff for a husband - there would never be a match there - and she cannot look to those she so often is treated as an equal by". I paused briefly then, just to draw breath, but Thorpe took the opportunity to take my arm and lead me over to a bench which was nearby. Brushing the few leaves off before we both sat and without saying a word, he slipped his arm underneath my cape so he could wrap it around my waist, he turned to me and smiled, which I knew was my cue to continue, after taking a deep breath I did just that.

"What I am saying Thorpe, probably by using far more words than I really need to, is that I had forsaken and given up on the hope of finding a husband when I came here, but that fact does not in any way counter or mean that I can stop being who or what I am. Perhaps I have learned a little more about who I am, or maybe more about who I could be, but the only way I could ever make those discoveries was with a man who was mine, and only mine. I can see only hollow pleasure in what your evenings would offer me should I embark upon them without that. I see only joy and true happiness in the giving of myself to a man who would treasure that gift, nurture it, care for it and together with me tread a path together, a path which only includes the two of us". I sighed and allowed my body to melt against his, the feeling of him being so close was again quite intoxicating, I felt in us both a sense of huge disappointment. I turned my head to look at him.

"You see my Lord, some might say if you have nothing, you should accept something, but I could not, perhaps with a lesser man, but not with you, with you, it could never be that way".

Finally I had finished, I felt as though there was so much more to say, but that I couldn't find the words right now. I knew that sat here like this with him, was more than very likely the last time I would be this close to him and I willed myself to make the most of it.

The look on his face when I now glanced up was one of sadness; I could see behind his eyes some kind of battle going on. Of course his next words surprised me perhaps more than any others would have done.

"Tell me about your life Cassandra, your parents who they were? I saw your father you know, more than once when I attended a concert, he was a fine conductor, but tell me about your mother, tell me about your memories, your favourite foods, your favourite books, tell me about you Cassandra. I shall in turn tell you about me, and in that we shall put off what is perhaps inevitable, let me court you as we are sat here, I will impress you with my wit and my charm and you will beguile me with your beauty and your intelligence, and then maybe we will find a way through, an answer could spring up in front of either of us".

And so that is what we did, just the two of us sat outside on a bench, for what became hours, at some point a footman arrived bearing a flask of steaming tea and some sandwiches, which we ate gratefully from greaseproof paper. We found a way to talk and to laugh, to learn about each other and to grow closer as we did, there was a tinge of sadness of course, it ran through my body like ice, chilling my veins. Thorpe's words following my revelation had made it clear that I was correct he was not looking for the word that neither of us had said, or I had really even allowed myself to think about. So I entered into the conversation enthusiastically, I held his hand, I allowed his arm around my waist, and his fingers to snake over my belly, and inside I began grieving for a love I hadn't even started to know yet.

CHAPTER TWENTY-ONE

Thorpe

Exactly how I had gotten here, I didn't really know. Asking Cassandra to go for a walk had started out in my mind to be a good way to escape Sybil and Poppy and their infernal giggling and gossiping. The way Sybil kept looking at Cassandra and then at me with a knowing grin plastered over her too pretty face was beginning to seriously annoy me. However as soon as we stepped outside I realised that had been a foil, my own mind had been tricking me, all I really wanted was to be alone with her, we had walked and talked, enjoying each other's company, and then I had gone and done it. For some reason deciding it was a good idea to kiss her, it was not a good idea at all, it was a terrible plan, it meant that reason and logic got flung out of the window replaced by ridiculous feelings and emotions, and of course she couldn't help but be honest and adorable with it.

I knew before she said the words that she wasn't going to tell me that she wanted to be a plaything, that she would submit to me tonight, allow me to take her virginity and fuck her into next week. Of course I bloody well knew it, but still I should have been kicking myself, should have been kissing her again softly, escorting her back to the main house and saying a goodbye to her as anything other than my children's beloved governess, but oh no, idiot that I must bloody well be, we sat there, in the cold talking, and I told her things I have never told another soul.

It felt so very good with my arm about her waist, she wasn't a skinny woman, and so she felt warm and soft pressed next to me, almost familiar and yet so new, a discovery I probably wasn't going to be able to complete of course. The cool air had brought out a blush to her cheeks, and her hair had spilled out from her hastily placed pins, she looked to me almost pre-Raphaelite, ringlets spilled over pale perfect skin, whilst her cheeks and her lips were almost the same rosebud pink. As she opened her mouth to speak I could see white teeth in a perfect row, she had a habit I had noted of flicking out her tongue as she spoke every now and again to lick and moisten her lips, the desire to grab her and crush her plump lips with mine each time she did this was almost overwhelming. Despite the fact that I could sense a deep growing sadness from each of us, still as I watched her I became aroused, my cock hardening pressing against my clothing, tonight I was going to need to fuck someone, in fact more than one. I was going to fuck as many women as I possibly could, take away the taste of this woman sat next to me, remove her from my mind, by groping, tasting and fucking as much female flesh as I possibly could. In fact Sybil and Poppy were going to be first on my hit list, I knew Sybil would let me beat Poppy, and Poppy would get down on her knees and beg like a slut for it, that girl was an amazing fuck I mused, the moment you touched her cunt she was dripping wet and begging, legs open wide hips thrusting. Poppy did needy and horny like few women I had ever met. Sometimes she only wanted to be fucked in her delicious slightly fat arse and would get up on all fours and reach around spreading her arse cheeks for you begging for a cock to fill her, there had been times in the past when Sybil and I had used her for hours, Sybil had a streak of cruel in her which would leave Poppy sobbing and begging to cum, her arse red and bleeding from the whip she had begged Sybil use on her.

I filled my mind on purpose with such thoughts, because I thought they may purge Cassandra from my head, however I knew it wasn't going to work, and I cursed myself for missing some of what she said.

We sat outside on that cold bench for over two hours, the offering of tea and sandwiches had been readily accepted by us both, and now the flask was empty, and I could feel her starting to shiver a little as she sat next to me, it was time to go inside, but I knew I couldn't abandon her, I wasn't ready yet to send her back to the world on the other side of those huge doors.

I stood up, uncurling my arm from around her, which I then extended to help her stand.

"Time to go inside I think my Cassandra, I am certain we would both like to sit out here for hours more, but I think we might both freeze to the spot if we did, and they will find us both in a few days frozen looking much like ice sculptures". She laughed softly and rose up.

"You are right of course, but I am reluctant, it's rare don't you think that two people will be quite so honest with each other and still walk away friends", I couldn't help but nod and agree.

"Oh yes, that is very true, and I do hope we are friends Cassandra, you are a joy, and if I could give you what you needed we could be so much more than friends. I am not sure I can, if I am honest, I don't know how to, but I also find myself unable here and now to send you away, to say it could never be, because if I do that we will become what we were before, employer and employee and that, well that Cassandra, seems awful".

We had by now made our way to the house, and were both paused outside of the main entrance. Giles came slowly out, opening the door for us; the damn man must have people stationed all over the house, so he knew exactly the coming and goings.

Once inside the lobby we both raced over to the roaring fire, and after I helped Cassandra off with the huge cape, which had done such a good job of keeping the frostbite at bay we both stood for a moment or two silently warming our hands. It was Cassandra who spoke first, doing what she seemed to manage always to do - she surprised me, with her presence of mind, and her ability to take control for herself. Even as she spoke I was regretting my earlier words, because I knew she was doing what she thought she needed to, to save herself.

"I will take my leave of you here Thorpe, you said just a few minutes ago that you could not let me go just yet, so let me make that job a little easier for you. I will not venture again to the West Wing, and I will never again speak to you of it. You of course have my absolute and utter assurance that I will never breathe a word to another living soul about what happens behind those doors. What we both failed so spectacularly to admit to each other earlier, was that however right you are about my desires, about the needs that have been awoken in me, the only man to whom I can give myself to in that way is my husband. I don't have a husband, and nor am I likely to". With those words she reached up placed a now warm soft hand on my check smiling.

"You really are the most beautiful man Lord Pembroath, and if that kiss is the only kiss I shall ever have, then at least my heart has been allowed to race at the thought of more and my lips have tasted a kiss".

I wanted to kiss her again, to crush those perfect lips to mine and kiss her passionately, but I didn't, how could I, she was right, the damn woman was always right. She wanted and needed a husband to offer her the protection and love that would allow her to give herself. I simply wanted her to give herself to me, with no promise of any more, what an idiot, what a damn fucking idiot I had been, to have even thought I could play with her in the manner I had been planning.

"Do me one thing please my Lord" she asked her voice already changing back to one of respectful dutiful governess to her employer, I nodded and gruffly said.

"Well yes, what"? The gruffness came out without me realising and straight away I regretted it. She almost recoiled from me, seeing a woman so hurt would have normally elicited nothing but a raised eyebrow and a small smug sense of satisfaction, but with this woman I couldn't bear it. Grabbing her hand which had dropped like a small stone from my face, I kissed it, before moving to kiss her cheek, cradling her face in both my hands.

"My sweet Cassandra, I am sorry these are not emotions I would normally expect, what, what can I do if it is in my power I will do it", she smiled relieved, however the tears gathering in her eyes, making them appear full and shiny were not going away and I assumed that once away from me she would let them flow.

"Please, would you tell Sybil and Poppy how much I have loved meeting them, and beg their favour that if they are ever here for a gathering and have time to please call upon me, I would so love to see them. Perhaps the next time the children visit London I may be permitted to go with them and if I would be welcome at Sybil's home I would love to visit – to call upon them, then I shall be so very pleased to". With that she stopped, her hands were still grasped in mine, and she made no attempt to move them, and of course neither did I. I nodded my head slowly;

"Of course, you can consider it done". She smiled and then with a boldness I would never have associated with her, or a woman of her upbringing she leaned up, snaked her arms about my neck, pressed her body against mine and kissed me. She truly kissed me, the urgency and passion in her kiss was like nothing I had never experienced before, without any conscious thought on my part, I wrapped my arms tightly about her waist. My hand reached up to her back, I pulled her even closer to me, and returned the kiss, our tongues dancing together, her lips so soft and perfect pressed against mine. I opened my eyes briefly to see hers closed, the lashes that frame those perfect soft eyes were spiked and I could see a tiny tear running down her cheek. My heart hammered as we pulled away, her lips were slightly swollen and reddened, and I wanted nothing more than to pull her to me again, kiss away every tear she might ever have, wrap her up, make her safe forever and never let a tear fall again. She smiled weakly and I saw her fingers go up to her mouth, brushing over her lips for a moment.

I forced myself to calm down, reasoned with myself that forever was never a word I would use rationally when thinking about a woman. She had now dropped my hands and had taken a step back, the gulf between us now seemed huge, and it took all the self-control I possessed not to reach out and grab her again, yank her roughly towards me, and bruise those red lips with my kisses.

She turned to walk away, pausing just for a moment.

"That was a kiss to remember, thank you Thorpe. No doubt I will see you soon, perhaps we can breakfast while the children are away, I hope the company of a woman who promises not to chatter too much first thing in the morning may not be too tiresome. Enjoy your evening Sir".

I stood speechless as she walked away, her steps at first were slow and seemed almost laboured, but as she reached the staircase she seemed to find her feet and ran all the way to the top of the first flight, and I watched as she turned and continued her way up the second flight, obviously heading to her room and the nursery.

Deciding the cold air was just what I needed to clear my head and perhaps knock some sense into me, I turned now and walked out of the front door, climbing down the couple of steps with a very heavy heart indeed. I walked at a brisk pace, heading back to my beloved West Wing, where I knew there would be people, friends and warmth and later in just a few hours I could wipe her from my mind totally. I had every intention of using as many women, enjoying them to the fullest, until she was gone, a tiny blip, simply another woman.

CHAPTER TWENTY-TWO

Cassandra

Managing to make it through my bedroom door and just about onto my bed, before I finally crumpled and allowed the sobs to come was a feat of human endurance, but once I had started, I didn't think I would ever be able to stop. My heart was broken that was for sure, in the space of a just a few days, I had managed to get my heart broken. I felt strangely utterly cheated as if heartbreak should at least entail before it occurs a little time and a lot more happiness. Since I had met Thorpe Pembroath my emotions had been on a crazy up and down, but mainly if I was honest with myself, down, and now I felt in the depths of despair. After a good thirty minutes of doing nothing much more than sobbing, I stood up and removed the damn dress, the one I had been so happy putting on this morning. It was now all but ruined, the hems was sodden and muddy, throwing it into a corner, I instead put on my old dark blue dress, the one so much more suited to a governess knowing her position. The sleeves were just a little frayed, and the hems were mended so many times you could see visible lines and stray ends of cotton. But this was who I was, wasn't it, and I should just get used to dressing that way.

After dressing I made myself sit, rather than lay. I sat down at the small desk in my room, gazing out over the garden. The view from my room was nowhere near as nice as the view from the West Wing, it was slightly obscured by walls, and trees, although if one stared very intently into the distance, you could see the moors, bleak and uninviting as they were, their beauty was undeniable and they seemed to perfectly capture my present mood. As I sat, I realised the source of my grief, my heart wasn't broken because of love lost it was broken because I hadn't ever had the chance to fall in love. The hope and promise of love had been so close and then it was ripped away from me, and that was the source of my grief.

Despite my angst and desolation, I knew I had made the correct decision, had I gone that evening to the West Wing, what could have happened? I knew I wouldn't allow myself to become a real physical part of it, so I would again be on the side-lines, just watching waiting for a scrap of conversation or kindness from someone. They themselves would just be waiting to get away, find someone real enough to satisfy their lusts rather than a tiresome dull young woman too scared to become a part of their reality. And of course Thorpe would be there, I assume dinner would be the same affair as the previous night, with him at the head of the table with some young plump woman, panting and chomping at the bit for him to pay her some attention. When he did, which of course he would, she would give him her all, everything that I could not, and how could I bear to see him kiss, touch hold and even have sex with another woman again.

I gasped at those thoughts, and my fingers reluctantly touched my mouth, I could almost still taste him, could still remember the kiss, it had been an impulse that had shocked me, but one I knew I couldn't regret. To kiss him in that manner had felt beyond my wildest dreams, I had the capacity for passion, the capacity to love and need and desire, but now I would never get the chance to fulfil that potential. I guessed that as time went by I would slowly forget how it felt to have him so close, to feel his arms around me, his breath hot on my skin, to taste him on my lips. I would forget the closeness of sitting next to him, with an arm around my waist pulling me ever closer, the whispered words in my ear which caused me to shiver and goose pimple.

And I would forget what I had seen, forget the women able to be on their knees, delighting in every way in the power they held because I saw now so clearly that with the need and desire they showed also came liberation and power. It was they who gave and they who could take away, it had been made clear to me that the women chose to give themselves and I could see how absolutely true this was, but also it was their decision, and theirs alone when if ever to revoke that. But all of this, in time would fade from me, I would forget, my blood would cool and I would be nothing but a well-mannered governess, whose future was set, going from family to family, until I retired with hopefully enough money to spend my last days somewhere near the sea.

The thought of this caused me such great pain, that I indeed did fling myself upon my bed again, thumping the pillow with my fists, sobbing into the pillow to muffle the sound, as much from myself as from anyone else. Finally the need to cry subsided, and I lay on my back looking up at the ceiling, tracing the cracks in the plaster with my eyes. Following one particularly active crack all the way from the ceiling and down the wall, my gaze came to alight upon the now empty and upturned tin bath. I cringed and pulled my legs up remembering him as he had been when he had entered my room unannounced or invited. How he had watched as I touched myself, exploring and discovering places that would now go untouched or explored by anyone else.

That I resolved was the real Thorpe Pembroath, that rude and chuckling man, the man for whom manners were reserved for those below him in social standing, whilst he, the Lord in his castle could behave exactly how he pleased with little regard for the feelings of others. It must have all been a great game for him, see how much he could fool the governess; could he charm her enough into believing his affections were real so that her corset would be like paper in his hands when he ripped it from her, and her virginity given to him. But no, he hadn't been able to, I was still a virgin, but now I was a virgin in whom feelings, lusts and needs which could not be sated, had been created.

I murmured now in grief, as my mind wandered mixing the time when his eyes had raked over me laying naked in the bath, to those women, in fact just one woman. The woman whose husband had held her leash so tightly and who had begged with such love and need it had caused my heart leap and my stomach to flip. In my mind's eye, it was me, naked and wet from that bath, knelt at the feet of Thorpe, his fist was the one around a chain wrapped so very tightly, attached to this chain was a collar, fastened about my neck denoting me as his, owned, wanted and desired.

The murmur turned to one of need as I felt a warmth between my legs, trying to wipe the image from my mind, I crossed and uncrossed my legs, squeezing my thighs together, this did nothing to help only making it worse. The feeling of arousal kept growing; my hands with fists bunched were crossed over my chest, in an attempt by me to ignore what was happening. My mind however had other ideas and I could not remove from it the picture of me naked and dripping wet kneeling at the feet of Thorpe. He was fully dressed, wearing shirt sleeves and I could see the strength in his arms and hands as he held onto my leash, my imagined self, had no more control than I because she was leaning up, wrapping her arms about his legs, nuzzling her face to his groin, panting slightly, she was begging of course, begging that he do something about the need between her legs. His face was unmoving, but his lips were slightly parted and gave away his emotions, his tongue was running over his teeth and lips and his breath had quickened slightly.

I opened my eyes in an attempt to rid myself of the images, but although I could no longer see them, I could feel them and their effect on my body was apparent. I was breathing heavier and I could feel my nipples pressing against the rough material of my corset, between my legs now felt on fire and unable to stop myself one hand started to pull up my skirts. Finally able to reach between my legs, I quickly pulled my bloomers down, so they were just below my knees, meaning I could pull my knees up and let my legs fall open, after two days of pent up and hither before unknown sexual arousal and frustration my fingers fell upon a very wet and hot vagina, this time I was not gentle or reticent, I had a need and I was going to very simply do what it took to lessen that need.

Unpractised fingers found their way inside me; I had parted my lips with one hand and used the other to delve deeply inside. Using the knowledge I had garnered the previous night, I slipped the tip of a finger inside me, my hole was so tight that for a moment I was unsure if I was in the correct place, but quickly this resolved itself, as I relaxed. I allowed myself the luxury of just slipping a now very wet finger up and down over the lips of my sex, up to that small nub which now felt so very sensitive and swollen, rather than force my fingers inside. I just slowly rubbed, and as I did that my body relaxed and I was able to slip the first inch or so of my finger inside myself, so now on every stroke my fingers rubbed over my swollen clitoris and then down delving inside me slightly more each time. The sheer physical pleasure of this action gave me some respite from my grief and upset, as I allowed my mind to wander again this time focussing on the kiss, and my pleasure in his touch, imaging his hands cupping my full breasts fingers pinching softly at hardened nipples. I knew instead of crying, I was whimpering and moaning. The fingers on and in my vagina were now soaking wet, a by-product I assumed of my arousal, I had seen the women last night also had been as wet between their legs.

I shifted slightly on the bed, my breathing was now at a low pant and I had moved both hands between my legs, my clitoris was so sensitive and swollen I couldn't touch it with too much pressure now, so one finger was rubbing it, the faster I rubbed the better it felt, and I arched my back with the joy of it. Gulping slightly as I did, the other hand was also now between my legs and my middle finger was slipping inside me, my body was relaxed and aroused enough for me to move my whole finger in and out of my body, over and over again.

All of this I did by instinct, and the knowledge that I needed to continue, and eventually some relief would come. Which of course it did, all of a sudden I felt as though I had reached the top of a very large hill and just over that hill is where I had to be. My hands moved quicker and hips thrust upwards, I straightened my legs and curled my toes, holding my breath and then as quickly as it appeared on the horizon it overtook me, my whole body seemed for a few seconds to convulse and I cried out in pure pleasure. My orgasm sent shards of intense pleasure throughout my whole body radiating up through my belly, my tongue was flicking over my lips and I laid whimpering for a moment as the feelings gently subsided, my hands fell naturally away from my body. Without bothering to pull up my bloomers I instead kicked them off and onto the floor, I smoothed my skirts over my naked sodden flesh. After a few minutes to catch my breath, and understanding exactly why people did what they did with each other, I turned over and sobbed, mourning the loss now more acutely than ever.

As the day turned slowly into evening I didn't move, and the tears didn't stop, but eventually I slept, it was fitful and restless, full of grief, unresolved feelings and more than anything fear.

CHAPTER TWENTY-THREE

Thorpe

So that was it, it was done and I had to be glad, I was again a free man, no nagging feelings of guilt or worse having her here with that look on her face, watching me, stifling me. Nope, this was good, this was what the carnal set was all about, and I was the centre of it all, it was my idea, this was my house and these were my friends. She was just the bloody governess for god's sake, a woman whose father was a drunken conductor, hardly the material one should be thinking of more than quick fuck.

I had decided a long time ago that I was never again going to be shackled to a woman, and away from Cassandra's annoyingly intoxicating presence I reaffirmed this to myself, knowing what is right for you, and sticking to it I decided was the most sensible thing any man can do.

As I walked back through the terrace doors, I was surprised at how late in the afternoon it was, and normally I would have been relaxing thinking about the evening ahead, with one eye on the staff, making sure each was doing what they should be doing. I immediately spotted Sybil and Poppy, they had of course moved by now, and were part of a large group of people sat near to the fire. Someone, and I couldn't see who it was, was playing the piano rather beautifully and the group were all but silent listening, I smiled instantly feeling more relaxed.

Not wanting the third degree from the two women just yet, I wandered from room to room, checking to see all was in order. There were two smaller saloons, both were furnished as opulently as the main hall, however being smaller the atmosphere in both was so very much more intimate. One of the rooms I had allowed Sybil, after she had asked me so very nicely every day for about two weeks to furnish, and I had to admit the woman had done a fine job. She had created what she called an "exotic tent", the entire ceiling was covered in silk, which was hung down from a large jewel encrusted ring in the centre, the silk was swathed and pleated, fastening all the way around the room to long thin strips of wood. The effect was exactly as she had wished, the material continued over much of the walls, and covered both of the windows. Sybil had had an artist friend of hers paint two large murals on the walls, and the silk curtains parted over this, to give the impression of looking out over a dessert, complete with camels and a palm tree covered oasis in the distance. The carpet had been removed, and over the highly polished wooden floor boards were a myriad of small rugs and large soft silk covered cushions and in the corners of the room were large daybeds, covered in bright jewel coloured satin.

The only part of the room Sybil had not been able to change had been the fireplace, and the woman had sulked for days at my flat refusal to nearly rebuild an entire part of my house, so she could have a fire in the middle of the room. She had to settle for leaving it exactly where it was, and simply adorning it with jewels and candles. That was where I was stood now, by the fire, warming my legs, and drying my feet, I hadn't realised until I had looked down and seen a soaking wet patch on the floor that my feet were as wet and in fact as cold as they were.

Assuming I was alone, I reached down and removed my shoes and socks, placing the socks so they were draped over some of the glass jewels which I knew after listening to Sybil drone on explaining it to me, were supposed to look like they were dripping over the fireplace. I chuckled to myself thinking of how annoyed it would cause Sybil to be if she saw my slightly grubby wet socks hung up there. My feet very quickly turned back from having a rather bluish tinge, to their normal shade of pink. The bottom of my trousers which were as wet as my feet, also started to quickly dry out, feeling much happier and enjoying the quietness of the room, I didn't move at all for a while just standing comfortably by the fireplace. It was only then that I heard a small rustle, and then another, and before I could blink again up sat one of the kitchen maids. I knew her name to be Martha, and she was a sweet girl whom I had on more than one occasion enjoyed, she saw me and grinned, I swear she was more freckled every time I saw her.

"Bloody 'ell" she exclaimed looking up at a small clock which hung from one of the walls.

"I woke up at about 7 am, grabbed a cuppa, and then decided that I really should make the most of having the day off, so threw me'self down in here and would you just look at the time now Sir it's nearly 4.30 in the afternoon, ain't it. I have slept right through breakfast and lunch, I swear I don't think I have ever been this hungry in all me days". Martha's turn of phrase never failed to illicit a grin from me, and still smiling I said to her.

"Well make haste then girl go and find something to eat, when I passed the dining table there was still food set upon it". She nodded and quickly stood up, her hair was all over the place, and her clothes wrinkled and creased, making no attempt to smarted herself up, her hunger obviously more important than anything else. As she rushed past me, I grabbed a hold of her wrist.

"Martha, this evening come find me." I didn't say any more than that, I didn't need to, she knew exactly what I wanted, and she grinned again broadly.

"Yes, Sir oh yes, I will", and with those words she finally hurtled off, I stood at the door watching her, laughing, as she went speeding off she was simultaneously now trying to tidy herself up a little, smooth her skirts down and ineffectually pat her hair. I liked Martha, she was funny, intelligent and sweet, why would I want to give up enjoying girls like that, and I wasn't going to.

Dinner was in full swing, tonight no one joined me at the head of the table, where Lucy had been sitting the previous night, I had them instead, set just one place. For some reason I wasn't in the mood for making small talk with a woman who was swelled up to twice her normal size with some kind of strange pride. A pride that she felt chosen, simply due to the fact of where she was sitting. I had looked about and seen absolute nobody I wished to spend that amount of time sitting next to and presumably making conversation with. Martha for all her amusement was far too annoying to spend any time with whilst actually wearing one's clothes. No, I ruefully and frustratingly admitted to myself that the one person who I would like to be sitting next to, was probably up in her room, either asleep or reading. I suspected there may have been some tears, but I was fairly certain by now she would have decided that I was an awful man who she was extremely lucky to have escaped from.

Every now and again I looked down the table and would catch the thunderous glances of Poppy and Sybil, both had been furious with me. It had taken very little time for them to realise that Cassandra was not with me, and that she would not be joining us for the evening. Even less time for them to both hurtle over, give me a dressing down in very loud tones, declare me an absolute waste of time human being, and the kind of man who shouldn't really be allowed out after dark alone. They were right, of course, how could I deny anything they said, but what irked me more than anything was the only reason they were so annoyed with me, was because they both had themselves fallen for Cassandra's charms. Her intelligence, humour and personality had charmed both of them as much as it had me. If I stopped and gave it a little bit of thought they were a couple of hypocrites, Sybil more than anyone, she who hired her staff based purely on how much she wanted to bed them. She kept Poppy her mistress in rooms, bringing her out like a plaything when she felt like it. Granted Poppy's personality was always such, that it felt very much as if it was the other way round, and Sybil could be the one dropped at any moment. Nonetheless the facts were plain and Sybil kept Poppy in a way she had made it clear she would not approve of me doing with Cassandra.

They had said there was a good chance that Cassandra or Cassie as they called her was the one thing I had been waiting for all my life, because I was such a fucking horrible monster, I couldn't possibly see it, and would live for sure to regret my actions. I let them both rant,

I didn't feel I had the energy to add further fuel to their fires, and eventually they both did run of out steam. Sensing there was no fight to be had, they stalked away giving me furious backward glances as they went. I had plonked myself down at the end of the table, and sat drinking red wine at speed, scowling at anyone who glanced in my direction.

My friend Raj was again sat at my left hand side; he took in my mood, and knowing me rather better than most, didn't ask me why I was so damn angry. He was not stupid, and would have seen the furious looks passing between Sybil and Poppy while they glared at me. Instead of giving me the third degree, he berated me good naturedly about not arriving last night to help him with the twins, who were both tonight sat alongside him. Looking as absolutely stunning as they both had done the previous night, their skin seemed to almost sparkle as much as the jewels which adorned their bodies. I had to admit as my eyes skimmed over them both, that they were the most stunning creatures I had seen in many years. One of the women, neither of whose names I knew, caught my eye and smiled, before lowering her eyes and speaking so softly, I had to lean a little forward to catch her words.

"We were a little disappointed yesterday, my sister and I were both so looking forward to enjoying some time with the infamous host of the carnal set. Raj took such good care of us both, but could we implore you, or do anything to persuade you to part with a little of your time tonight. I am sure it would be time you would consider very well spent". With that her sister looked up, and graced me with a smile almost identical to her sister's, she said nothing but merely nodded her head in agreement, it was Raj who added his two pennyworth.

"Yes my brother, you really must, I am an old man now, and after last night I feel even older and very tired, I think your help is needed". I couldn't help but crack a smile, Raj almost always was able to make me grin. I snorted...

"Raj you are one of the fittest men I know, and if you are old, then that makes me also a very old man, but yes, yes, tonight I am looking forward to getting to know", I paused and turned to the women.

"I am sorry, I do not yet know your names, Raj was so excited to introduce you both last night, extolling your many virtues, however he forgot the basic manners of a name"? With that, both women smiled, and it was again the same twin who spoke.

"I am Prabhati, which in your language means of the morning, but please call me Hati everyone does, and my sister here she is called Tarakini which would translate as starry night, but you can call her Tara, we are simply Hati and Tara, and so you see in us you have it all, night and day, what more could a man desire"?

Both women looked over to me smiling, and I had the distinct impression that I had just heard the same short speech that many, many men had done, however I grinned at the appropriate time and nodded my head.

"What beautiful names, and yes, you are right what more could a man desire, I hope then, Tara and Hati that tonight I will indeed be able to assist Raj, poor old man that he is", I looked up then briefly seeing Sybil and Poppy staring over, with looks that would sour milk and turn a lesser man to stone, I sighed, shrugged and arose, making eye contact with Sybil. I first of all turned to Hati the talkative twin and leaning down, wrapping my arms briefly about her warm, silken soft body I kissed her, she was surprised but quickly regained her composure and returned the kiss. Her body smelt of musk and rosewater and my hands ran over her shoulders and my fingers up to her chin as I broke off the kiss and looked into her eyes.

"Yes Hati, you are going to be a treat aren't you", with those words said I stood up and again staring straight at Sybil turned to Tara, who was slightly more demure than her sister, but no less beautiful or alluring. I slipped my hands over her shoulders and bent down, as I did my lips finding her collar bone. I kissed softly feeling her shiver and shudder slightly as I did, like her sister, she smelt of musk and rosewater. I could see goose bumps rising on her oiled skin as I kissed further up her neck, she turned her head upwards as I reached her lips and we kissed softly this time, her lips fitting mine perfectly, her tongue flicking over my teeth for a moment. I broke the kiss and made my way back to my seat, throwing myself down, pausing to visibly adjust the erection under my trousers. After I sat down I looked up and over to Sybil and Poppy and nodded slightly it was a challenge, and one they knew better than to act upon. Both women would now realise the game was done and over, this was what it was, I was who I was, just as were they, there was no room for daydreams or perfect endings, we rutted like sophisticated pigs and we loved every moment of it.

I grabbed my wine glass and took a huge mouthful of wine, I knew I was trying to remove the taste of the women from my mouth, but it didn't work, still all I could smell was musk and rose. The scent and taste was heady and made me feel a little sick. Raj turned and slapped me on my back laughing as he did.

"Ahhh welcome back my brother, after last night, there was a tiny bit of me worried you might be losing interest". I snorted and laughed, holding out my wine glass as I did, talking as it was refilled.

"Bloody hell Raj, you have known me too many years to think that, they will cart me out of here in a box, with my cock still hard", Raj laughed again, speaking almost just to himself as he then set about eating the huge pile of food in front of him.

"Isn't that the truth my brother, isn't that the truth". I watched Raj for just a moment, for a man brought up with the highly spiced and delicious food of his home country, he was certainly able to turn his stomach to eat pretty much anything. I remembered at school when for the rest of us the food had at times seemed almost totally inedible, he had tucked in with gusto seemingly finding something to like in every meal served to him.

I looked down at my own plate, which I had filled with roasted chicken pieces, potatoes and buttered carrots, I didn't feel terribly hungry, but still forced myself to partake. I paused only to look around me a few times, spotting Martha the kitchen maid halfway down the table I had to stop and smile. She had managed to find some time to straighten herself out, her hair was now piled atop her head in a mass of red curls, in which flowers had been placed, I recognised the tiny daisies as being from the massive flower arrangements I always had set upon the tables in the main hall. She was a resourceful young lady because they made up for the lack of jewellery or finery on her dress. She had changed into a low cut, but plain deep purple gown, the bodice was tight fitting and her breasts were pushed up and almost spilled out and over the top. I saw she had made a small corsage from the same daisies and this was pinned upon her dress. Her cheeks were ever so slightly rouged and I could see her animatedly chatting to the people next to her, a young man who I knew to be the son of a Countess who was a rare attendee. She was getting on in age, and came now only to enjoy the meal and the company afterwards of those who were happy to sit and watch. She wasn't a voyeur herself, in her prime she had been one of the grand beauties of the day, but time and tide waited for no man and she was now, however well preserved too elderly to really be a part of our activities. There was no chance I would revoke her invitation, she was as welcome today as she always had been, but this young man currently talking ten to the dozen to a very over-excited Martha I knew to be her eldest and most favourite son. It was very unusual I surmised for a mother to introduce her son to such things, but as I understood the case to be, after listening to Sybil chatter on about it at length, he had been as young men so often are, found to be spending far too much time in whore houses. He was seducing the serving staff at his family home, so much like a dog on heat that his mother had decided that the monthly gatherings were his best hope of 'discharging' some of his excess spirit whilst thoroughly enjoying himself. She had been right, he was more than often in attendance, his manners were impeccable and again according to Sybil who had, as she put it 'sampled' him, he was a jolly good mover in the bedroom. Martha it seemed was more than happy to be the centre of his attention, I doubted very much I would see her tonight as instructed, but I really didn't mind, I had promised myself now to Raj and the lovely twins, and I knew time with Raj was never rushed, he enjoyed everything at length.

Finally dinner was over, I admitted to myself that I hadn't enjoyed any real part of it, my heart felt heavy in my chest, and I wasn't really sure why. Sybil and Poppy had made it very clear if I was to go near either of them that evening, then my penis was likely to be removed via means I would not enjoy. Young Martha was in the thrall of a young man who was giving and would give her the kind of attention she would never be likely to have received from me, and I was beholden and promised to Raj and the two twins, both of whom were gorgeous women the likes of which most men could only dream of being with.

I must be tired, age really was starting to catch up with me, I had not had a lot of sleep, very often I mused I would take a short afternoon nap, which would set me up for the evening. I just wasn't rested enough, that was it, I had spent all afternoon with that damn woman and she had put my routine totally out. She really had gone some way to ruin my entire weekend, what a stupid man, I had been temporarily charmed by the creature, it would not happen again, of that I was very sure.

As I had been the night before I found myself almost the last person at the table, Raj had escorted Hati and Tara away, planning on sequestering himself and the twins in the tented room, they were not he mused to me earlier the kind of women one flung on crosses and chained up. Instead he made sure he had a good supply of silk scarves and gags, the women naked and tied up with such things apparently was a sight to behold, and one I knew I could no longer put off.

Making my way to the tented room somewhat slowly, I was accosted by Sybil and Poppy, I sighed thinking for sure that I was in for another tongue lashing. I held my hands up in mock surrender as they surrounded me.

"Poppy, Sybil come on now, how can you be quite so angry with me, you know me and you know what we do, the pair of you are as guilty as any one of us in this room, so if you have come to tell me yet again what a terrible man I am, then save it, keep it to yourself. I am not interested, Cassandra is a very nice woman, she is my children's governess, and will continue to be so, she was shown this world and she decided it was not for her. That is her choice". Instead of berating me again, Sybil leaned forward and planted a kiss on my cheek, she looked almost contrite, as did Poppy, Sybil then reached down, grabbed my hand, and she spoke in tones which were far removed from her earlier anger.

"Thorpe, my dearest, dearest friend, you are right, and we are sorry. Both Poppy and I saw something in you, and in Cassie when you were together, something you can wait a lifetime to find and we were amazingly jealous, we wanted to see more of it, know more of it, and indulge ourselves by basking in what the two of you could discover. My anger my old friend was just because it feels like you are throwing away something amazing simply because you cannot or will not admit that you could live your life in a totally different way, that happiness might be there for the taking", she paused and smiled, leaning over to grab Poppy's hand.

"But who am I to judge you, I cannot myself commit to a life with just one love, and do you think I do not know that Poppy would, if I asked her she would happily and faithfully commit to me and us. That she lives life the way she does simply because I ask it of her, is something that weighs heavily and forever on my heart. I love you Thorpe, and for a while it felt as though you might have had a spark lit in you, and I was angry, angry with us all, for being who we are and reverting somewhat to type, which is what we always end up doing......does that make sense, you know what I am saying Thorpe, will you forgive me"? She stepped back holding Poppy's hand, Poppy was smiling and I had seen the truth in Sybil's words in Poppy's reaction, I had never stopped and thought about it, but yes I realised, everything Poppy did was for Sybil. She could sacrifice and realise that Sybil would never be able to be just hers. I smiled at Poppy, instantly feeling a little sorry for her.

It took me a few moments to digest what Sybil had said, and my reaction could have been one of many I guessed, anger that the women had been so virulent in their earlier anger, or contrite that I had thrown away what they perceived to be a chance at happiness, but instead I felt myself sanguine, and understanding. Sybil's words had cut me deeply but at the same time had almost been like salve to the very same wound, she had voiced what my head and in fact my heart was refusing to acknowledge. Perhaps a spark had been lit, perhaps Cassandra was a woman I should be courting, pursuing, adoring and loving but I was, who I was, and that meant that I was going to stride into that room, rip the clothing and jewellery from both of those gorgeous Indian women and fuck them both until I couldn't even remember the name of my children's governess.

I smiled and turned to each woman in turn, wrapping my arms around them both and hugging them tightly, I know I could have kissed either one of them. I could have wrapped them up in my arms and kissed them, could have done what I had been planning to do earlier, but there really was a time and a place for everything and this was a time to show understanding and friendship, plus of course I knew Tara and Hati were waiting, and I feared I didn't have the requisite energy for them all.

I could see both were grateful and happy to have balance restored, pulling a back from the hug, Sybil pecked me on the cheek and smiled.

"We are all we can be Thorpe, for the good, or the bad, we are who we are. I love you my darling, always will, but damn she was a nice dream wasn't she, pure as a spring day, with the promise to be as a dark and hot as a summer's night." I nodded with some regret but said no more, and stood still where I was. Poppy and Sybil turned and made their way across the room, heading no doubt for a pre-arranged assignation, or perhaps simply to go sit and talk and enjoy some company. If the time with Cassandra had taught me anything, it was that actually simply doing nothing more than enjoying the company of friends happened more than I realised each weekend, and there was nothing whatsoever wrong with that.

CHAPTER TWENTY-FOUR

Thorpe

I was still dragging my heels, and I damn well knew it, Raj was going to be fuming if I didn't turn up soon, and so with as much enthusiasm as I could muster, I made my way through the hall and to the tented room. The door was closed and the small curtain which hung over, was pulled across . Although for most of the time, it was an open house, there was always the option of some privacy, and Raj was someone for whom sex was never a performance or a spectator sport. I was not surprised at all to see he had chosen to drop the curtain, which was a visible signal to all that the room was in use and the occupants were not happy to be watched. I tapped on the door, I took an uncharacteristic deep breath, opened the door and strode in. Raj, Tara and Hati were as I knew they would be, the only occupants of the room. They were not though as I had assumed would be the case, engaged in anything more erotic than a glass of wine and what appeared to be amusing conversation, as all three were laughing loudly. On seeing me, Raj stood up and quickly crossed the room, grasping me by the top of my arm, patting affectionately and smiling.

"Ahhh my brother, we feared it was yet another night when you would not be here to help your ageing old friend, the girls and I were just contemplating a night of chess before you arrived". I laughed out loud, hearing him speak, knowing it would be a very dark day indeed when Raj decided chess was a better prospect than the pleasures of the flesh. Slapping him on the back I walked into the room, and over to Hati and Tara.

"Well do not fear my old friend, help is here", I said laughing as I sat between both women, placing an arm around each of them, drawing them close to me, looking from one to the other, I frowned and speaking to them both I said.

"Tara, Hati, Hati, Tara, right now I confess I have no idea which one of you is which, tell me, there must be some way of telling you both apart". One of them nodded and they both smiled, it was Tara, or Hati, who answered,

"Well yes, there is a way, but you can't see it with our clothing on, we must be naked for you to be able to tell us apart", neither of the women moved, both sat still, giggling softly to themselves, I looked over to Raj who grinned and shrugged.

Slapping both women at the same time on their plump rumps, I said.

"Well come on we haven't got all day, naked Tara and Hati at the double". They both sprung up almost in unison, Raj took the place of one of them and sat next to me. I looked around at his smiling face, and for just a moment was instantly transported back to our school days. Raj's grin and enthusiasm hadn't waned or changed with the march of time. I knew his face would change soon, both Hati and Tara were standing giggling, apparently suddenly falling shy, despite all their promise earlier, I had a feeling they were playing with us and knew exactly what Raj would do. They didn't know me however, and suddenly I decided it was time they did.

Springing up from my seat with a face set in a grim line, I grabbed the first one of the women, pulling her towards me, I grabbed a hold of her clothing; she was wearing a sari which was worn in such a way as to expose much of her flesh, neither of the twins wore blouses or any other covering under their sari's. I was fairly certain I knew there was a long strip of material so I surmised it should come off in one long strip. Happy to test my knowledge, I grabbed the skirt of her sari and simply pulled, she struggled for just a moment, I could see she was surprised. I only had a certain amount of patience for coy, giggling sluts, it soon became old news and bored me, and I had no intention of allowing these two gorgeous creatures to disappoint me in such a way.

She quickly gave in and raised her arms, after reaching to release the sari, which seemed fastened with just one tuck of the material. The sari fell to the floor then in one quick action and she was stood there finally in front of me naked. Her arms, neck and shoulders were adored with jewels, and she quickly wriggled and moved under my grasp so as to free herself, she was stood just a step back from me, smiling slightly victoriously as she watched my approving eyes raking over her perfect body. I set my face with a grim look, and didn't break a smile or change my harsh tone as I spoke to her.

"Oh no, no, no girl, I think you have entirely the wrong idea here, I call the shots in this room, in fact in this house, if that does not suit you - then your sari is there, put it back on and I am sure you will find many in the hall more than happy to spend time with you and your sister. In fact I will happily sit and talk by the fire with you. However, if we are actually on the same page, then let's stop playing silly games. Remove your jewellery, unpin your hair and kneel at my feet where you belong".

I stopped speaking, took another step back, and waited. I looked over to Raj, whose demeanour had also changed, together we understood each other well, and would always work as a team. The twins were also obviously a team, and I saw a look pass between them, with a slight nod and a shrug.

Slowly after the shrug, the twin who I had not grabbed, reached around and quickly removed her sari, it took just seconds to unfasten it, and allow it to fall to the ground. Both sisters then stood in front of each other and removed the other's copious amounts of jewellery, carefully setting every piece aside placing it all upon a low table. Finally each reached up and unpinned their own hair from the intricate and bejewelled creation, again placing the jewels and pins on the small table. All of this took at least ten minutes, but I knew neither Raj nor myself was bored, watching them was fascinating and arousing, for me they grew more stunning the less adorned they became, and when finally they both stood before me, completely naked, free from all adornment, I was struck by the perfection of them. I nodded my approval, just a short sharp bob of the head, but it was all that was needed, both women in unison then fell to their knees, it was a practised move, and one I was fairly sure had been done many times before.

Raj moved and came to stand next to me, and I turned to him.

"Very nice Raj, I prefer them like this, and on their knees like this is a sight for my world weary eyes", turning to the twins, I spoke in a calm but slightly, I hoped, severe tone.

'So, Tara, Hati, even though I may just refer to you both as sluts, girls or in fact anything I want tell me, how do we tell which one of you is which"?

They looked up and smiled before speaking, and then both almost spoke together in unison.

"Hati has a birth mark, on her left buttock", I nodded and raised my hands in front of them, well come on stand and turn around, this they did, and spinning on their heels, I could see that Hati did in fact have on her bottom almost where her thigh started a large round birth mark. I smiled and stepped forward, placing a hand on each of their round, smooth, warm and very pert bottoms, I could feel each one shiver under my touch, pulling my hands back in one swift movement I spanked them each just once, it was a hard slap, and both yelped, taking my hands from them I spoke in a more gentle tone.

"Good girls, now turn around and back on your knees, but open your legs, I want to see exactly what you have hidden between your legs, now quick on your knees both of you, I want legs as wide open as you can, thrust your hips forward and place both your hands behind your head." They moved quickly, and I knew they were mine, I walked over to a large chaise and sat down, loosening my trousers and my shirt as I did, my erection had faded somewhat, but I wasn't concerned, knowing I could quickly and easily regain it. Raj then took up the mantle, walking about the women inspecting them like he might a racehorse. It was only then as I sat down that I really took a good look at them both, they both had very large full breasts with extremely large dark nipples, their bellies were not flat, but were perfectly rounded, and down to a dark thatch of hair, which I noted with some disappointment was unshaven. I knew it was an unusual thing to expect and one which most women would never ever dream of, but despite the copious triangles of dark hair between their legs, I could still see the plump lips of their sex. Both women I noted with some sense of satisfaction were already aroused, and the lips of their cunts were split open, a strip of pink wet flesh could be seen, I grinned my erection was back and I decided to waste no more time.

I stood and leaving my shirt on, kicked off my shoes and quickly removed my trousers, allowing my now very erect cock to be free. Raj looked around, quickly following suit. He was wearing a long jacket with thick embroidered leggings underneath, and I sensed he was only too happy to remove the heavy clothing. Within minutes, he too was stood wearing nothing but a white silk shirt and a large erection. It was amusing in many ways, Raj and I never actually looked at each other's manhood, we had fucked together so many times, in fact we had on more than one occasion fucked the same woman at the same time, but still somehow we managed to not touch or look directly at each other's cocks.

We stood in front of the women, I knew now I was standing in front of Hati, and I bent down, grabbing her hair from behind, pulling her neck back, launching my lips to her neck, I again smelled the heady and slightly sickly smell of musk and rose. Pushing that from my head, I let my lips trail over her soft silken skin, I heard her murmur almost silently as her body relaxed a little, I flicked my tongue out and licked my way to her lips, which she opened quickly, kissing me deeply and passionately. Our tongues dancing together, my eyes were shut, but I could feel her now trying to straighten up, to lean up on her knees but I wasn't about to let her, and I kept one hand very firmly wrapped about her hair, pulling her neck back just a little, and keeping her down on her knees.

My other hand wend its way down her body, pausing to cup her heavy breasts. I had been surprised when both women were naked at the size of her their breasts, from within their saris it had been impossible to see, but now naked, they were weighty and soft in my hand. I felt my erection grow a little as for a moment, I saw her on her on all fours with me pounding her so hard from behind it made these large full breasts swing almost like pendulums. I knew instantly how this evening was going to finish, and I almost then couldn't wait to reach that ending, my hands cupped around full breasts, pinching hard nipples as I fucked. But for now this was just the beginning and there were some delicious parts to come before that crescendo.

Her nipples were very hard and erect and I pinched each one in turn, without any hint of being gentle, she moaned loudly and I appreciatively continued to pinch them, loving the small sounds. I hadn't stopped kissing her and I could feel her continuing to kiss me, but with each sharp pinch having to stop for a second, moan and then kiss. It was almost amusing to feel her trying so hard, finally my lips moved from her mouth and down for just a few moments to join my fingers pinching her nipples, it was then I noticed her hands had moved from behind her head and she was about to wrap them about me. I paused, and moving my lips to her ear, I whispered.

"Hands back behind your head slut, you do not touch me without permission, and I haven't heard you ask for permission".

She murmured quietly and obediently placed her hands behind her head, she learned quickly and her body was delightfully responsive, I knew she and in fact her sister, who was knelt close enough next to me, for me to hear her murmurs and groans as Raj played with her, were both perfect finds. Intelligent, beautiful and submissive, my ideal women and yet despite the fact that my cock was doing what it always did, and despite the fact that Hati was playing her part so well, I knew something was missing. I was feeling strangely empty, never before had my mind skipped ahead to the end of an evening the way it had, with me almost longing for that time to come. I was wishing for that release so I could go, be alone, I knew exactly what was wrong, but there was no way in the world I was about to admit it to myself, or do anything about it. Instead I concentrated my efforts back to the beautiful woman in my arms, reaching down now with both my hands between her legs placing them on her thighs, pushing just slightly to widen her legs a little more, I knew it would make her more uncomfortable, but that was the point. With one hand still firmly grasping her thigh, the other made its way very slowly between her legs, I looked up and fixing my eyes with hers, I started to stroke about her pussy, my fingers never actually touching her lips, instead I stroked the top of her thighs, and her bottom, she was whimpering was quietly, lifting her arse from the floor. She pushed her pelvis forward as finally my fingers brushed over her pussy with the lightest of touches, just simply grazing over her lips, stroking softly, I grinned as she moved her hips trying to anticipate my movements. My fingers would delve and sink deeper into that pink delicious hole, but I had no intention of letting her off so easily; and I pulled away quickly, standing up and towering in front of her. She looked up not saying a word, but whimpering instead softly, her hands then moved from her thighs, and onto my hips, imploring me.

The very moment she moved her hands, I froze, stood stock still and looked down, Hati instantly knew what she had done, and her hands flew back to interlace behind her head, she also pulled her shoulders back, and straightened her back, the imploring look was still on her face, but now for a different reason.

But it was too late, and taking two steps back from her, I turned and crossed to the middle of the room, where there was a large thick pole. After Sybil's plan for a fire in the middle of the room had been dismissed, she had had to settle for a large pole, which had the appearance of holding the 'tent' up, but it also served as the only piece of restraining apparatus in the room. Having large rings attached to it at various places, with other rings, attached to the floor boards, in a circle around it, they were mostly hidden by small rugs and cushions. Having initially been left out standing proud, the broken bones and sprained ankles had soon proved tiresome, so we covered them up and it was only if you knew they existed were you ever likely to find them. Standing in front of the pole, I looked over to Hati who, to give her her due, had not moved a muscle, but this was not going to sway me in any way from my chosen course of action, and I knew it was one she was not going to be expecting.

I looked over to her and without smiling simply said.

"To the right of you is a large silk bolster cushion, stand up, grab the cushion and come to my feet," this she did of course without needing to be told again. Before I almost had time to blink she was there, back on her knees with the bolster cushion to the left of her. She kept her eyes down, her gaze was lowered and I knew the way she had touched me had been a calculated move, and I didn't blame her, she wanted a firm hand and knew if she pushed me that is what she would get. I looked up briefly and I could see that Raj was engrossed, Tara was gagged by a silk scarf, and he was currently busy using two more to tie her hands behind her back. I looked away and back to Hati, Raj and I would act together sometimes or we would break away from each other. Normally however at some point one of us would request the other's help or would swap, something which a submissive found at certain points to be an incredibly stressful situation. But for now we would continue as we were, the four of us paired off.

I looked down to Hati and smiled, I knew she would not be expecting what was coming and there was never any telling how each person would react.

"Place the bolster on the floor, in front of the pole, sit on the bolster, and wrap your hands around the pole", I told her, as I leaned down and removed some cushions and a small vivid purple silk rug from the floor. I revealed four large metal rings sunk into the floor boards, with a small amount of effort, I pulled them so they were all upright. Hati quickly did as she was bid and was sat on the bolster within seconds, it was firm enough to stay solid as she sat on it, and yet soft enough to provide moulding comfort. After I had unwound one large length of soft silken rope from the pole, and tied it securely to a metal ring about halfway up from the floor, I stood behind Hati and placed my hands on her shoulders, my lips briefly brushed the top of her head and she relaxed into me. This time when I spoke my voice was purposefully more commanding, if she was going to falter it would be now, and I didn't want that, and I knew neither would she.

"Now, release your hands, and fall back, I will catch you"; she did so instantly and already having my arms around her shoulders I eased her fall backwards, until her head and shoulders touched the floor, she gulped slightly, as I then let go, so she was effectively laid backwards over the bolster.

"DO not move", I told her, as I grabbed both her legs, and having done this many times over the years I was able to swiftly tie a soft silk scarf around each of her ankles, this was purely for comfort. It was one thing causing a girl to be uncomfortable, and even in pain, it was another to be slapdash and cause her injury whilst playing, that was not part of the deal. Once the silk scarves were secure it was not an easy job, but one I had perfected, to grab each leg in turn, take the end of the silk rope and tie and fastening it about her ankles. Once I had done this, and was certain they would take her weight, whilst still keeping a half hold on her, I fell down to the ground grabbing cushions, I used them under her head, and behind her shoulders, ensuring she was well supported, and that her neck would not bend and cause her chin to press into her chest. I stood up again and grinning to myself, I took two more shorter lengths of rope and hooked each one through the rings in the floor, I then quickly threaded each one through the rope on her ankles and whilst supporting her body, taking the left one first, I pulled, which had the effect of splitting her legs open wide, tying both of the ropes off, but leaving a little loop with some slack, I prepared the final and most impressive part of the my plan. I had just two shorter lengths of silk rope and after looping again, one through two metal hoops, this time set a little nearer to her, and further away from the pole finally, I tied them behind her knees.

It was now that I needed to be careful, and standing, with my arms around her waist, supporting her, I slackened off the ropes on her ankles just enough and said to her.

"Bend your knees, slut open those legs as widely as you possibly can", this she did with surprising ease and agility, I had the ends of the ropes which were attached behind her knees in my hands, and I pulled them into place, so she was secured with her legs wide open, unable to really move at all. Her back was still arched over the bolster and her shoulders and head were supported by cushions. The brilliance of this tying up meant she had the feeling and appearance of being upside down, but wasn't actually completely, instead she was sloped somewhat, this meant she could stay like it for so much longer than you could with a girl totally upside down, who would soon start to feel gravity pushing against her eyeballs and making her nose water.

I smiled looking down more than very satisfied with what I had created. Hati for her part was silent, her hands and arms which were unbound and grasped together tightly in front of her. My eyes for a moment roved over her body, not touching her or even being close enough to, simply watching her aware she was unable to move and was at my mercy gave me my erection back in seconds. I took the two or so steps back to the pole and started to stroke by fingers down her legs, pausing as she shivered and moved slightly, finally my hands reached between her legs and again I spent a over a minute stroking the top of her thighs, my fingers brushing over the prize there. I could see exactly how aroused and wet she was with each stroke, as my fingers got closer and closer, I could see her quivering, and even as she was so very trussed up and unable to move she was able to jiggle and move her hips slightly and this was exactly what she was doing. It made me grin and tease her even more, finally, I licked my finger knowing this was wholly unnecessary seeing how visibly sodden her needy little cunt was, but it was a habit, leaning down I blew gently over the puffy swollen lips of her sex, just as I was about to delve my fingers deep into her wet pink hole I heard Raj chuckle, and I looked up to see him staring over and grinning. It was Raj, who had shown we how to tie the knots needed, and in fact him who had first introduced me this particular position.

"Ahhh Thorpe", said Raj

"So many women, so may poles, and so many of them upside down like that, every time I see it, I feel very proud of you". He left Tara for a moment, she had been on her knees with Raj's cock in her mouth, but with a click of his fingers she sunk down and waited patiently whilst he strolled over and slapped me on my back.

"You never tire of it eh brother, and this one certainly looks stunning that cunt is worth a dip for sure". It was at that absolute split second, that very moment that I realised that I was extremely tired, and actually I had tired of it all, my cock went limp and I felt my shoulders droop, I took a deep breath and knew without a doubt what I had to do. People changed and lives changed, new people came into your life and it was simply never the same again. Someone had come into my life and I knew now suddenly with such perfect clarity that my life was never going to be the same again, but I didn't mind I realised with a grin, I really didn't mind.

Turning to Raj, I grabbed a hold of his shoulders, and pulling him towards me I planted a huge somewhat wet and sloppy kiss on his cheek, he laughed and wiped his face.

"Hey my brother what is that for, I know these girls are gorgeous but really...". I laughed and shook my head.

"No no Raj, you have freed me, you don't know it, and will probably never understand it, and as I stand here about to do what I am about to, I also know you are going to be angry with me, but that cannot be helped". Raj looked confused but said no more, it was only as I turned and spoke to poor Hati, who was going to be abandoned I knew in the most awful of states, at the most terrible of times, but what could I do, cupids arrow had struck, and if I myself did not strike now whilst the arrow was still embedded deep in my heart, then there was a chance I never would.

"Hati, Hati I am so sorry, you are a delight, an absolute unprecedented delight, you together with your sister are most probably and more than likely the two most beautiful women we have ever had attend our evenings. My dear I am well aware that I am about to run out on you, leaving you in possibly the most indelicate situation possible, what with you being trussed up like the Christmas turkey with the delicious petals of your flower on show, but I am comforted knowing that Raj has already spent a night with you . He has already no doubt caressed and plucked that flower so I am not abandoning you to the wolves, please forgive me, and your sister Tara, I am sorry I didn't get to sample your delights at all. I know together you will please Raj, and perhaps from the many men outside in the hall another could be found worthy enough to assist Raj, he will know who and send a servant no doubt. So you see ladies, I am not running out on you, more running into my destiny". I wasn't one for long flowery speeches, Raj just stood there silently I could see a vein in his temple throbbing, and knew he was fuming. The two women, well Hati, I could see suddenly was very uncomfortable and began to almost start to struggle, her sister was the only one with a wry smile on her face and she looked up to me, grinned and said softly.

"Well then you big bad man run, run now and find her, before you are devoured alive by the anger in this room.".

So that was exactly what I did, grabbing my trousers from the floor and hastily pulling them on, I ran from the room, I ran across the hall, not stopping even for Sybil and Poppy, both who beckoned me to. Running out of the huge wooden doors, I finally stopped for breath, finally stopped and thought about exactly what I was doing. It was about 1.30 am, I was not drunk by any means, but I had had enough, Cassandra would no doubt be asleep and suddenly I was aware, I was not even sure what I was offering her, and actually what I could offer her. But I knew I had to try and find a middle ground, be what we both needed, but darn it would she even accept me. Would a more sensible man wait, wait until the morning, do the right thing. I couldn't wait however, I just couldn't, what if the cold light of dawn came and I lost my bravado, the reality the morning might bring was something that I just couldn't risk, no I had to do it now, and so I broke into a run again, heading to the governess's room.

CHAPTER TWENTY-FIVE

Cassandra

Sleep had come, after I had lain sobbing for so long, utterly convinced it never would but heartbreak was a good sedative and my mind and body were exhausted enough for me to fall into a deep sleep. It was from this deep sleep that I was suddenly awakened, I lay for a moment or two trying to work out what was going on, someone was hammering on my door, and when I say hammering they really were, they were slamming their fists against it with some passion and strength. I was immediately scared and sniffed the air initially scared there was a fire, that the house was ablaze and they were trying to wake me, but smelling nothing and finally coming round from my drowsy state I heard him calling as he was banging.

"Cassandra, Cassandra, it's me, it's Thorpe, please I need to talk to you, it's important, I know you will say it can wait until morning, but it really, really can't, I need to talk to you now, please Cassandra".

I sat bolt upright in bed, and hugged my knees. I was still wearing my old dress, with no underwear, how could I answer the door like that, but answer it I realised I must. If I didn't he would eventually assume something was wrong and would go get his key, and let himself in, or worse break it down, which would wake the entire household. I realised with a start he was making such a damn racket, I was surprised the whole house was not awake, they probably were, so my next course of action simply had to be getting off of this bed and open the door. I briefly thought about getting undressed and at least answering my bedroom door to him wearing a nightdress instead of as I was, dressed in an old day dress with the hair of a crazy harridan. There was however no time and so I took a deep breath, wondered briefly if the pain and embarrassment caused by this man was ever going to lessen or if in fact I was simply now an amusement for him. Deciding actually I was really rather angry after all, I stood up and strode over to my door purposefully; this bravado didn't last and I slipped the bolt with more than a small amount of trepidation. However, I did my level best to disguise this, and yanked the door open with as much aggression as a tired and crazy looking heartbroken young woman could muster.

On the other side of the door stood Thorpe, wearing just a white un-tucked shirt, and his dress trousers, I noticed that even his feet were bare. His face was soft and warm, he was grinning broadly with what I could only describe as an extremely hopeful look on his face.

I said nothing, I was, I think momentarily struck dumb, and it would appear that that didn't matter as he started to speak the very moment the door was open, in fact speak was almost an overstatement, he actually garbled his words out.

"Cassandra, Cassandra my Cassandra I am sorry, I have woken you, I know I have but there comes a time in a man's life when he must follow his heart, and that is what I am doing, I am following my heart to your bedroom door, please may I come in, I must talk to you properly".

Again, I was struck dumb, I decided, he must look crazier than me, which all things considered was a fairly damning indictment. He was slightly out of breath, his hair was all over the place, I noticed his shirt was buttoned incorrectly at the bottom, and there were some very hairy toes poking out the bottom of his trousers. The look on his face was so very earnest and so very unlike his usual stoic trait. While I digested not only his appearance, but his words, he stood there like a cat on a hot tin roof, hopping from one foot to the other. It was then that I started, and I really don't know where it came from, if someone had told me a few hours ago that I would be standing laughing my head off I would have declared them mad and stupid, but that is exactly what happened, I started to laugh, and once I started it was clear, that nothing was going to stop me.

This was most definitely not the reaction he was expecting, his face instantly fell and he just stared at me incredulously. However this was the kind of laughter that nothing short of being run over by a train was going to stop, brought on by being over tired, over emotional and purely the sight in front of me being so very funny. I laughed until my sides started to hurt and I had to lean on my door handle, I was laughing so very hard, that I couldn't speak, I kept trying to say that I was sorry, that I didn't mean to be laughing so, but the words were not coming out.

As my hysteria reached its peak, I saw the starting of a smile breaking at the corners of his mouth, and then that hint became a full grin and finally he joined me. Thorpe was an extremely intelligent man, and I suspected it suddenly struck him, in the way it had done me the utter ridiculousness of the situation. Of course there is nothing like a bit of shared mirth to knock down walls and remove barriers, and so when he moved forward to grab me around my waist I did nothing to stop him. I did instantly stop laughing as did he, without waiting to be asked any further he stepped over the threshold of my room, pushing me in with him, I let go of the door, and it slammed shut with a resounding thud.

Once he made it to the middle of the room, he stopped with his hands still around my waist, he looked at me with a huge grin on his face, I grinned back, having him in such close proximity was making my heart beat loudly in my chest and the laugher had been replaced with the same mix of anxiety and excitement I had become accustomed to over the past few days.

Whilst still holding my gaze one of his hands reached up and stroked down my face, and over my unruly messy hair and he smiled again, this time he looked more like the Thorpe I had got to know over the past few days. Confident and together, I sighed with relief, without saying a word, he leaned forward and kissed me. It was most definitely he who was kissing me, it took me a second or so to realise and return the kiss, but by then my lips were crushed against his and his tongue was forcefully in my mouth. I murmured and was unable not to just fall against him, he pulled away for a few seconds and looked at me, his face as now set hard and he almost growled as he again leaned forward and kissed me. It was as passionate as the first kiss, only this time I was more ready for it, and so I managed to hold my own, our lips melded together, tongues dancing in and out of each other's mouths. When he finally pulled away, I was panting and so very aroused I wanted nothing more than to rake my fingers through his hair and be as close to him as I possibly could, but I could see the time had now come for talking.

Thorpe dropped his hands to his side and turning, he walked across the room to the fireplace, the fire was dead in the grate, only a few cinders were glowing red showing the fire that had been lit earlier in the day when I had been out walking with the man who was currently attempting with some success I might add, to coax it back to life. With the help of some paper faggots, a little dry tinder and then a sprinkling of coal in just a few minutes, a fire was dancing merrily again in the grate sending out welcome light and warmth. He then sat himself down in one of the well-worn armchairs set next to the fire. After lighting the gas light on the wall, which added to the warmth, I went to sit myself on the other armchair, smiling happily but wishing then it was a sofa, so I didn't have to be so far from him. Just as my bottom was making contact with the cushioned seat, I heard him say.

"No no Cassandra, not the seat, it will only ever be the seat when there is company or I deem it fit, you may sit at my feet on a cushion. I think if you are going to be mine, and you are going to be mine, then it is the right time to start your training". I gulped instantly knowing he wasn't joking, and also instantly knowing that my decision here and now was going to affect possibly the rest of my life. My thoughts went instantly back to a little earlier when my head had been full of images of me kneeling at his feet, here I was now being offered almost exactly that, what I needed to work out was if I was brave enough.

I was, of course I bloody was, I nearly skipped over to the bed and grabbed one of the copious number of brocade cushions placed upon it, keeping my steps even, I returned to the chair, and threw it on the floor, with me landing upon the cushion just a few seconds later. With my back to him leaning slightly on his legs, I felt perfectly comfortable.

He stroked my hair for a moment or two before speaking again.

"Good girl Cassandra, my good girl, you are probably wondering what is going on, well of course you bloody well are", he said for a moment losing the seriousness out of his voice. I smiled and nodded my head, speaking for the very first time since he had hammered upon my door.

"Well yes, yes Thorpe I really am, I thought the world was how it was, you were who you were, and that was it. Yet you come hammering on my door in the middle of the night, find me looking like a crazy woman sleeping in my old dress, you kiss me with a passion I couldn't have known existed and now I find us here, with me happily sat at your feet, but puzzled and not a little worried at where this will lead. If my reputation, dignity and respectability will leave the room with me in the morning, or it will be lost somewhere in this room, never to be found again. Because you see Thorpe, I think you know against you I am fairly weak and unable to fight, despite knowing how something should be, it seems I am unable to actually do what is required to make it that way, so I have to rely on you and your hopefully kind feelings towards me and ask you not play with the poor governess too much. She simply cannot take it, she is a woman in love you see, and she simply cannot see beyond that". I heard a low chuckle and then felt lips briefly on my neck before he spoke again.

"You are safe Cassandra, so very safe, tonight I had every intention of doing what I always do, in fact, I started to do what I normally always do, one of those two beautiful twins Raj brought along was left in a most revealing position. Raj will take good care of her, but luckily before I really delved in, shall we say, I realised". I knew my body had stiffened at the mention of the twin, of course I knew exactly who he was talking about, I had seen those beautiful women the night before, and wondered at their poise and elegance. No wonder Thorpe had wanted to spend some time with them. Feeling me tense, Thorpe's hands moved to my shoulders and he started to caress them gently as he spoke.

"No Cassandra, you see I realised that in these few short days my life had changed, that my needs, wants and desires had changed, it doesn't make what was irrelevant or any less perfect for its time, but for now and from now on, I admit I want something different, and someone different. I am a man who takes what he wants, but from you Cassandra, I will only take what you want to give. So can you? Can you give yourself to me Cassandra"?

I took a deep breath and rose up on my knees, I needed to look him in the eye for this, and so I spun about to face him and as I did Thorpe leaned forward and grabbed both hands, holding them tightly in his.

"Really give yourself to me Cassandra, I will make you mine, take care of you, love you and yes I will marry you. I didn't know it until the moment you opened the door, nothing in truth had been formed in my mind, but now I do, because I know I must have you, and only you, and to do that, for you to be happy then we will be married." My face must have, even in the dim light, gone ashen because his hands ran to my cheeks, cupping my face he leaned forward and kissed my lips softly.

"Cassandra, marry me, be mine, mine in every way, give yourself to me, I want to know and own every part of you". I knew deep inside what the answer would be and my body knew it before my mind could speak it. I reached my arms up, and flung them around his neck laughing and grinning.

"Yes, yes, yes I will marry you, it's probably lunacy, it could be doomed to failure, but I have never wanted anything so much in my life". As I clung to him I whispered words which came from the deepest part of my being, so I was almost speaking from my very soul.

"Keep me in your thrall my love, own me, every part of me, keep me in the strictest, deepest bondage, make me earn your love, and beg for your touch."

EPILOGUE

10 months later
Thorpe

As I looked about the hall, I was as always so very pleased, fires were just being lit, and it would be within the next couple of hours that my treasured guests would arrive. It was the last carnal set before Christmas and so the rooms absolutely glowed with candles and seasonal décor, a huge tree was set near to the window, under which there gifts for everybody.

It had taken the staff hours to wrap them all, and all where tokens to remind our friends of their fabulous times here, a picture or a statute, perhaps some scented oils or a silk scarf, of course the presents hadn't been my idea, my wife had insisted it was a 'perfect thing to do', and being only seven months married and still like first teenage lovers what could I do, but acquiesce.

I smiled then, seeing her walk into the hall and over to me, my Cassandra was dressed in a gown of green velvet which accented her perfect breasts. When she reached me, she turned and I could see that the ribbons which fastened the bodice of her dress were untied, she spun back on her heels and moved a little closer, I smiled and inclined my head giving her the permission to reach out and press her body against me, her breath was warm on my neck as she whispered.

"My new dress, its perfect thank you so much Sir, but I don't seem able to tie it, perhaps if we went to the tented room, you could assist me, I think maybe if you took the whole dress off again and we started again from the beginning I may be more successful". As she pulled away her lips grazed over my neck and I shivered slightly, taking a step back from me, she stood demurely waiting for a decision, for just a moment I looked about the room again, a final check. The table was laid with mine and Cassandra's places at the head of it, now a permanent fixture. We also had a large chaise in the hall, which placed near to the fire was always in the middle of any conversation, and I grinned knowing that later on, after dinner I would sit and hold my wife close whilst my nearest and dearest friends moved and chattered around us. Some would move away for some privacy, some would be intimate near to us, and some like us would spend the evening in company, holding the one they had chosen close whilst drinking wine, with laughter peeling out.

But for now, for right now my girl was begging me silently with her eyes and I knew what for, with everything ready and in place I could think of nothing I would wish for more. Leaning down I took her hand and together with walked to the tented room, on the way, as she moved I could just see the swell of her belly, it seemed to now grow every day, and I had started to be more and more careful. The cargo she carried in her belly, the product of so much love, it seemed more precious than life itself.

As we reached the tented room, she waited for me to enter first, and after pulling the curtain down and closing the door, she came to me, stripped herself naked, knelt at my feet and begged for her collar.

I hope you have enjoyed Cassandra!

The short story which follows tells the tale of how the Carnal Set came about, it gives a little more insight into Sybil and Poppy, and their relationship.

Set well before Cassandra and Thorpe met, be prepared for Thorpe to be at his rakish best!

Lottie

The Inauguration of the Carnal Set

Lottie Winter

Grapes were nice, they were sweet enough to satisfy the taste buds, but yet with enough sharpness to not to be totally boring. I mused on this briefly as I lay back on my chaise lounge, deciding I would consider myself to be rather grape like, sweet enough to satisfy anyone's cravings, but sharp enough to be used with some caution. I couldn't help but chuckle at my own analogy, of course I was utterly aware how self-centered I was, it was hard not to be, born into such total privilege, and as the only daughter amongst a sea of brothers, I had been brought up awash with attention, and affection. Adulthood turning up had done little to abate my desire to be adored and the centre of attention. Being self-aware had not in any way served to change my ways, I was quite happy to stamp a little, shout a bit and/or sulk when needed as long as my needs were met, and I was happy; after all, that was all that really mattered.

I was Lady Sybil Lilliana Charlotte Troughton, and at 24 years old and unmarried (a subject I knew my family were getting rather itchy about) I was a fairly constant source for the gossips, the fact I had moved from the family estate to a property in London, had caused more than a little bit of tongue flapping, 34 Edgingham Terrace was a perfectly acceptable address, in fact one many would have run over hot coals for, but it was a house that my family had owned for many years, but had never really used, the main residence in Newham Square was twice the size and kept with full staff all year round. But I had wanted a little freedom, and my father was a wise man knowing had he refused my request I would have gone anyway, and then he would have absolutely no control whatsoever over my life. By allowing me to live in this house, and behave like it was mine I couldn't hide!

So I was happy, I had what virtually no other well bred young unmarried woman could ever have – freedom, and of course I absolutely and utterly abused that freedom as often as I could, with as many people as I could.

I felt the cotton sheet covering me move slightly and I turned and stretched, seeing Charlie, the young butler I had employed return with a tray of drinks. He was stark naked, apart from his feet, which were well encased in very shiny black lace-up shoes.

He snorted seeing me staring.

190

"What!! This whole house is covered in tiles, hardly a rug in the place, do you know how cold me bleedin feet get going all the way down to the kitchen and back"! I carried on laughing as he passed me a large glass of champagne.

"Well stop bleating about it, and come here I will warm them up for you". He grinned and kicked the shoes off.

"Yes M'Lady". I took a large mouthful of the Champagne, and Charlie downed his glass in one, before leaning down, and ripping the sheet from my naked body and almost hurling himself onto me. I laughed and wrapped myself about him, warm hands snaking over his smooth cool skin. Reaching down, I pulled the sheet over us both and grinned.

"There is that better? Now be a good boy and fuck me will you, I have been laying here thinking about things, and you know how tiresome one's own head can be".

He didn't speak, actions speaking louder than words, I felt his cock harden against my thigh almost immediately. He really had been such a good find, for one so young he was an acceptable butler, and also of course, someone who enjoyed the simple carnal pleasure of a good fuck without the need to become emotionally attached. He was formally betrothed to a young cook a few houses along the street, he had made this clear when he came to apply for the job, he had lost his previous job because of this relationship, and subsequent engagement. I couldn't care less, and as I understood the girl was a half-decent cook, had offered them both a room for after they were married.

Taking a deep breath, which was a habit of mine just before sex I grinned looking up at Charlie. That delicious cock of his was pressing even harder against my thigh, he leaned down, just as I reached up and we met somewhere in the middle, his lips pressing against mine and for a few moments we did no more than kiss, it was a delicious starter for what was coming, his tongue pressed through my lips and twirled and danced with mine, tasting each other. I pulled back and smiled softly gazing for a short time over his features, my fingers coming up to stroke briefly over his eyelids and cheeks, before I reached up and ran my tongue over his lips, our mouths then again came together and this time our kiss was more urgent, his lips and tongue almost assaulting my mouth. I whimpered as his hands started to rake over my body, and in one swift movement, he sat up and grinned at me, I knew I was squirming about desperate now for him to touch me, but he waited a while longer, just simply watching me, as I wriggled about reaching my hands up to try and touch him but he merely "tut tut'ed" at me and dodged my grasp. Finally after what seemed like a small age he reached down and behind grabbing ahold of my ankles and pulling my legs wide apart, he let out a low growl while moving his hands to my knees, he pushed them upwards so my legs were spread wide with my very neat and well trimmed pussy on show.

I knew I was aroused, I could feel the warmness spreading about my body. I guessed I was wet, so I put one hand down between my legs, and for just a moment slipped my fingers inside, licking my lips and whimpering as I did, I was so wet and turned on that just my fingers felt delicious slipping over the soft, warm and wet flesh. My eyes were closed, and my back was arching just a little as I in those few seconds, almost become lost in my own pleasure, Charlie's low growl and him batting my hand away brought me back to reality but only for a few moments and quickly my rubbing exploring fingers were replaced by his searching, licking and lapping tongue, I moaned loudly as his initially cool tongue licked at first slowly up and down my lips, pausing for a brief second to blow cool air over my hot flesh, causing me to shiver and whimper. I put both my hands behind my thighs, so I could pull my legs open as wide as possible, holding them there, so my pussy hole and arse hole both pulled slightly open, which of course meant that the lips of my pussy spread open, and his tongue now delved there, as he lapped up and down pausing each time to press the tip of his tongue hard against my now swollen and pink clit, twirling the tip of his tongue round and round my little nub.

I was, of course, by now stretching my toes out and tensing my muscles, my hips rhythmically moving; thrusting slightly up and down with each lap and lick of his tongue. I felt one warm, dry and slightly work roughened hand on my belly, stretching out and pressing his palm down, with just enough pressure to keep me in place. Where his other hand was very quickly became apparent as I felt two fingers push quickly and instantly deeply inside me, his mouth and tongue never left my clit, lapping and twirling with more insistence, as he now matched the licks with thrusting his fingers in and out of my pussy quickly, each time pushing his fingers in as deeply as he could finger fucking my cunt while he licked me.

Now lost to my own pleasure, my back was arching, the pressure of his hand on my belly never lifting, I was held securely in place, my movement restricted so I couldn't wriggle or move away from that insistent tongue or those thrusting fingers. I knew I was going to come, my orgasm was building up ready to flood me with ecstasy, my whole body stiffened as I stretched out, and knowing what was coming, Charlie lapped at me quicker his fingers fucked harder and the room was filled with the sounds of my whimpering and the fabulous squelching sound of a dripping pussy being pounded by large rough fingers. My neck stretched out as I finally came, and as I did, I let go of my legs, so they fell down to rest on the arms of the couch while my body shook with each wave of my orgasm, Charlie quickly pulled his fingers from me, and seemed to almost slide up my body, wordlessly he shoved the two fingers which were dripping with my juices into my mouth and at the same time as he thrust his large very hard cock into me.

I screamed and caught my breath, his fingers were in my mouth and I sucked and licked them, tasting myself on him. He of course now took his pleasure, his cock was large and very hard. He certainly knew how to fuck a woman, he grabbed ahold of both of my hands and pulled them above my head, whilst I rounded my hips and wrapped my legs about his torso, which allowed him to push deeper inside me, that fabulous noise was back, this time with every hard and needy thrust of his cock inside me. I felt him more urgently fucking like an animal rutting, we locked eyes and together we rode those last few thrusts, the last three of four thrusts so hard and deep, it felt almost as though he was cutting me in half. Finally he came with a loud grunt, he pulled out swiftly and his seed spilled onto my belly, his cock almost having a life of its own quivering and pulsing as he pressed himself against my stomach.

We laid back on the chaise lounge languidly, Charlie staying with me for just a few moments, he was never one for too much cuddling or warmth afterwards which didn't bother me, often it was so nice after the crowdedness and intimacy of sex to have a little time to one's self to gather thoughts and so on. So when after he had wiped away what he had produced from my belly, and wrapped me up in his arms for no more than five minutes, he leaned up and kissed my forehead and smiled.

"Well M'Lady you have guests this afternoon and I have a whole house to whip into shape, so I will be off, to earn my wages"

A man of few words he was, and that was it! He got up, went to the stand where there was large jug of water and a bowl, grabbing a cloth and a towel, he stood stark naked washing himself. He really was a beautiful man; well muscled with just a smattering of hair on his chest, a very firm bottom and long legs. Having my fill of him and not really wanting him to think he was too Adonis like, I turned over and pulled a large patchwork eiderdown from the side of the couch, wrapping it about myself before standing and moving to pull the large velvet cord, calling for Nessie. Nessie was my lady's maid, she was about my age and had been with me since she was a teenager, moving when I did, something I had been rather surprised about when she agreed to it so readily. Nessie was a sturdy young woman, plain faced and rather dour at times, she had seen every dalliance and indulgence, knew everything that went on, but still chose to be my maid, she never commented and if she judged I wouldn't have known it.

Nessie arrived, just as Charlie left. He was now dressed as a butler, and he stood a little straighter and obviously in work mode he nodded to Nessie as she entered the room she didn't acknowledge him, but instead came straight over to me and smiled her efficient little smile before speaking.

"Ready to get dressed Milady? Lord Pembroath and your other guests will be here in a few hours, I know cook has been fussing in the kitchen as none of us are too sure how many people you are expecting". I nodded, somewhat absent mind-idly, thinking about exactly how I was going to cater to my guests, finally I turned and addressed Nessie.

"Hmm, yes getting dressed, now that is a good idea. My blue gown I think, the one you very obviously think is too low cut for daytime wear, but a little bath first, this morning has been fun but I do now feel rather grubby." Nessie nodded as I carried on speaking.

"As for how many guests, I am not too sure either, Thorpe errr Lord Pembroath's note was rather cryptic, and so I also have no idea if they want feeding, and whether it be afternoon tea, or dinner. So, let's just say to cook to cater for ten people for sandwiches and cakes in the library, with the possibility it might become dinner so she should have a plan in place should that be the case! Even if it be cold cuts and salad. If we make sure there is plenty of wine, no one will mind what they eat". Nessie, who had by then pulled the same red velvet cord I had a few minutes earlier, and had arranged for hot water to fill a bath, had been nodding as I spoke, pulling out the blue dress, and laying out clean underwear and stockings for me.

About fifteen minutes later, I was happily dunked in a warm bath scented with some rather gorgeous rose oil, musing on Thorpe's rather cryptic note which I received yesterday. I had spent the day with my parents being, of course, bored rigid by the idle chit chat. The most important subject it seemed was which unmarried men were in town! I had no real intention of getting married, it seemed to be a pointless exercise. I had four brothers, two of whom were already married and the eldest, Thomas, had managed to produce two sons, well Ethel his dull dull wife had, so the line was secure, the other two brothers, were seen as extremely eligible, and marriage for them would be an easy matter. The family was swimming in money, so should I decide to remain a childless spinster, I could see no possible reason why anyone would care, but my mother had made it her current career to try and get me married off to someone suitable. I knew they felt this would lessen the chances of me bringing a huge scandal to the family.

So yesterday, when I had arrived home I been laying in a somewhat exhausted over dramatic fashion in the summer room, when the note had arrived. It simply said:

Have a brilliant idea, must discuss, will be round tomorrow afternoon, will bring Sabine, Nadia and a couple of others, have plenty of wine ready! You are going to love it.
Yours
Lord Thorpe Pembroath

Thorpe Pembroath was possibly my oldest friend, we had been friends since childhood and fucking since adolescence. He shared my take on all things sexual, carnal and physical, and there was much we had discovered together. I know there had been a huge hope from my family that he and I would be married, but after his family had applied plenty of pressure and then threats of being cut off, he had married the vile Esther Carlisle. The only thing Esther had liked was her horses, so there was some irony in the fact that it was one of her beloved nags who, after just four years of marriage, kicked her in the head and killed her instantly. She had managed to spit out two children before she died, so no one was particularly concerned about her death, or Thorpe remarrying, and as I knew he had never really had any intention of marrying me, I never mentioned it, and our relationship carried on the same as it had done before, during and now after his marriage! We were the best of friends, and always had fun in the bedroom but I knew his true passion lay with a submissive woman, and I was fairly certain, knowing him almost better, I thought, than he knew himself, that should an intelligent, attractive woman who thought wearing a collar and doing as she was told in the bedroom was a fabulous proposition arrive on the scene, then Thorpe would be able to leave the rest of us deviants behind, and live happily ever after.

But until that happened, if it ever happened, we enjoyed each other, the same way we enjoyed others. I did hope though that our friendship would always endure. For a man, he was terribly good fun!

Dressed in my favourite blue dress, with my hair neatly piled up on top of my head by Nessie, and jostled and messed up so tendrils fell out down my neck and shoulders by me, I was waiting patiently (well almost) in the library for my guests. They were late, of course, and it was well past 3.30 pm when I finally heard a pull on the front door bell, and the slow footsteps of Charlie answering the door. It felt like a small age, before the library door opened and bypassing Charlie without giving him the chance to announce, in strode Thorpe followed in quick succession by Sabine and Nadia, always together and very often quite literally joined at the hip! Katherine Harrington-

Brown, with a young man I didn't recognise followed in rather more slowly, and then I was rather over excited to see Earl Thatchingham – Simon stroll in, he was accompanied by the extremely handsome Rajmata Vishwanah, an Indian Prince, I loved being intimate with him almost for one reason only – which was that my pale skin and dark hair looked utterly divine when wrapped about him, his dark skin seemed to glow and his beautiful liquid brown eyes were full of fake emotion!

The final entrant to the room was a young woman, whom I had known for many months, she was the nearest I had ever come to a true love affair, Poppy Clements was an ex-prostitute, whom I had found and 'rescued', she was older than me and at 32, her only memories were of the brothel, and then the streets where she worked, she started so young, there was nothing before that for her. Many thought her name didn't suit her, countless years on the streets being beaten, raped and neglected had taken their toll and she looked older than her years, her voice was rough and hard, and her face, which had obviously once been beautiful was scarred not only with the years of that rough life, but also a few years ago she had been attacked, raped and the man responsible had had rather a liking for knives, and sliced down her face, flaying open her left cheek. Had a doctor with a little skill been employed to sew her face back together, the scar may have been a lot smaller, but as it was, she was given a bottle of brandy to drink, and the madam in her brothel had sewn her back together again.

After the attack work was scarcer to find for Poppy, and I came across her on one of mine and Thorpe's fun incognito trips, dressed as though we didn't have a shilling between us we loved to frequent the roughest parts of London, it got a little hairy sometimes but it was fun. On this occasion, Thorpe had fallen in deep lust with a barmaid at an Inn we would sometimes frequent, and had persuaded her to step outside the back with him for as long as it would take for him to deal with that lust, by bending her over some empty barrels and giving her what he liked to call "a damn good seeing to", but of course I was left alone at a table with nothing but huge mugs of awful ale to keep me company. Now as brave and brazen as I may be, I do hope I am not stupid, so I as very well aware that the three men I saw making their way to my table with a determined look plastered on each one of their faces was not a good thing!

If I tried to bolt, I would put myself in a worse predicament, ending up outside on the street with these men intent on either robbing or raping me, or perhaps both staying in the Inn would offer a little in the way of protection, if I made enough noise perhaps Thorpe would hear the commotion.

The men had wordlessly arrived, sat down and smiled at me, one of the placing a hand in a painful claw like fashion around my knee, and right at that moment, up stepped Poppy and without a second glance to me she gave them a verbal bashing.

"Oh no no, lads, I wouldn't if I was you, she is the latest purchase by Mrs Murphy for South Street, you can imagine no doubt exactly what would happen to you if you messed about with her property".

At those words, the hand was removed instantly from my knee, caps were doffed and the men were gone in moments.

I looked up and smiled, just as Poppy plonked herself down at the table.

"Thank you so much, my heart was about to pop out of my chest I think". Poppy looked me over up and down before she spoke.

"Now look 'ere, you and your toff friend might think we are all stupid, but let me assure you, we ain't, despite the clothes you both stick out like sore thumbs, a fun game it might be, but you will end up in a gutter." She paused briefly, her hands spread out on the table before she spoke again, this time with a strangely engaging slightly lopsided smile, her eyes I noted were the most beautiful green I had ever seen.

"This rescuing lark is thirsty business isn't it, and it builds up a mighty big hunger doesn't it." It took me a moment to understand the meaning of this, but finally it dawned on me.

"Ahh ahh yes yes, of course" I said as I scrambled to my feet and made it to the bar in less than ten steps, where I ordered fresh jugs of that awful ale stuff, plus some wine, not being sure what she would drink, finally I ordered large plates of roasted meat and vegetables. I hadn't ever dared to eat here, but thought I should probably at least have a plate of food in front of me, if she did.

I sat back down at the table, just as wine and ale was arriving, Poppy looked up and grinned, and that was it, from that day to this, I have taken care of her and she has me. I found behind the scars, attitude and the terrible life experience, was the sweetest, kindest most intelligent woman. She asked for so very little from me, which may seem laughable considering she lived in rooms paid for by myself, and wore clothes I had bought for her. But it was all so much less than I had wanted to do, I had a wild fantasy about keeping her like a man might a mistress, but she settled for modest rooms in a slightly less rough part of town than she was used to and had laughed her head off when I suggested a housekeeper.

Most the time we spent together was at her home, but she would visit me here, and sometimes we would take trips together. She had never seen the sea, so we ventured to Brighton together, staying in a wonderful guest house with a fabulous landlady, who had made us huge vats of tea and toast and had not battered an eyelid at our obvious 'togetherness'.

I had enjoyed spending time with women before, but it was different with Poppy, she challenged me and she never wanted to possess me. Despite the fact I was the one who paid out all the money to keep her, I always got the feeling it was Poppy who called the shots and if tomorrow she decided she didn't want to see me again, she would disappear off without a whimper.

Not having seen Poppy for over a week, it was her of course I ran over to, flung my arms about and kissed passionately, nuzzling into her neck my arms wrapped about her. It was only after hearing some throats being cleared, that I actually remembered my other guests, I had been lost for a few moments in the delights of my Poppy, her smell was always like honey and musk, in equal measure and I could never get enough of the pleasure of just being wrapped up all naked and warm with her. I hoped whatever happened in our lives that Poppy would always be a part of it and that I could always make sure she was taken care of.

Poppy and I took a step back from each other, and I grinned broadly at the rest of my guests, racing over, one by one to plant kisses of varying degrees upon each one of them, and ushering them to large comfy seats and sofas. Charlie was on hand and he handed out glasses of wine, whilst Sarah, the housemaid, who helped cook and did just about everything else was whizzing about with plates of tiny delicate sandwiches.

Once everyone was looking comfortable and well taken care of, with drinks and sandwiches, I dismissed Charlie and Sarah and plonked myself down on a sofa in between Thorpe and Poppy and turned around looking at Thorpe expectantly.

"Well come on you send me a cryptic note, turn up, drink my wine and eat my sandwiches, I suggest you tell me exactly what this 'brilliant' idea is?"

Thorpe looked over and grinned, always one for the dramatic, he stood up and went over to the fireplace in which a small fire was burning and for a moment, he warmed his hands before turning around to face us all, addressing us as one.

"All of you here are my friends, a few of you are my lovers and we all share one common passion, it is what glues us together, and if we were put in a room, and told to spend a few hours talking about things which didn't involve sex, lust and everything carnal, I would wager we would struggle rather a lot."

We were all listening somewhat avidly, I could see Sabine nodding her head in agreement at his words. Thorpe for himself was getting into his rhetoric and he now turned to each one of us in turn.

"Sabine and Nadia, I adore you both, your love for each other, your beautiful home and Nadia's amazing artwork make you two of the most interesting people I have ever met. But we have little else in common but our love of submission, Sabine and I delight in the dominant, and Nadia when your Mistress has been gracious enough to allow you to serve me, your submission has been a joy, you are a fabulous creature, so our ties are bound in the carnal." I could see Nadia wriggling about delighted at his words, while Sabine continued her nodding.

"Katherine, oh Katherine, there are few women in this world as sensual as you, it seems as each year goes past, you just get more and more perfect. Afternoons in London would not be the same without your wonderful presence, and your soirees have left me more satisfied than all the brothels in the whole of London could. But imagine us without the knowledge of each other's pleasure, what would we have?"

Katherine Harrington-Brown had been married at 17, to a man much older than herself and she had simply bidded her time, and when at 24 she had been widowed, she had never again remarried and after selling the family estate much to the horror of the rest of the extended family, she had moved herself and her two at the time very young daughters to London, where she had lived since in absolute luxury and decadence, bringing up her daughters to be well educated, beautiful, independent women, both had married well, and after they had left home, Katherine's home had become an even more delight of the decadent and she herself was never seen without a man at least half her age on her arm.

I could see she agreed with what Thorpe had said as she sat with a small satisfied smile on her face. I loved and disliked Katherine in equal measure, I almost saw her place in society and London almost as mine should be, but at the same time I admired her lust for life and her obvious kindness more than I disliked her, so that side always won the day.

Turning his attention to the two men in the room, Thorpe grinned that smile men have, the one of shared triumphs and lust.

"Raj and Simon, your company and your friendship is one of the most important things in my life, we have been friends since collectively fighting off the older boys at school, ensuring we kept our bottoms intact and unviolated, it is both of you that have helped to formulate who and what I am. We each lost our virginity together, have all made bad brothel decisions and suffered the itching from it. All of us have made bad marriages to women, we haven't liked much. But collectively, this is what we are, we enjoy together the carnal and the lust." The two men grinned almost conspiratorially at Thorpe's words, I knew the three of them, when together were a fairly unstoppable combination.

There was just me and Poppy left on Thorpe's speech list, and Poppy came next.

"And there is Poppy, Poppy you are somebody who I would have never come into contact with normally, beyond paying some money to your brother keeper and doing whatever nasty things I contracted to be able to do to you. Of all the people here, you are the one who makes me think, my dear friend Sybil has found in you something she seemed to be searching for in all the wrong places. Your sharp wit and intelligence make you someone I love to spend time with, and add in Sybil and remove all our clothes and what fabulous times we have".

In Poppy's normal fashion, it was hard to really see what emotion the words brought out in her, she did however give Thorpe a beaming smile, and I found my hand suddenly grasped in hers, and I knew she had been touched.

So that just left me.....

"Sybil, oh my Sybil I think you and I possibly understand each other more than anyone else I have ever met, I love you from the bottom of my heart, and the time we spend together always means so much, to have someone in your life from whom judgement never comes forth is a rare gift and if I believed there was a god, I would thank him daily for your presence in my life, however as I am convinced religion is just a way to keep the masses under control, I shall simply thank you and hope our friendship never lessens or wanes, and whoever or whatever comes into our lives, we never lose each other." I felt some rather uncharacteristic emotion rise in my chest and I swallowed hard, having no intention of allowing anyone to see a tear fall, instead I just looked up and smiled.

"I love you too Thorpe, but come on now, this uncharacteristic show of truth and emotion is rather unsettling, however nice. So come along now, and let get to the point"

Thorpe looked over to me and narrowed his eyes, with a look of indignation I had seen play over his handsome features many times over the years.

"Ok, yes yes yes, it would seem that I am rather enjoying my time in the light too much, so yes yes yes"

At this point, the collective breath in the room was held, and we all leaned forward just a little bit. Thorpe after a pause for even more dramatic effect started speaking.

"I have a huge estate, and more money than I can spend in one lifetime. At my aforementioned huge estate, I have a wing, the west wing, which is never used. As you all know, my late wife was a woman for whom any pleasure really wasn't an option and so I want to use the money I received on her death to create a haven for pleasure. We will become The Carnal Set, and the west wing will become our haven, and a haven for all those who enjoy what we do, with no barriers as to class or money, simply that they are trusted to be able to enjoy what we have on offer without shock or histrionics! I would propose creating a house within a house, the west wing will become a dwelling within my home, and will be used only for our pleasure. My thoughts at the moment have moved as far as to suggest monthly weekends, devoted to nothing more than the delights of the flesh. It won't be a brothel, no one will be paid to attend, it will be invite only and the invite must come via one of the founder members, and the founder members, my dear friends are us. I would wager one of the best horses in my stables that right now each one of your minds is racing with thoughts of those who would love and enjoy what I have proposed. If we are clever, and do it right, an invite to one of our weekends will become the hottest ticket in London, we will be celebrated and famous, or perhaps infamous...."

As Thorpe finished speaking, we all let out a breath collectively, and I could tell by the atmosphere in the room that all of us were excited and thought Thorpe's plan to be perhaps almost perfect.

Thorpe looked around the silent room and grinned.

"Well.......what do you all think? Shall we do it"?

Three months later

It was a languid summer's day and Poppy and I were outside, in a beautiful hidden grotto in my garden, the ground had been cleared and the sun was shaded by beautiful ash trees, which stood tall and strong. On the ground were blankets and cushions, creating the most beautiful space to just lay back and relax, we were chatting and sipping cool fruit juice when we were interrupted by Charlie, who announced that Lord Pembroath had arrived. Before giving Charlie permission to bring him out to us, I turned to Poppy.

"What do you think darling, do we have the energy for him?" She smiled and nodded.

"Why not, let's hope he has the energy for us". I gave Charlie a nod and told him to bring Thorpe out here.

Poppy and I grinned and quickly stood up. We managed to strip ourselves down totally naked in less than the minute or so it took before we heard Thorpe's familiar footsteps coming across the garden.

We both laid down, propping ourselves up on cushions, so when Thorpe appeared he was faced with the two of us apparently ready for him grinning with our legs wide open, as soon as he opened his mouth to speak, we turned to each other and after a look of lust passed over our faces, we started kissing, our warm soft mouths meeting, lips pressed against each others and when Poppy's tongue made its way into my mouth I murmured happily with delight. Our arms wrapped about each other, her hands cupped my breasts and pinched my rosy pink nipples which were rapidly becoming like hard little pebbles under her touch.

It was at that point that Thorpe, who I knew had been standing watching must have knelt down because all of a sudden I felt fingers slide inside my already very wet pussy, I knew it wasn't Poppy and so of course Thorpe had taken us up on our obvious invitation to join in.

We broke the kiss off, and both again laid back so we were propped up on our elbows, Thorpe was knelt in front of us both, one hand buried deep in each of our cunts, I could hear Poppy's breathing becoming a little faster, as his thumb moved to press and rub our clits. I leaned over and took one of Poppy's perfectly hard nipples into my mouth, biting softly, she moaned gently and let her head fall back so her perfect beautiful neck was stretched out, looking up I could see the pulse in her neck quickening and my lips very quickly made their way from her breasts to her collarbone and up her neck, pausing briefly to nibble on her earlobe my lips were soon back to hers and we again kissed deeply, our tongues dancing and rubbing against each other.

I felt Thorpe's fingers leave my pussy, we broke off the kiss and looked over to him, he was standing up and quickly removing his clothing. It was just seconds before he was stood over us both wearing nothing but a huge erection, his body was hard and well muscled but with just enough softness about his middle to make him almost normal and a little vulnerable. He came and stood in front of us, so his erection was between our heads. Poppy looked up and both of us quickly scrambled to our knees, and together we sucked him, starting by licking at hard cock, our tongues running up and down the length of his shaft together, over and over, it was my hand that reached up and grasped around him, whilst it was Poppy's mouth that first took him, his large penis filling her mouth, the very moment he felt her lips around him and as she sucked him in deeply he started to thrust his hips very softly. As Poppy sucked him, I let go of his cock and she wrapped her hands about his shaft so her mouth and hands moved together in perfect rhythm, I moved so I leaned around and reached under him, I quickly took his balls in my mouth, and heard him gasp as I did, I reached up and placed both my hands on his buttocks, which gave me the purchase I needed to continue to suck and lick, my tongue making its way to that little sensitive patch between his cock and balls, Thorpe was grunting a little bit now, and I guessed he was struggling to control himself, being launched upon by two naked, wet and horny women didn't happen every day I assumed.

Just as I could feel him really start to move quicker, he stepped away, pulling his cock from Poppy's mouth and leaning down he moved her so she was on all fours, she leaned down so her elbows were on the ground giving him the perfect position to place his hands upon her well rounded hips and drive his cock in one swift action inside her pussy, which I could see was wet and swollen, her generous pussy lips dripping with her juices. Once inside her, she started to whimper softly as he without any thought to be gentle started to thrust deeply. He looked over to me and grinned.

"Get on it Sybil, the slut loves to suck pussy you know that", not needing to be reminded again, I quickly moved and laid down in front of Poppy, spreading my legs in each reach of her mouth, she almost gratefully launched her mouth to my pussy, licking and sucking as quickly as Thorpe was fucking her, she moved her hands so she could get fingers inside me, slipping one finger deep inside my soaking cunt, while the other moved to sit just inside my anus. It was my turn to be the one to start whimpering loudly, Poppy's tongue was insistent, lapping over my clit over and over, whilst the force of Thorpe thrusts inside Poppy meant her fingers were just forcefully and quickly thrusting inside my pussy and arse.

All three of us were lost for those final moments in our own version of utopia, with not a little bit of holding on and some serious timing on Thorpe's part, we all managed to come together, sweaty, warm bodies shuddering in unison, as we rode the waves and thrusts of our respective climaxes, Thorpe had pulled out of Poppy, and I could see the thick streams of his semen running down her back. Poppy looked up at me with a happy grin, her mouth and face were wet with my juice, and I leaned down to kiss her passionately, tasting myself.

   ...

After calming down and calling for more drinks, we were laid down on the cushions enjoying the sunshine and the smell of lust and sex emanating from all three of us, when Thorpe looked up and grinned, leaping to his feet and grabbing his breeches, which were still strewn on the ground, he rifled about pulling out a black card which he flicked delicately on to the ground next to me, looking down I could just make out the outline of what looked like a gold embossed key, picking it up for closer examination while at the same time letting my eyes wander between the card in my hand and Thorpe standing there in all his glory, the words "Invite......The Carnal Set" could now be clearly read, looking up at Thorpe once more and uttering excitedly,

"You masterful man, you did it you did it". Saying nothing he just stood there with that grin of achievement which from men of his standing meant 'I told you I would '.

Proof

Made in the USA
Charleston, SC
18 November 2013